About

My background is as a practitioner in business and information technology in various management roles over four decades. In more recent times, I have specialised in strategy and analytics as an independent consultant.

I was an active sportsman, playing cricket, football (the round ball), golf and squash. A few years ago, I took an interest in horse racing and have had shares in a number of horses, some more successful than others. I am a member of the Melbourne Racing Club and attend race meetings whenever possible with my daughter.

I am also a keen theatre goer, a member of the Arts Centre Melbourne and the National Gallery of Victoria. Now, in semi-retirement, I have turned my hand to writing. This is my first publication after a number of drafts.

OPPORTUNITIES

Vanguard Press

ALEXANDER NEILSON

OPPORTUNITIES

A CIP catalogue record for this title is
available from the British Library.

ISBN 978 1 784658 20 5

*Vanguard Press is an imprint of
Pegasus Elliot MacKenzie Publishers Ltd.*
www.pegasuspublishers.com

First Published in 2021

**Vanguard Press
Sheraton House Castle Park
Cambridge England**

Printed & Bound in Great Britain

Dedication

Help others take advantage of their
Opportunities and grab Opportunities that
come along for yourself.

Chapter 1
Chance Meeting

It was the last day of March 2001.

Robert Black had finished the work he needed to do in his room and decided to go for a swim before lunch. However, he had forgotten to pack his swimming trunks. So, he went to the little mall near the hotel. Trunks in hand, he started heading back towards the hotel.

As usual Asha Ranjiv Sharma was hopping around on one leg, using a long pole for support, meandering through the outdoor shopping area in a Mumbai suburb called Powai.

Robert saw this young man in the near distance, stumbling along. He froze and immediately thought of Yung-Su. Yung-Su is a Korean polio victim, whom he had helped for a number of years before they had a falling out. Robert mused that Yung-Su had been like a son to him and he was his father figure, providing encouragement as well as financial assistance. Robert really enjoyed being involved in his life, mapping out a future for him: university, wheelchair tennis and eventually a career. But he had been too pushy.

Seeing this young person with a disability made Robert think if this was another opportunity to help someone in need. Perhaps a bit presumptuous of him as he knew nothing about that person.

As Robert came out of his reverie and looked up that person was about to hop past him. Robert called out.

Asha heard a Westerner called out to him in English "Excuse me!" Asha stopped in his tracks and the Westerner came closer to him, looking at his right leg.

"Sorry to interrupt you and my apologies for being nosey. But I was intrigued by how you were walking and wondered about the reason for you using the pole," Robert explained.

"My right leg is affected by polio and I cannot walk on it. So, I use the pole for support to get around," Asha responded.

Their discussion continued for a short time and then, out of the blue, the man offered to help him get treatment for his leg. He said he had experience with people with polio and felt that there were medical procedures that could help. This offer seemed very sudden as they had only just met. But Asha was curious. If something could be done, that would be wonderful.

Robert asked Asha to go back to his hotel so they could discuss this further and then to find out about options for appropriate treatment. For some reason, Asha trusted him and they made their way to his hotel, which was nearby.

As they were walking back, Robert was deep in thought. Had he been too quick to offer help? Did he really want to get involved in someone else's life again, particularly after what had happened with Yung-Su? Why take him back to his hotel? Why not a street-side cafe? Robert rationalised that the hotel would be fine, just sitting in the lobby area or in the restaurant, which was very public.

By the time they reached the hotel, Robert had persuaded himself that helping this young man was the right thing to do. Just take it easy, one step at a time.

Asha is seventeen years old. He contracted polio as a very young baby. He comes from a farming family in country Maharashtra, India, and did not get any treatment for the condition. As a result, his right leg is locked at the knee, meaning he cannot straighten it. So, the only means of mobility is crawling or hopping. Nobody knows how or when exactly he contracted polio. A few months after birth, his family noticed that he was not moving his right leg. They took him to a doctor but he was not able to provide much in the way of constructive advice. He did recognise that Asha had polio. But he said there was no cure and that there was nothing that could be done. So, his parents just accepted that and they all got on with their lives. Asha's is a little different to most other people.

He is from Nagpur in Maharashtra India, about 700 kilometres east of Mumbai. He was visiting his aunt and uncle, who live in Powai, for the school summer holidays.

Asha understood what the man was saying in English as he was studying that language in high school. Although physically disabled, his brain does not seem to have been affected by polio as he is doing very well with his studies. He had finished his Standard XI exams and had achieved good results in all subjects, including English.

On the way to the hotel, they did not talk much. But Asha was thinking a lot. Why did the man stop me? Why did he want to help me? Was he taking a chance going back to the hotel with him?

When they entered the hotel lobby, Robert noticed that the seating area on the left was vacant. So, he signalled to Asha to head over there where there were two, two-seaters at right angles to each other, with a low long table in front and a square table with a large vase and big flower arrangement in the corner. They sat down on each side of the corner table.

Asha pulled his hoodie back and Robert could see his face more clearly. He had deep brown eyes with a smallish straight nose and narrow mouth. His hair was jet black atop a head that was not too big. He was very good-looking.

Asha's little right leg, all bone and skin, could be seen below his three-quarter length pants, with his small foot dangling below.

Asha was looking around the lobby and up at the high ceiling.

The man looked very presidential, with brown thinning hair receding from the temple, green eyes and a slightly bent nose. He also was a bit podgy. Asha thought he was handsome.

The man introduced himself as Robert from Sydney, Australia. He said he was in Mumbai on business and would be there for a couple of more days on this trip. He told Asha that he ran his own company providing consulting services on strategic planning and had a number of clients in Mumbai.

Then Asha gave Robert a brief background about himself.

Asha borrowed Robert's mobile to call his aunt and uncle to ask them to come over to the hotel. He explained that he wanted to introduce them to someone.

Robert then started telling him what he had in mind. He suggested that Asha could get an operation to straighten his leg and then he could be fitted with a full-length calliper that would allow him to walk unaided without a pole or crutches. Asha was not sure what a calliper was. However, it sounded interesting. But...

While they were waiting for his aunt and uncle to arrive, Robert asked about his family. Asha told him that his father, Ranjiv, runs an orange orchard just outside Nagpur. He is quite successful allowing him to provide good support for the family. But times have not always been good. They have been lucky, whereas, in bad times, some farmers have committed suicide. As a result, his father has lost a number of close friends and acquaintances. His mother, Anji, is primarily a housewife, looking after the family. She is also a very good cook and likes to try recipes from the various cuisines across the country. This started off the taste buds in Asha's mouth. He told Robert that he also has an older sister, Visha, and younger brother, Bishu.

"Mr Robert, what is that over there and what are they doing?"

"Asha, just call me Robert. That is the reception area." But before Robert could finish, Asha announced the arrival of his aunt and uncle.

Robert rose to greet them and ushered them to the two-seater where he had been sitting and then sat down next to Asha. They looked very smart, his aunt wearing a brown and yellow sari and his uncle, an off-white shirt, brown pants and sandals. They seemed to be around the same age as him.

Asha introduced Robert, who proceeded to explain to them, using Asha as an interpreter, what he had already told Asha about the operation and calliper. Robert put his left hand on Asha's locked right knee and his right hand on Asha's right leg, moving the leg backwards and forwards as a way of demonstrating what the operation would mean, giving Asha more flexibility and movement, depending on the remnants of the muscle power in his leg.

Asha, his aunt and uncle still seemed a little perplexed. So, Robert suggested that they go into the restaurant for some refreshments and have a more detailed discussion.

Asha felt a little nervous about this as he had never been in a hotel like this before, never mind its restaurant. Nevertheless, they made their way there and were shown to a table. Very impressive, thought Asha. Robert ordered drinks and some snacks.

Naturally enough, Asha's aunt and uncle were a little suspicious about a foreigner approaching their nephew and asking to help him. They were not sure if he could be trusted. But they were willing to listen to him.

Robert told them not to rely on his layman's assessment of the treatment for Asha's leg. He recommended that they consult with a specialist. Robert also explained, in a little detail, that a calliper is a device that would support Asha's leg from foot to thigh to help him walk. Sounded good.

Asha asked Robert why he wanted to help him.

"I have helped a teenager with polio before. And when I saw you hopping around, I felt that this was another opportunity to help someone. Also, I have a son with a mild disability, which has strengthened my resolve to help those who are not as able."

Asha's aunt asked Robert what he expected to achieve from the visit to the specialist. She seemed happy with the answer. After some more discussion, the aunt told Asha that she felt more comfortable with Robert and his motives. Was this because Robert was a good salesman or because they were desperate to grab the opportunity for me, Asha pondered?

Robert thought it was interesting that it was Asha's aunt who was asking all the questions while his uncle just watched on, looking at him and seemingly weighing him up.

Robert also told them that he would pay for any expenses. Very generous. Asha thought that it also took any financial concern out of the picture as he was sure that his family would not be able to cover the costs.

Asha then borrowed his uncle's mobile and called his parents, going through the same scenario with them. Naturally, being so far away, and not really understanding what was being proposed, they had some concerns. The aunt then took the mobile and gave his mother her views on what they had been discussing. In the end, his parents and aunt and uncle agreed that they ought to meet a specialist to get his opinion on what Robert was suggesting.

The hotel's front desk helped Robert get details of a specialist who treated those affected by polio. He called the specialist and made an appointment for them to see him the following day, which was a Sunday.

Asha then went back to his aunt's and uncle's place about 400 metres from the hotel. When they got there, the aunt made some tea and they talked some more about the surprising events of the day. The uncle was still a little sceptical.

The next day the aunt and uncle accompanied Asha to the hotel where Robert was waiting with a wheelchair that he had borrowed from the hotel. Robert wheeled Asha to the hospital near the hotel where the specialist, Dr Semoy, had rooms.

Dr Semoy examined Asha's polio leg and recommended corrective surgery to straighten the leg. He explained the procedure, the risks and expected outcome.

Robert thanked Dr Semoy for his consultation and told him that Asha and his family had a lot to think about before deciding to proceed with the surgery. Also, he was about to go back to Sydney. But, told him that he would call him as soon as he found out what Asha's and his family's decision was.

Robert told Asha to think long and hard about the recommended operation and the possibilities beyond that and discuss it with his parents.

They went back to Robert's hotel, had some refreshments and then said their good byes. Before that, Robert took Asha's telephone number and told him that he would call him in a few days to find out what the collective decision was. He also told Asha he would be back in Powai in two weeks' time.

Chapter 2
Decision Time

Asha's aunt and uncle drove him to Nagpur two days after that chance meeting with Robert. On the long journey he had plenty of time to think about what had happened. His aunt and uncle seemed positive about the operation but were also concerned about the risks.

Asha had already decided that he wanted to take the opportunity. The possibility of him being able to walk on two legs, even although he would need to wear this thing called a calliper, made him feel very happy.

But there was a nagging feeling in his mind. Robert had returned to Sydney. Out of sight, out of mind! Would he really call to find out about the decision?

But Asha still needed to convince his parents that the operation on his leg was the right thing to do.

When Asha got out of the car, he was excited to see his family again. But that was not the only reason for his excitement. He just wanted to have the operation that would hopefully change his life for the better.

Over dinner, his aunt told his family about the meetings with Robert and Dr Semoy. She was quite passionate about recommending to his parents that they let him have the operation. Yes, there were risks. But the positives outweighed the negatives, she suggested.

Anji said that she had watched him hop from the car to the house and had felt sad. She said that she had always wanted things to be more normal for him. But she had not known what could be done.

Once Asha explained to his family what the operation would mean for him, being able to be more mobile and be more actively involved with his friends and family, Ranjiv agreed for him to have the operation. What a relief. I can't wait to tell Robert, Asha thought.

The following day, Asha met Rajesh and Manosh, two of his best friends from school, at a coffee shop in the city. He excitedly told them about his meeting with Robert, a businessman from Sydney, and the examination by Dr Semoy. They would not believe that a stranger would offer to help him the way he had told them. They made a bet with him that Robert would not call. This made Asha angry and he left abruptly with tears streaming down his face.

Asha wondered why Robert had not called him. It had been a few days since he had gone back to Sydney. Perhaps Rajesh and Manosh were right. Why had he not asked Robert for his telephone number, Asha pondered? Then he could have called him.

It was good to get back to Sydney and to see and spend time with Andrew, my son.

The night Robert got back, Andrew and he went out to the local Thai restaurant and had a good chat, mainly about Andrew.

The university term had just finished and Andrew was getting ready to go to Japan to play in a wheelchair tennis tournament after the Easter weekend.

Andrew told Robert that he had enjoyed the challenges of the first term at university and thought that the end of term exams had gone well.

Andrew had a new girlfriend, Elisa, whom Robert had never met. Andrew talked at length about her, with his face lighting up every time he mentioned her. It was good to see him so happy.

He was looking forward to the Japan tournament and had been practising hard. He was moving up the rankings and had set his sights on getting to the number-one position. Naturally enough, it would not be easy. But he was determined. Andrew had never stepped away from a challenge.

Robert talked about business in India and how successful the trip had been, particularly winning a major project with a very large corporation to review and fine tune their three-year rolling plan. But he was hesitant about mentioning Asha.

On the Saturday morning, after breakfast, Robert decided he could not wait any longer to talk to Andrew about Asha. He sat down with his son and told him about his meeting with Asha, the discussions with his aunt, uncle and himself and the consultation with Dr Semoy.

Andrew seemed a little taken aback.

"Dad, do you really want to get involved in the same way you did with Yung-Su? Remember how disappointed and upset you were when Yung-Su fell out with you. I do not want this to happen to you again."

"Andrew, I thought about the very same thing on the flight back. It is a risk that it could all go pear-shaped. But that is a risk I am willing to take. First things first, Asha and his family need to decide if they want to go ahead with the operation."

"Dad, you know it will not end there. You will want to stay involved and help plan his life the way you did with Yung-Su. Anyway, you have my support with whatever you decide to do with Asha. From what you have told me, he seems to be a lovely person. But, just be careful."

This sounded like such mature advice coming from such a young head. Andrew was right. Robert didn't want to invest time and money into Asha and be let down again. Hopefully, he had learned his lesson.

Thoughts were running through Andrew's head. He was worried about Dad. Once he grabbed hold of something, he poured all of his energy into it. This has been more so since Mum died two years ago. We both miss her so much. When he had not been travelling, he had focused all of his attention on me, which has been great. He made sure I concentrated on getting a high score in the Higher School Certificate so I could get into a top university to study law. He is my biggest tennis fan and comes to see me play whenever he can. But, perhaps, he does need another outlet, a cause to make his own! Just hope it turns out well for him.

Robert was eager to call Asha. But he left it until Tuesday afternoon. That gave Asha and his family more than a week to discuss the operation and, hopefully, make a decision.

"Asha, this is Robert. How are you?" Robert could hear sobbing. "Asha, what is the matter?"

"I did not think you would call and I am so happy to hear your voice."

Asha said that he and his family had discussed the operation at length and had decided to proceed. A smile broke out all over Robert's face. A great decision.

"Asha, I am so happy for you."

"Me too, happy with the decision and very happy to hear your voice."

Robert told Asha that he would let Dr Semoy know, agree a date for the operation and call him back.

Dr Semoy fitted Asha into his schedule for the operation on Wednesday, 18 April 2001, which worked in well with Robert's return to Powai.

Chapter 3
The Operation

Robert was able to get time away from his work to be with Asha for the operation. On the Wednesday morning, Asha met Robert at his hotel, where he had borrowed the wheelchair again.

They had a long talk before they set off for the hospital.

"Asha, how do you feel?" Robert inquired.

"I am a little nervous about what is going to happen. I have never had an operation before, never mind being a patient in hospital. So, I do not know what to expect."

Robert followed up with some comments to ease Asha's mind. "I did some research on Dr Semoy and he seems to be an excellent surgeon. He has done the procedure he is going to perform on you many, many times. Do not worry. I am sure everything will go well. Andrew has had operations on his legs and each time he has pulled through without any problems. Even I had an operation when I ruptured my left Achilles tendon. The whole experience was interesting from the anaesthetic through to resting in the ward after the operation. So, I am used to what you are going through. You will be given an anaesthetic to put you to sleep before the operation and when you wake up it will be all over. So, just try to relax."

At the hospital, Robert and Asha were ushered into a changing room for him to prepare for the operation. Asha had to get weighed and confirm his particulars, such as name, date of birth and address, to the nurse. Asha then got into a bed, wearing only his underpants and a hospital gown. He was still feeling a little nervous. As Robert recommended, he tried to relax. But he just wanted it to be all over.

Asha's right leg was shaved. He was then given an injection, an anaesthetic, to relax him. After a short time, Asha thought he was floating on air. He felt so calm. This settled the nerves.

Asha lay there looking at the ceiling and thinking. Thinking about the past, a life as a pole hopper or crawler. Hoping the future would bring more mobility and ability. He did not really know how the operation was going to affect him. He'd put his trust in Robert and Dr Semoy that his life would not only be different but better as a result of the operation.

"Robert, I am frightened," Asha said.

But before Robert had a chance to say anything, the ward staff arrived to wheel him to the operating theatre. Asha waved to Robert and he waved back.

"See you back here after the operation," said Robert.

Asha forced a smile.

Asha was wheeled along a corridor, into a lift and down to the operating theatre. On entering, he could feel a chill. He could see a few faces. One of them said, "Hi Asha."

Asha was lifted onto a table, an oxygen mask placed on his face and a needle attached to his arm. Amidst all the voices, he was asked to count backwards from ten. "Ten, nine, eight, seven…"

Asha opened his eyes and he was alone in a corridor lying in a bed with the oxygen mask still on his face. He felt a little woozy but overall fine. A short time afterwards, he was taken to a ward where there were a number of other patients and rolled into an empty space.

After the attendants had gone, Asha pulled the bed sheet back to discover his right leg flat on the bed covered in some white chalky substance from his toes to his thigh. His leg did not feel sore. And it was no longer locked at the knee. Asha smiled to himself.

A nurse came to see him and asked how he felt. "Fine. But my mouth feels a little dry." She gave him some water to sip and helped him sit up a little. She then gave him a sandwich and some juice.

A little while later Robert arrived to visit Asha. He told him that he had been allowed to be with him during the operation and he had stood by his head as he watched Dr Semoy use a "hammer and chisel" to break the bone at the side of his right knee and then straighten his leg before putting it in a plaster of Paris casing from toes to thigh.

"So, the white chalky substance is plaster of Paris?" inquired Asha.

"Yes. Your leg has been wrapped in cotton bandages, combined with gypsum and water, which then hardened. The cast is there to keep your leg in place as it recovers from the operation," Robert explained.

Robert had watched a similar operation before, standing at the head of the patient, watching the surgeon do his work. He was so close that he ended up with a speck of blood on his shirt. Such operations were organised by an NGO and were funded by public donations. They are just a great benefit for polio sufferers from poor families, as they mostly seemed to be in India.

Dr Semoy arrived to see how Asha was and to confirm that the operation had been successful. Asha was relieved that all had seemed to have gone well.

Robert left soon afterwards and Asha nodded off to sleep. He must have slept for over an hour. It was now dark outside.

So, this is what hospital is like, Asha thought. It did not seem too bad to him. The staff were helpful. They asked him if he needed a bottle or pan to use for the toilet. He was glad that they asked because he was not sure how he was going to be able to go to the toilet. Brief panic over.

Then it was time for dinner, which was a vegetarian curry. It tasted very good.

After dinner, Asha relaxed, looking at the ceiling again. He felt restless and his mind kept wandering. Were his pole-hopping days over? He hoped so. He was still feeling tired, which was probably due to a combination of anxiety and anaesthetics.

Asha could hear a voice. "Would you like a drink?" It was morning and the drinks trolley was doing the rounds of the ward. He asked the ward assistant for an orange juice.

A nurse pulled the curtains round Asha's bed and brought in a basin with water. She helped him sit up and proceeded to wash him down. She called it giving a bed bath. She left another small bowl with toothpaste and a brush to clean his teeth. All done and Asha felt quite refreshed. A good sleep and a clean body.

Then the trolley was back delivering breakfasts. Asha had an omelette and toast with some milky tea. Once his tray had been cleared, he slid down the bed and nodded off again. But not for long.

Dr Semoy arrived for his rounds and told Asha that, as there had not appeared to be any negative reaction to the operation, he would be discharged that afternoon. Asha telephoned Robert to let him know so he could come to get him. Before Robert arrived, Asha got dressed and was given a pair of crutches to practise walking, including going up and down stairs. Crutch hopping not pole-hopping. It was different but comfortable.

Robert brought the wheelchair again. Asha felt odd with his leg sticking out straight ahead. His aunt and uncle came to meet them at the hotel. Over a late lunch, Robert asked Asha how he felt.

"I am relieved that the operation is over and pleased that the doctor told me that it had been successful. But now I am impatient, having to wait three weeks for the cast to be taken off to see what my leg looks like."

Robert said he would make an appointment for Asha to get fitted for a calliper after the cast came off. He would be back in Powai to oversee the process from Asha's leg getting measured for the calliper to learning to walk with it. Asha would also need extensive physiotherapy to mobilise his ankle and knee as much as that would be possible.

Asha told Robert how grateful he was for his help. Words could not really express how he felt about what Robert had done for him.

They parted company and Asha crutch-walked back with his aunt and uncle. The following day Robert flew back to Sydney.

Asha became very contemplative. What different lives? A chance encounter brought us together. What did the future hold?

Robert sat on the plane feeling relieved that all had gone well with the operation. He could see Asha's huge smile as they parted company in the hotel. Everybody seemed to be looking forward to the next stage of Asha's mobilisation.

Chapter 4
Asha's First Calliper

Asha's aunt and uncle drove him back to Nagpur once again. This time with him sitting in the back seat, right leg stretched out a little uncomfortably.

His family was very pleased to see him and were very inquisitive about the operation and what would happen next. He told them about the anaesthetic, being put to sleep and waking up with his leg in plaster. After the operation, the surgeon had visited him in his hospital bed and said how well the operation had gone. Asha then outlined the process as Robert had explained to him and they all, except his father, cried with joy. Ranjiv just smiled, wide-eyed. He was not very good about showing his emotions. But Asha could tell that he was excited about Asha's future.

Asha had not seen Rajesh and Manosh since that time in the cafe. Now, when they saw him, leg in plaster and on crutches, they seemed very surprised and asked him what had happened. He told them how stupid they had been to doubt that Robert would call. Robert had called and had come back to Powai where he had arranged for a surgeon to operate on Asha's leg to straighten it. So, you lost your bet said Asha to the two of them. Even though they were very apologetic, Asha did not tell them any more as he was still annoyed with their behaviour previously in the cafe.

For the next three weeks, Asha led a new but pretty normal life, getting about using the crutches, which turned out to be much easier than hopping around with the pole. He just wanted to keep busy so that the time would pass quickly and he could move onto the next phase of his rehabilitation. Asha spent time with some of his friends. They played some cricket while Asha watched, a little frustrated, because he still could not participate. And sometimes, they watched television or went to the movies. Just an ordinary existence. But Asha was enjoying life.

Anji was so happy and kept smiling at him and hugging him when she got a chance. Ranjiv was more reserved but still clearly happy for him. Bishu helped him whenever required, particularly when Asha had a shower. And Visha kept offering words of encouragement. Such a beautiful family!

After the three weeks, Ranjiv drove him back to Powai.

Robert had returned to India and took Asha to see Dr Semoy to get the cast removed. His leg felt strange, no longer being locked at the knee, thought Asha.

They then went to see an orthotist where Asha was measured for a calliper. It would run from the top of his thigh and be held in position by a slot in his footwear. Its technical term is KAFO, which is an abbreviation for knee-ankle-foot-orthosis. It would take about two weeks to make the calliper. Asha also had to have special boots made with a build-up inside the right one as his straightened right leg is four inches shorter than his left leg. One pair of boots was for normal day-to-day use, black in colour. The other pair was similar to basketball boots.

Robert also arranged for Asha to get a proper fitting wheelchair to use when he did not wear his calliper.

During the period when he was waiting for the calliper, he also had physiotherapy on his polio leg just to get rid of the stiffness caused by being in the cast and to loosen up his knee and ankle.

Robert was to be in Mumbai for three weeks on this trip. Asha was still on school holidays staying with his aunt and uncle and Robert was staying at his usual hotel in Powai. So, they were able to spend time together, particularly at weekends. Robert would take Asha shopping for clothes. He even bought Asha a mobile phone. They would eat in good Western-style restaurants, a far cry from Asha's normal diet of curries and rice.

Asha was looking forward to getting the calliper, although not really sure what the experience would be. D-day arrived, the calliper was fitted and Asha took his first steps. A little weird. But after walking up and down the corridor using crutches, it felt good, comfortable and, best of all, he was mobile. Another strange thing was that this was the first time that he had worn any kind of footwear on his right foot.

As Asha took his first step, a huge smile lit up his whole face. He seemed very happy and Robert was very happy with tears of joy moistening his eyes.

As Asha got out of the car at the hotel, his family was waiting for him inside the lobby. He was still using the crutches for support while getting used to walking with the calliper. Anji hugged him as tears of joy ran down her face, seeing him walking using both legs for the first time. Ranjiv smiled proudly with Visha, Bishu, aunt and uncle looking on with apparent happiness for him.

They went to the hotel restaurant for some tea and then to Robert's room where he explained to the family the ins and outs of the calliper. Seems quite complicated but effective.

Asha's parents and sister as well as his aunt and uncle left to go shopping.

Asha spent time walking around the hotel room getting used to walking with no crutch support. Then they went for a swim. Asha's father had taken him to the local swimming pool when he was about five years old and had taught him how to swim. This time would be somewhat different with a straight right leg. On the pool deck, Asha took off his calliper and crawled to the edge before falling into the water. Very refreshing. Robert and Bishu, joined him and they swam and played around. Back on deck and dried off by the sun, Asha put his calliper back on. Shorts on, and they walked back to the lift and then down to the room.

After Asha showered in the bath, he started getting dressed. Once he had put on his calliper, he just sat there and looked at his small leg encased in metal and leather.

"Asha, what is happening with you? Robert asked. "It looks like you are in a trance!"

Asha started to cry and Robert came over to him. Asha hugged him tightly in silence for a while.

"I am just so overjoyed that I can walk," Asha uttered.

Asha thought more about the changes to his life. It might seem a bit of a nuisance and effort to put on and take off the calliper. However, it was really worthwhile. The calliper gave him the freedom and mobility that he did not have before. Also, for some reason, he felt good about himself, even although he was still limping a little. Asha even felt good wearing shorts and not hiding his polio leg in long pants. Mind you, his long pants had to be modified so he could get them on over the calliper and built-up boot. This meant inserting a zip on the inside from the leg bottom upwards for about nine inches.

While they were waiting for his family to return, Robert explained to him the importance of using his polio leg, not only through swimming but by doing different exercises. This was mainly to keep it active. Robert showed Asha the exercises he had in mind.

Robert told him not to overdo the exercising and suggested doing them only every second or third day.

The telephone rang. The rest of Asha's family had arrived in the lobby, where they joined them to go into the hotel restaurant for brunch or, as Robert called it, linner — lunch and dinner. It was three o'clock in the afternoon.

Asha could hardly stop smiling. There he was walking on two feet for the first time in his life. He did not need any help to get his food from the buffet. He was independent.

Anji told him how happy she was watching him walk backwards and forwards between their table and the buffet. She said she could hardly believe her eyes.

Ranjiv leaned over to Asha and told him to thank Robert for all his help and hoped to see him again.

Then they got up from the table. Robert, Bishu and Asha went up to Robert's room to get all Asha's things: clothes, wheelchair and crutches. Back downstairs they said goodbye to Robert at the hotel's entrance.

"Asha, you look fantastic," enthused Robert. "No stopping you now."

"Robert, thank you very much. My family and I can never repay you for what you have done for me. When will you be back in Mumbai?"

"No plans at this stage. But I will let you know. Stay in touch by email and let me know how you are doing."

Asha was very sad leaving Robert again. They had forged such a strong friendship, not just between Robert and himself but also Robert and the rest of his family. Asha tried to hide his tears to no avail. Robert hugged him, turned around and walked back into the lobby.

"See you soon," shouted Robert.

They strolled back to Asha's aunt's and uncle's apartment. Yes, walking and no longer hopping. Asha felt so good and full of energy. Bishu had the task of wheeling the chair, luggage and crutches while Asha walked along, more like floated, without a care in the world.

Ranjiv drove them back to their home.

What a wonderful day, particularly for Asha, reflected Robert!

However, a disastrous end to the day for Robert. After Asha and his family left, Robert went to the ATM to get some money out. But all his requests to withdraw money were rejected.

When he got back to the hotel, he contacted his bank in Australia regarding the problem with his credit card. They told him that his credit account had been drained of funds through some kind of scam. However, there was a positive balance in his savings account that he could access.

When he got home two days later, he called his bank. He was told that all the money that had been scammed would be credited back to him within two weeks once they had gone through their processes.

Chapter 5
Getting Used to a New Life

Things were now very different for Asha. He was able to help Ranjiv pick oranges to go to the processing plant to turn them into juice. He spent more time outside with his friends and Bishu rather than being shut away inside. It was the start of summer. So, it was hotting up. But that did not stop him going for long walks in the beautiful countryside. He wanted to make the most of his freedom.

Asha returned to high school for his final year, which would culminate in him taking the Standard XII examination in order to get the Higher School Certificate, which would make him eligible for university admission.

On the first day, when Bishu and Asha caught the school bus, the driver was shocked to see Asha without his pole. He told him that he looked good. Great for Asha's self-esteem, which was growing day by day.

Asha's classmates were surprised and, seemingly happy, to see him walking without the pole.

Asha was now able to join in some sports, particularly cricket. His running was not very good, more of a hobble, dragging his right leg. But he could bowl some right hand off-spin from a two-pace hobble up. And, he could bat right-handed, using his left leg for balance and strength. As for fielding, he could stand in the slips so he did not need to hobble much. Fortunately, he had big hands with good hand-eye co-ordination so it was a good place to field.

Asha managed to get a game for the local club's third eleven and really enjoyed it. He took a few wickets and catches but did not get many runs batting at number eleven. And they won their fair share of matches without setting the world on fire.

Bishu, at 15 years old, also played cricket for the same club's first eleven. He was a talented fast bowler and spearheaded their attack. Bishu had been playing cricket since the age of ten and had already represented Nagpur in the Maharashtra under-fifteen District tournament, finishing fourth out of eight teams. But he competed well, ending up with the most wickets in the tournament.

Life was now very different for Asha. He was no longer the freak hopping around. He was accepted as just another human. Girls started to talk to him and he was becoming more interested in them. Nothing serious initially but it was a start, mixing with the opposite sex.

During the rest of the year, Robert returned to India a number of times.

However, there was one occasion when Robert called Asha and told him that he had to cancel his visit to India.

Robert was working in his study one morning when he got a call. It was from the Accident and Emergency Department at the local hospital. Andrew had been injured in a car crash while driving to university when a car crossed over to his lane and collided head on.

Robert rushed up to the hospital and found Andrew lying on a stretcher. He said he was fine, just a few bruises and scratches.

A short time later, Andrew was examined fully. As it turned out, it was a little worse than Andrew had suspected. His right wrist had been broken. Fortunately, he is left-handed. It was a simple fracture. His arm was put in a plaster cast up to his elbow. He would need to keep it in a sling for a few days. This meant that he could not push his wheelchair properly and, definitely, could not walk using both crutches. So, Robert decided to cancel his India trip to be on hand to provide whatever care Andrew needed.

Andrew had been driving along his normal route to the university. It was a bright sunny day and he did not have a care in the world, happily listening to a pop music channel on the radio. Then, all of a sudden, a car had veered over into his lane and hit him head on before he could react. He was shaken. He did not feel that he had been too badly injured. But he could not reach his wheelchair on the back seat to be able to get out of the car. The other driver came to see how he was. Andrew explained his situation and the other driver kindly called for an ambulance. He was fine. But both their cars needed to be towed away. Two tow trucks and the ambulance arrived almost simultaneously. Andrew was able to exchange particulars with the other driver and give details to the tow truck driver. One of the paramedics carried Andrew out of the car and onto a mobile stretcher, which was wheeled into the back of the ambulance, before being carted off to hospital. Fortunately, Andrew is pretty light at around fifty kilograms.

Dad arrived in a slight panic and was relieved to find out that Andrew had not been badly hurt.

Andrew felt disappointed for him that he decided to cancel his India trip. But he was also very happy that Dad was going to be around.

Until it happens, you do not really know how incapacitating it is to not be able to use one arm. But his dad was a blessing. He helped with all the basic care, such as dressing, undressing and bathing. Fortunately, this was only required for a couple of days before he was able to use his right arm again.

Andrew could still push his wheelchair clumsily, moving his left hand from one wheel to the other. And that was fine around the apartment. Other than that, his dad would push him. He could also move around the apartment a little using a walking stick or one crutch. So, not too bad.

Then, once he did not need to wear the sling, it was back to normal, pushing the wheelchair with both hands but no walking with both crutches until he got the cast off and had some physio on the arm.

Also, Elisa was able to come over after class during the week and at weekends and she helped him whenever possible. Andrew liked that.

He got his car back after ten days and was glad to be able to return to driving. Mobility was important to him.

When Robert made it to India and Asha could spend time with him, they did many interesting things together.

One time, Asha was on school holidays in Powai, coinciding with Robert's stay there. Robert suggested that they go to the horse racing. Robert was a big fan of racing and had a share in two horses in Sydney. Asha had never been to the races. So, he thought it would be another interesting experience. Interesting experience? It was brilliant. For each race, they stood by the rail as the horses ran down the home straight. They just flashed past at what Asha thought was supersonic speed. He was thrilled and excited. Robert had a few bets and did all right. Asha did not bother with betting. But he was hooked on racing.

On Robert's final trip that year, Bishu accompanied Asha to Mumbai. Robert was staying at a hotel near the Gateway. He had arranged a room for them there for a few days to spend time together after he had completed his business activities. When they arrived at his hotel, he surprised them with tickets to the first day of the test match between India and the West Indies. Asha was happy but Bishu was ecstatic. Bishu had but dreamed about seeing the Indian cricket stars in real life.

The following day, they walked to the ground from their hotel. Very handy. Bishu was so excited as they entered the ground and made their way to their seats. Bishu could hardly believe his eyes as he watched the players practise before the start of play. He kept pointing out the Indian players and their names.

India won the toss and chose to bat. Here was Bishu's opportunity to watch his heroes, not only Tendulkar but also Sehwag and Dravid. By the close of play on that day, India was well in command, with Sehwag scoring 147 runs and Dravid and Tendulkar still at the crease.

As they were leaving their hotel to go out to dinner, some of the Indian players were entering the lobby. Cheekily, Robert stopped one of them and asked for an autograph, which was duly given. Robert handed the piece of paper to Bishu, whose eyes lit up when he recognised Rahul Dravid's name. Over dinner, Bishu could hardly stop talking about the day.

The next couple of days were spent by the pool or shopping as well as trying different restaurants. One that fascinated Asha and Bishu was a revolving restaurant. They could hardly concentrate on their food as they slowly moved around. The view of the city and the Arabian Sea was splendid and the Chinese food was very tasty.

Then it was time for them to go their separate ways. Robert had enjoyed his time with the brothers, particularly sharing in Bishu's enjoyment of the cricket experience. Robert was sure Bishu will never forget it.

Robert had a relatively quiet Christmas and New Year with Andrew, Elisa and her parents. Robert had grown to like Elisa and they got on very well. Andrew seemed very happy in her company and fortunately he also got on fine with Elisa's parents. They had accepted him for the person he is.

Christmas dinner was at Elisa's parents' place, not the hot and fulsome roast but a selection of seafoods and salads. Most delicious. Robert had them all over to his balcony for a New Year's Eve barbeque and to watch the fireworks, which Robert thought would become something of a tradition for him. Great view and no need to travel. At least not for him.

Chapter 6
A Surprise

On another visit to India in February 2002, Robert made the trip to Nagpur and stayed for a few days. It was during that visit that he suggested that Asha move to Sydney to study at university after he had finished Standard XII. This was a surprise to Asha and a shock for his family. Robert explained the advantages of life in Sydney, the opportunities for a good degree and work thereafter, earning a better salary than Asha could in India.

Robert told Asha and his family more about his son who was two years older than Asha. He had been born with a very mild form of muscular dystrophy. He had worn below knee leg braces on each leg until the age of ten when he was fitted with full length (KAFO) braces. He now uses crutches with his leg braces or a wheelchair for mobility.

Asha pondered why he called what he wore a calliper and not a leg brace. Same thing. Maybe the Indian way!

Robert said that Andrew had been very mobile, even with below knee leg braces, albeit sometimes a little unstable. But he persevered. They would kick a ball together and go swimming. When Andrew moved onto the full-length braces, he had decided to take up wheelchair tennis and was now one of the top male wheelchair singles tennis players in the world.

Robert's wife, Pauline, had died about two years previously of cancer. So, he was the sole parent, raising Andrew.

Asha already knew all this so it was mainly for the benefit of his parents.

Whenever Robert came back to India and Asha met him, Asha would ask how Andrew was. Robert would tell Asha about how Andrew was doing at university, his wheelchair tennis exploits and his girlfriend, Elisa, as well as other things that were happening in Andrew's life. But not much about himself. When Asha asked Robert about his business, he merely said that it was going well. Same sort of conversation every visit.

When it was just Robert and Asha together, Robert put all his energy into Asha, particularly encouraging him to do his best at school. Robert would ask Asha what he was doing at school and if there was any help that he needed. They were in sync on that as excelling in the Standard XII exams was Asha's highest, in fact the only, priority. So far so good and Robert did not think Asha needed extra coaching.

"Asha, I have a poem I want you to read and understand," Robert stated.

Robert handed Asha a piece of paper and Asha read the poem.

IF

If you can keep your head when all about you
Are losing theirs and blaming it on you,
If you can trust yourself when all men doubt you
But make allowance for their doubting too,
If you can wait and not be tired by waiting,
Or being lied about, don't deal in lies,
Or being hated, don't give way to hating,
And yet don't look too good, nor talk too wise:
If you can dream– and not make dreams your
master,
If you can think– and not make thoughts your
aim;
If you can meet with Triumph and Disaster
And treat those two impostors just the same;
If you can bear to hear the truth you've spoken
Twisted by knaves to make a trap for fools,
Or watch the things you gave your life to,
broken,
And stoop and build 'em up with worn-out tools:
If you can make one heap of all your winnings
And risk it all on one turn of pitch-and-toss,
And lose, and start again at your beginnings
And never breath a word about your loss;
If you can force your heart and nerve and sinew
To serve your turn long after they are gone,
And so hold on when there is nothing in you
Except the Will which says to them: "Hold
on!"

If you can talk with crowds and keep your virtue,
Or walk with kings – nor lose the common
touch,
If neither foes nor loving friends can hurt you;
If all men count with you, but none too much,
If you can fill the unforgiving minute
With sixty seconds' worth of distance run,
Yours is the Earth and everything that's in it,
And – which is more – you'll be a Man, my
son!
– Rudyard Kipling

Asha read it again and again.

"Robert, that sounds like wonderful advice on many fronts, Asha said. "I will keep this and refer to it to give me confidence."

Robert had made a habit of giving Asha motivational quotations and poems.

If it is to be, it is up to me. No more blaming someone else or relying on them to get things done for you. You need to make the effort.

Carpe diem. Seize the day. Make the most of every moment.

Go confidently in the direction of your dreams. Live the life you've imagined. Henry David Thoreau

Life is a song – sing it.

Life is a game – play it.
Life is a challenge – meet it.
Life is a dream – realize it.
Life is a sacrifice – offer it.
Life is love – enjoy it.
Sathya Sai Baba

If a child lives with…
If a child lives with criticism
He learns to condemn
If a child lives with hostility
He learns to fight
If a child lives with ridicule
He learns to be shy
If a child lives with shame
He learns to feel guilty
If a child lives with tolerance
He learns to be patient
If a child lives with encouragement
He learns confidence
If a child lives with praise
He learns to appreciate
If a child lives with fairness
He learns justice
If a child lives with security
He learns to have faith
If a child lives with approval
He learns to like himself

If a child lives with acceptance and friendship
He learns to find love in the World.
Dorothy Law Nolte

Asha felt they were all very thought provoking, offering great advice. From time to time, he'd go back to them and reflect on his life and how he was behaving. They gave him encouragement to do better.

After a lot of soul-searching, Asha's parents agreed for him to go to Sydney to study. This was partly influenced by the fact that Robert had experience dealing with someone with a disability. Also, they had all learned to trust Robert.

It was at that time that Asha asked Robert if he could communicate with Andrew by email as he thought it would be good to get to know each other a little before they met in Sydney the following year. So, Robert gave Asha Andrew's email address and Asha started the ball off by writing to Andrew.

Andrew was pleased that Asha had started communicating with him by email. He was keen to understand Asha first hand and not just through the eyes of his father. Asha told him about his family and how school was going as well as his social life, which seemed to be quite limited. Andrew kept Asha up to date with his life at university, wheelchair tennis and with Elisa.

Asha had decided that he wanted to study law and Robert provided the names of a couple of suitable Sydney universities.

Then the long process began: medical, Australian visa, applications to the colleges. However, everything was dependent on Asha's Standard XII results. Fortunately, there were no hurdles to overcome. Asha got excellent marks in all subjects, his student visa was approved and he was accepted into the University of New South Wales to do a double degree over five years, comprising Bachelor of Arts and Bachelor of Law. Asha's ambition was to join a law firm after graduating from university and to become a solicitor.

Asha was very excited about the prospect of moving to Sydney. However, he had some sadness about leaving his family. They had looked after him and nurtured him through his challenges. Yet, they recognised and accepted that his future lay elsewhere.

As the year came to a close and Asha's departure became imminent, he spent more quality time with his family, engaging in deep discussion with Ranjiv, playing games with Bishu and cuddling up to Anji and Visha. He felt so happy.

Chapter 7
Leaving Home

Robert came to India in January 2003 to take Asha to Sydney to acclimatise before starting university towards the end of February. Exciting times ahead!

Asha's parents, siblings and his aunt and uncle said goodbye to Robert and him at Robert's Powai hotel. Asha had mixed feelings. Sad about leaving his family behind. Excited about what lay ahead but also a little apprehensive. Asha knew that Robert was there to support him. But, for the most part, Asha had to make it on his own in this new world.

Asha's mother and aunt were in tears. But his father was his normal stoic self, not showing any emotion. His brother and sister both looked sad as they hugged him. But Asha kept his cool and quickly turned his back on them to get into Robert's car for the driver to take them to the airport.

As soon as the car was out of their sight, Asha started to cry. Robert put his arm around him.

"Asha, it is OK to cry. In fact, I think it is pretty natural." The sobbing continued for a few more minutes as Robert held Asha. By the time they reached the airport, Asha was fine, at least on the outside.

This was to be Asha's first flight. He was not sure what to expect. He had asked Robert what it was like up there in a plane. Although Robert had flown many times before, he found it difficult to explain the experience of flying.

Robert tried to explain it. "After take-off and once the plane has reached its cruising altitude, it is just like floating on air usually, unless, of course, there is turbulence and then it could be a nightmare. I am a bit of a nervous flyer. I don't know why. But every time there is a shudder or slight drop, I grab for the armrest."

Now Asha was about to find out for himself.

They checked in at the business class counter: Robert's bag, Asha's suitcase and wheelchair.

The process was straightforward for Robert but very new for Asha: customs control, security, lounge and finally boarding.

Going through security was particularly interesting. As Asha waited his turn, he observed that the X-ray machine made a sound and the light went red every time someone walked through. Yet nobody in security appeared to be concerned. The X-ray machine seemed like a waste of time. The whole process was relying on the security officer after a person passed through the machine to pick up any problems using his handheld scanner.

When it was Asha's turn, he walked through the arch of the X-ray machine and stepped up onto the platform in front of the security man. Asha put his passport and boarding pass down and raised his arms to the side as told. As soon as the handheld scanner was put beside Asha's right leg, it went off. The man asked Asha to raise his right trouser leg and Asha explained, in Hindi, that he was wearing a full-length calliper attached to a belt around his waist. Asha was then asked to raise his shirt. All very intrusive, Asha thought. Then Asha was told it was OK to go. So, Asha picked up his passport and boarding pass and stepped down from the platform, stumbling as, absent-mindedly, he had put his left leg down first instead of his right leg.

Robert had gone through before Asha and was waiting by the escalator for him so they could go down to the airline's lounge. Asha was not sure about the escalator as he had not been on one before. He walked down the stairs instead. "Asha, you need to get used to escalators, I'll help you next time, if needed." Robert suggested.

They had some refreshments in the lounge while they waited for their flight to be called and then they made their way to the aircraft.

Asha had a window seat with Robert sitting next to him. Very comfortable seats with a lot of leg room.

After the plane took off, Asha was focused on looking outside, watching the Mumbai night skyline disappear as they made their way towards Singapore.

The cabin crew came round with drinks and Asha had a glass of French champagne for the first time and really liked it. But Robert had told Asha before to drink in moderation. So, Asha only had one glass of white wine with dinner. The Indian food was great. Asha felt so excited that he did not want to sleep.

"Asha, what do you think about flying?"

"I am lost for words. I know you tried to explain to me what it is like up in the air. But I still did not know what to expect. So, I am just trying to take in as much as possible. I could never have imagined what Mumbai would look like from such a height! The city glowed with all the sparkling lights."

"It is so new for you. You will get used to it the more you fly and become blasé about the experience. What has been the best part so far?"

"I am not sure. Probably the views. But, overall, the incredible experience. Here we are in a 'tube' moving through the skies over land and now over sea. Yet, it does not feel like we are moving!"

"Enjoy it."

They had to change planes in Singapore and the scheduled connecting time was about an hour. Their arrival was ahead of schedule and they were able to make their connection comfortably. Unfortunately, there was no time to look around at all the shops.

This was a daytime flight. But Asha managed to get some sleep after breakfast.

Sitting beside Asha encouraged Robert to review where he had been in recent times and, perhaps, more importantly, where he was going.

Inside Robert's head he felt like he was interviewing himself.

Robert, tell me briefly about your recent career?

I have been in Business and Information Technology for many years. But a few years ago, I left the relative safety of corporate life to set up my own company, specialising in strategic planning.

In my earlier job roles, I had made many senior contacts across the Asia Pacific Region, particularly in India. So, it seemed quite natural to look to India as the initial focus to generate business. It was not easy. But over time, I built up a solid client base, allowing me also to branch out into other parts of the region, including China and Singapore.

I just need to continue to keep an eye on the business, maintaining growth in the current areas and branching out where appropriate in a controlled manner.

And what does India mean for you?

India, particularly Mumbai, still remained the beacon of my business and I have put together a very solid team to develop business opportunities and deliver projects there with my support. That support has ranged from executive contacts to hands-on. Depending on the level of my activities, that has meant up to six visits per year accumulating up to fifteen weeks, which was a really major but worthwhile investment of my time.

Depending on the client location, I have stayed in different parts of Mumbai, from South Mumbai, or SOBO as the locals call it, referring to South Bombay, the previous name for Mumbai, to Andheri, near the airport, to Powai.

India fascinates me. It is full of idiosyncrasies and contradictions.

Indians have a language all of their own, which is called Hinglish. They will finish a sentence with the word "accordingly". They will use the term "do the needful," meaning they will do what is required. They will add in the word "surely" stressing a positive action. For shorts and sleeveless shirts, they will say half pant/half shirt. Just some of the words and expressions that amuse me.

Bollywood stars are idolised much more than Westerners. A cricketer is treated like a god.

There appears to be more attention paid by the government to launching a flight to Mars rather than dealing with critical human issues such as poverty, sanitation and the safety of women.

Is India a focused nation or just full of distractions? Perhaps the focus and distractions are the same!

Each morning in India I would read a newspaper over breakfast. One time, every day as the Ganesh festival was drawing near, there was an article about the number of potholes found and repaired. Was that significant news? Perhaps for some.

Robert, I understand that something significant and fateful happened to you on one of your visits to Mumbai.

First some background. In March 2001, I was doing some work with one of my clients whose office was in Navi Mumbai, which is a rapidly developing city, hence my decision to stay in Powai. Even then, the travel time between the hotel and the client was at least thirty minutes. The roads were generally bumper to bumper with traffic lined up five abreast on a three-lane road, accompanied by the constant noise of drivers honking their horns. I worked out that there was some system to the honking. While at traffic lights or in a queue, the message was I'm impatient, let's go. While driving along, the horn sound signalled I'm coming through, stay where you are.

I generally worked at the client's premises five days a week from nine thirty am to seven pm and in my hotel room on Saturday mornings between breakfast and lunch.

Then the significant and fateful event. One Saturday, after lunch, I decided to have a swim in the pool on the hotel's rooftop. But I had not packed my swimming trunks. So, I went out to the nearby shopping centre in search of trunks. I walked past one shop that seemed to sell trunks but it was busy. So, I wandered around to see if there were any other suitable shops but without luck. So, I went back to the original shop, not much choice but they had trunks that I felt were to my liking.

As I exited the shop, purchase in hand, I saw a young man hopping around on one leg, using a pole for support. He was weaving in and out of the crowd like an experienced skateboard rider. As he came near to me, I stood in his path and stopped his momentum. I can still see the look of surprise in his eyes as he looked up at me. I can also hear the conversation and visualise the walk back to my hotel. What was Asha thinking? More so, what was I doing?

Asha had confirmed that his right leg was affected by polio. In the lobby of my hotel, we talked at length about my suggestion to seek advice about an operation on his polio leg. Then, when his aunt and uncle arrived, more questions and answers. And, finally, Asha's telephone call to his parents. Everyone agreed to take the next step and I arranged an appointment with the specialist at the nearby hospital.

Why did you do this? Firstly, stop Asha and then offer to help him?

I was still feeling guilt and shame for how I had shown no empathy for the difficult situation a high school classmate of mine had found himself in decades previously? All I had seen was his external arrogance and constant whingeing. I was blind to how different he must have felt and his lack of self-esteem. Paul, I think that was his name, had polio. He wore a full-length calliper on his right leg and used crutches.

At that time, I was ignorant of the effects of polio on individuals and how widespread it was. How my understanding and attitudes have changed, fortunately for the better.

I did try to track down Paul many years later. I contacted the high school to see if they had a record of the students for that particular year but without success. I also put a notice in the local area newspaper with details of the circumstances about Paul and me but nobody came forward. Such a pity. I would have liked to have said sorry to Paul for how I had ignored him in his time of great need.

More recently, I googled 'Buckhaven High School students'. But no Paul!

In the late 1990s, I had provided support for Yung-Su, a young Korean, who was affected by polio. This had been an interesting experience full of challenges, with the accompanying highs and lows. Did I understand what had happened between Yung-Su and me that ended in not such a good way? Why would this be any different? I was not sure.

Wasn't it enough just to look after Andrew, my son, helping him manage his own disability and get on with his life? Not that he needed much looking after now.

After all, he is almost twenty years old. I had been a sort of absentee father for many years due to travelling a lot on business. After the death of his mother two years ago, even although I was still travelling a great deal, when I was in Sydney, I endeavoured to spend quality time with Andrew, which I really enjoyed.

But I had decided that I wanted to help Asha get a better life.

Robert, what happened then?

As they say, the rest is history. I took Asha to see a specialist who discussed how he would be able to straighten Asha's leg and then Asha would be able to be fitted with a full-length calliper and walk.

The procedure was successful. Asha got fitted with a full-length calliper and went back to life in Nagpur.

And that was it?

I stayed in touch with Asha and we met occasionally when I visited India. And that was as far as I thought things would go.

The original intent had been to help Asha with his well-being. In other words, enable him to throw away the pole and walk, albeit wearing a full-length calliper. That accomplished, what was the next step?

Asha is such a bright boy and I was not sure what the prospects would be like for him in India to attend university and then find a professional job. Bang! The light went on. Why not invite Asha to Sydney to attend university there?

It took a while, firstly to persuade Asha and his family about the benefits and then Asha had to get good scores in his Standard XII exams, followed by the processes related to immigration to Australia as well as enrolment in a university.

It was a difficult decision for Asha's family to let him go. I thought about how I would feel if the shoe was on the other foot and Andrew was moving to India. Not sure how I would handle it.

But Asha seemed to be taking everything in his stride. Perhaps, having the operation and getting the calliper was just the starting phase of a new Asha and he intended to grasp every opportunity with both hands.

I had discussed supporting Asha with Andrew. He was a little reticent at first, not wanting me to be let down in the way that he felt I had with Yung-Su. But, in the end, Andrew told me I had his full support.

Robert, that was about Asha. Any other thoughts on India in general?

Over the years, I had grown to like India, even with all its contradictions and challenges. At one end of the spectrum are the extremely poor and at the other end the fabulously wealthy. I guess that Asha and his family would fit somewhere in the middle.

Meeting Asha and his family had made me think more about the inequalities of life. They were making the most of what they had and seemed happy. But just a little help can improve the situation and that is what Asha is experiencing. I am not wealthy. But I am comfortably well off. So, why not help someone in need? Why would the Indian billionaires not do the same!? Perhaps, some are but more can and more needs to be done.

I'll get off my soapbox and focus on what I can do.

Robert, what does the future hold for Asha and yourself?

Well for Asha, it is pretty straightforward, with a focus on university. Whatever else happens is mainly in his hands. Hopefully, a great future awaits him.

As for me, I still have a business to run and an extended family to support.

Asha and his family are putting a lot of faith in me. I am determined not to let them down. This is another opportunity to help a young person develop to his full potential, offering a sense of purpose for me beyond immediate family and business.

I need to make sure that I am not too pushy with Asha. Learn from my mistakes with Yung-Su. Perhaps, Andrew could be a good monitor and mentor!

Well, that was an interesting conversation with myself. It certainly put things into perspective, showing a balance of business and family.

I turned to Asha and smiled. His face was beaming. I was still in a very reflective mode.

"Asha, I am very impressed with how you have matured since I first came across you nearly two years ago. Early on, you were introverted and introspective. You kept to yourself a lot, preferring to concentrate on your studies. But you are now more outgoing. Your confidence level and self-esteem have really moved on. These changes ought to stand you in good stead for what is ahead of you at university and life in Sydney.

I still remember you hopping towards me on that fateful day at the end of March 2001. Your back was bent. Your head, which was covered by a hoodie that was hiding your face, was bowed. That body language told everything. There was a man who was very insecure. Now Asha you walk straight backed with head held high. Such a positive image."

"Robert, I too have very vivid memories from that day in March up until now. I can also see the positive changes in me that provide a solid foundation for my future. But…"

"Asha, sorry to interrupt. Look! There is the Sydney Harbour Bridge and the Sydney Opera House."

"Wow! What incredible sights! This is going to be such a fantastic experience."

Soon afterwards, they landed and taxied to the terminal.

"Asha, we are now going to do the reverse of what we did at Mumbai airport: get off the plane, go through passport control, pick up our luggage and exit the customs hall. I hope Andrew is waiting for us. I am looking forward to seeing Andrew again and introducing him formally to you. My wish is for both of you to get on well together, just like brothers, at least in a positive sense."

"I am also looking forward to meeting Andrew in person and I also wish for a close relationship with him."

"OK. Let's go."

Chapter 8
Sydney

Andrew got to the airport around the scheduled arrival time for his Dad's and Asha's flight.

According to the arrivals board, they were due to come out of Exit C. So, Andrew positioned himself between C and D to give a vantage point of both ramps just in case they came out of Exit D.

Andrew had plenty of time to people watch, those waiting and those arriving. Some of those waiting had balloons with various messages such as "Welcome" or were holding a bunch of flowers. Andrew had neither. He was concerned that he would be too distracted watching those waiting and miss Dad and Asha. But it did not stop him watching.

There were a couple of other flights that had arrived before his Dad's flight. There were passengers streaming down the Exit C ramp. But Andrew could not tell which flight they were off. Then some flight crew came on the scene but they were not from the airline that his dad had travelled on. More watching, more people excited as they met the people they were waiting for. Hugs and kisses all round.

Andrew checked his mobile phone for any messages. None. Then, as he glanced up again, he could see his dad. Andrew waved frantically and Robert acknowledged the greeting. Asha came into view, pushing his wheelchair just behind Robert, who was guiding the luggage cart. Asha looked smart, shortish black hair, white shirt and dark trousers.

Andrew let them come past some of the crowd waiting. Then he had his chance for hugs. First Dad and then Asha.

"Asha, welcome to Sydney."

"Andrew, thank you. It is great to be here."

"OK. Let's go," Andrew beckoned. "The car is in the short-term car park."

Andrew led the way. He was using his crutches as he said that there was no room for his wheelchair and their entire luggage in his car.

"Asha, jump into the front seat." commanded Robert.

Andrew drove them to Robert's apartment in Rushcutters Bay. On the way, Robert pointed out the building in the distance where his apartment is on the twenty-fourth floor.

"This is the first time I have been in a car driven using hand controls. Very interesting."

"Well, Asha, you will need to learn to drive using hand controls as well. Put that on your bucket list." commented Andrew.

"What is a bucket list," enquired Asha. Robert explained it is a list of things you are particularly interested in doing.

Asha could not help comparing their journey to those he had experienced in India. Here, the cars kept to the lanes, there were no potholes and no honking. The trip took approximately thirty minutes and they got there around eight p.m., just as it was getting dark.

Robert had recently moved in there after purchasing two adjoining apartments and having them converted into one three-bedroom apartment, each bedroom with en-suite facilities. After his wife died, Robert had decided to sell their mansion in Double Bay.

Andrew was fair skinned, blond hair and with blue eyes, compared to Asha's brown skin, dark hair and brown eyes. He had already finished his first of six years studying medicine at the University of New South Wales.

Andrew and Asha had been communicating for a few months by email and telephone and had got to know each other pretty well. So, meeting face-to-face was easy. Asha also thought he knew Andrew very well as Robert had told him so much about his son.

As Asha entered the apartment, he could see Sydney Harbour. Asha made his way to one of the balconies and was immediately overwhelmed by the views of the Harbour Bridge and Opera House all the way to the Heads and Manly. Asha knew all about the harbour because Robert had given him a picture book about it. But Asha had not realised how beautiful it would be in real life. He was really awestruck.

Robert showed Asha his room and left his bags there. Then they went out onto the balcony which had ramps on both sides of the French doors to enable easy access by wheelchair. They sat there, having snacks and a glass of champagne, the latter being to welcome Asha and to celebrate his arrival.

"This is incredible," Asha proclaimed. "I cannot believe that I am in Sydney."

Andrew assured him that he was in Sydney, which is your new home. "Are you tired from the travel? How long did it take?"

"Not too tired. I managed to get some sleep on the last leg. Overall, it must have taken around fifteen or sixteen hours from the time we left Mumbai until we touched down in Sydney."

Then it was off to bed. Beforehand, Asha did a little unpacking, mainly his toiletries and the clothes he would wear in the morning.

Asha was so excited and could hardly sleep. He just wanted the morning to arrive and for the journey to continue.

Asha got up around seven a.m. and had a shower. When he wheeled himself out into the living area, Robert and Andrew were already in the kitchen preparing breakfast.

Asha was surprised to see Andrew standing without leg braces. Then Andrew took some plates and, using one walking stick, made his way a little unsteadily to the balcony where they were to have breakfast.

Robert had gone down to the nearby bakery for croissants which they enjoyed with coffee or tea, whatever the preference was. Asha's was tea.

Asha commented on Andrew's ability to walk unaided.

"Mum and Dad always encouraged me to exercise my legs as much as possible and use them without support, particularly at home. However, they are still getting weaker and I may not be able to do this for much longer. I do not know how strong your right leg is. Perhaps, you can try walking without your calliper."

Asha was a bit sceptical. But decided to give it a go. He wheeled himself back into his room and put his boots on. When he got back to the lounge, Robert said he would hold his hands while he tried to walk. The first step was very awkward and Asha almost fell. But, as he persevered, he got used to it. Now for the big challenge. Andrew gave Asha his stick. With the first step, Asha stumbled and Robert caught him. Erect again, Asha took another step forward and stumbled again. He decided that this was too difficult for his right leg to hold his weight, little as it was.

Robert congratulated Asha on a good try and went on to discuss the day ahead.

"What shall we do for Asha's first day in Sydney? It is such a beautiful day, clear skies and sunshine. We can't just stay here. We need to get out and about."

Asha did not have a clue and Andrew was non-committal. So, it was left to Robert.

"Let's not try to do too much," Robert suggested. "We'll go for a drive."

Breakfast finished, they all got ready and made their way to the car, Asha wearing his calliper and Andrew using his wheelchair. And all three of them wore shorts, something that Robert had suggested to Asha. He had become comfortable wearing shorts in India. So why not here?

They drove round the beaches of the Eastern suburbs, eventually ending up at Watson's Bay.

They went up to a place called The Gap, which is a cliff overlooking the ocean on the South Head peninsula. Andrew stayed at the bottom while Robert took Asha up to the top of the look out. It offered a great view out to sea and down to a whirlpool of water lashing against the rocks below. As Asha was to find out, The Gap has been notorious for suicides, enticing people to jump off the ledge into the dangerous rocky ocean. More security measures are now in place to try to prevent such actions. Very sad that some people want to end their lives so tragically.

That exercise had given Asha an appetite. Robert got them some takeaway and they sat in the park on the grass relaxing while sharing the fish, prawns and chips. Most delicious.

"Robert, this was a great idea, such a breathtaking location looking out towards the city with the Harbour Bridge in the distance," Asha proclaimed.

"Well, Asha, get used to it," Andrew commented. "We are on the most spectacular harbour in the world, at least in my opinion."

Robert brought Asha back to earth. "Asha, don't get too used to this. Remember you are here to study. So, don't get too distracted by everything around. Mind you, you will still be able to fit in some time for pleasure.

"Asha, I am happy that you have come to Sydney. Now, I feel that I have a little brother."

"Andrew, thank you. But less about the 'little'."

"OK brother."

Asha was very pleased about what Andrew had said. A great start to their relationship, Asha thought. We have different personalities. For example, Andrew is easy going and I am a little uptight. Yet, I think we will be able to have a very strong relationship.

Andrew was so welcoming and Asha felt at home immediately. It could have been so different if Andrew had been the jealous type and wanting to protect his territory.

When they got back to the apartment, they decided to go down to the apartment's pool for a swim. No calliper for Asha, just his wheelchair like Andrew.

There were only a couple of people there. So, there was no difficulty finding loungers. Robert was quick to undress down to his trunks and got in the water first, while Andrew and Asha took off their shorts and T-shirts before crawling over to the water's edge.

"Slow coaches!" Robert shouted.

Andrew and Asha got into the water which Asha thought was not too cold and they threw a ball around for a while. Then Andrew challenged Asha to a race — one lap of the pool freestyle. Andrew was too quick for Asha. Obviously, Asha felt he needed more practise.

They sat on the poolside lounge chairs and chatted away. They were out of the sun but the temperature was still good, being in the high twenty degrees Celsius. Asha noticed that Andrew's legs and feet were small like his right leg. But, at least, his legs were the same length.

This felt like heaven to Asha, such a beautiful place with friends. But Asha was missing his family a little. He gave them a call to let them know that he had arrived safely and had settled in well.

Asha's family was very happy to hear from him. But the call left Asha with a sweet and sour feeling, happy to hear their voices but a little homesick.

It made Asha think about the changes in his life from India to Australia. Because of polio, he had been physically challenged for most of his life. He had not liked the situation that he was in. Why me, Asha queried to himself? A very profound question. But no useful answer. And then he had met Robert. That meeting had changed his whole life for which he was very grateful.

So, he needed to make the most of the opportunities that he had been given. There were more challenges ahead. But he was sure, that with the support of Robert and Andrew, he would face up to them and do his best.

"Asha, how is your family?"

Robert's question brought Asha back into the land of the living with Andrew and Robert sitting there looking at him.

"They are all fine and asked me to pass on their regards to the two of you."

Asha did not want to talk about his family and India. So, he changed the subject.

"Andrew, you have a great body. How did you get into such fine shape?"

"For as long as I can remember I have gone swimming. And now I try to do laps every other day, either here or at uni. Currently, I am doing up to twenty laps per session. On the other alternate days, I do weights, at least during the uni break. There is a gym here. I'll take you there tomorrow. Then, of course, there is tennis."

After breakfast the following morning, Andrew took Asha down to the gym. As they entered, there were two walking machines, a bicycle and a rowing machine.

"Let's go into the weights room. OK, we'll start slowly. First, arm curls with dumb-bells, right arm, then left arm. Just try a few. Don't overdo it."

Asha did five on each side. Not too bad, he thought.

"Next the bench press. I'll put ten kilograms on each side for you. See how you go."

Asha lay down on the bench with his head facing up towards the bar. Andrew showed him where to put his hands and what to do. And then, a deep breath, and Asha took the bar off the rack, lowered it towards his chest and lifted it back up until his arms were locked. Asha did five before Andrew added another five kilograms on each end. Another five and done, at least for today.

Andrew had brought a notebook with him to record each set of exercises.

Andrew added more weight, bringing each side up to fifty kilograms. He did ten lifts before asking Asha to increase the weights to sixty kilograms, another ten lifts and finally ten more with seventy-five kilograms.

The final set of exercises was on a device that Andrew called a pec machine. Three sets with light weights for Asha and much more for Andrew and they were finished.

"Well, we have worked on arms, shoulders and chest. Good effort. Let's go up to the apartment and have a shower."

"Hi guys. How was that, Asha?"

"It was good. Andrew did not push me hard. But I was happy to get back in the gym, particularly with Andrew's support and coaching."

Asha had done some work in the hotel gyms in India where Robert stayed and that had helped with his physique. He was in pretty good shape and continuing with this would be beneficial.

Over the next few days, they did some more sightseeing together. Sometimes Elisa came along.

They went to Manly by ferry. Robert and Asha sat out on the front deck, which Robert told him was the bow. It was a beautiful sunny day. They left Circular Quay with the Harbour Bridge on the left and the Opera House on the right.

"Look up at the Bridge, Asha," Robert remarked. "There are groups of people climbing it."

"Yes, I can see them, just like ants. Have you climbed it?"

"No. But I would like to. Would you?"

"Looks a bit frightening to me. But I think well worth doing."

As they made their way, Robert pointed out some of the landmarks, including his apartment. The ride was pretty smooth until they passed the gap between North and South Heads when the swell rose and the ferry rolled from side to side. Not in a bad way. Like being rocked to sleep.

There was so much to take in and remember. It was there and then that Asha decided to keep a diary. But he had some catching up to do. First the trip from India. Then his first busy week in Sydney.

Thirty minutes after leaving the city, they were disembarking in Manly.

"Let's head towards the ocean beach," Robert commanded. "Then we will get some lunch and sit by the water."

They found a bench overlooking the sea, where they shared some prawns, fish and chips. Seems like a standard seaside diet.

Robert added to Asha's education. "Asha, do you remember your first full day in Sydney when we went for a drive? One of the beaches we drove past was Bondi. People say it is the most famous beach in Sydney, maybe Australia and even the world. Yet, particularly on weekends, lots of people make the trek to Manly by road and by ferry to swim or surf. As you can see, the sands stretch a very long way here."

"This is wonderful. Sun, sea and seafood. I never had seafood like this in India. So fresh and tasty."

After lunch, they went for a stroll along the boardwalk to Shelly Beach. They passed a sea pool on the way. Shelly Beach was a little sheltered sitting in a sort of cove. There were many people sunbathing, swimming, playing games and having a barbeque. Looked like a great way to spend a day with family and friends.

On another day, they went down to Hyde Park, the NSW Art Gallery then through the Botanical Gardens to the Opera House, Circular Quay and The Rocks.

At night, they went to different local restaurants for dinner. Such a variety. All with very good food, originating from different countries: China, France, Italy, Mexico, Spain, Vietnam and, of course, India.

But, on Sundays, they had a barbeque, cooked by Robert's fair hands on his balcony. Sometimes sausages, sometimes steak and sometimes seafood. Asha's preference was prawns, so succulent.

"Robert, you certainly make the most of having balconies overlooking the water, enjoying breakfast, lunch, dinner or a drink or just sitting and relaxing while the world passes by. I really like this aspect of Sydney life."

"I like being outdoors, particularly when the weather is fine."

Asha had really settled into Sydney. Early days yet. After all, he was merely a tourist at the moment.

The wheelchair tennis circuit started in Australia each January and Andrew was due to defend his titles in tournaments in Sydney and Melbourne. Asha had never seen wheelchair tennis before, never mind played it.

The Sydney tournament was first and Elisa, Robert and Asha went along to watch and cheer on Andrew on all three days. It was being held at the Sydney Olympic Park, the location for the very successful 2000 Sydney Olympic Games. A most impressive venue.

Robert had not been that interested in going to the Olympics. It seemed to be such a huge expense that could have funded other important government projects. It was going to disrupt daily life, particularly with road closures. On the positive side, however, it was going to put Sydney on the world stage with tourists pouring in as well as worldwide television coverage that would deliver much needed revenue.

Residents were being encouraged to leave the city if they were not going to any events. Robert took their advice. He watched the opening ceremony with Yung-Su from the comfort of his hotel room in Seoul. He stayed in Seoul for the first week of the Games. The Koreans were very happy with the outcome of some of the events, particularly archery where they won a number of medals.

As it turned out the Sydney Olympic Games were a success, with very little negative press. Well done Sydney. Well done Australia.

Robert took Andrew to a number of the Paralympic events, particularly swimming, athletics and, of course, tennis. All very enjoyable and well attended, providing fantastic support for the athletes showing off their talents

At that time, there were other Australian tennis players ranked higher than Andrew. So, Andrew had not been selected to represent his country in tennis. If he continues to get the results he is achieving, he stands a chance of going to Athens for the next Paralympics. Fingers crossed. That would be a very interesting experience.

Watching Andrew and other players gliding across the court in their specially designed tennis wheelchairs impressed Asha immediately. The only variation to the rules in wheelchair tennis is that the ball can bounce twice, the first bounce needing to be in play correctly.

They stayed in one of the hotels near the courts, where the players were also staying, instead of driving backwards and forwards each day.

On Saturday, the middle day, Robert took Asha to the nearby Rosehill racecourse. They had a great day out, dining in one of the restaurants in the members' area overlooking the winning post.

Andrew won the singles final in a tense three set match and he won the doubles final a little easier.

At the end of the tournament, Andrew let Asha borrow his tennis wheelchair and a racquet to find out what it was like. It was very strange at first, needing to push towards the ball, while preparing the racquet to hit the ball, Asha reflected. Andrew sat in his normal wheelchair and hit balls to either side of Asha, making him chase them. To begin with there were more misses than hits. After some time, Asha got used to it.

"Asha, how did that feel?"

"Difficult. When *you* play, you make it look pretty easy. But I enjoyed the experience and I think I will take it up if you have the time and patience to teach me."

"Great idea. I will help you. OK. Let's go. Dad and Elisa are waiting for us."

Asha was excited about taking up tennis. He liked sport and had not had a chance to play any cricket for a long time, never in Australia. So, tennis could be a good opportunity to play some sport.

"Robert, Andrew is going to teach me to play tennis. Isn't that great?"

"Sounds good to me. Perhaps, a doubles team in the making?"

"I wish. If Andrew can teach me to be half as good a player as him, I would be very happy. I'm hungry. What are the plans for dinner?"

In chorus, Andrew, Elisa and Robert responded, "You are always hungry."

That night Asha lay in bed thinking how much has changed in a couple of years and how lucky he is. He is no longer hopping around using a pole for support. He is much more mobile. He has moved 10,000 kilometres from his home country to a land of opportunity, the lucky country. He misses his family but has a second caring family to nurture him. And, hopefully, he has a bright future.

Chapter 9
Melbourne

Robert, Andrew, Elisa and Asha flew to Melbourne for the Australian Open, which is the first tennis Grand Slam of the year. The wheelchair tennis event was part of the overall tournament.

Asha was getting used to flying and really enjoying it. Although this time they were back in economy class.

Travelling to a tennis tournament meant that Andrew had a lot of baggage: personal bag, tennis gear as well as his tennis wheelchair, which Andrew had to take to the oversized luggage chute.

At security, the alarm sounded, announcing Asha's calliper, as he passed through the scanner. And then he had to be scanned by hand, just like in Mumbai.

For Andrew, it was a little more complicated. He had to have his whole body hand-scanned while sitting in his chair.

No dramas for either of them.

Then they made their way to the airline's lounge where they had a light lunch. In Asha's case, mushroom soup, some salad and orange juice.

They went down to the gate in plenty of time to allow Andrew to get assistance with boarding. He had to transfer from his wheelchair to a smaller and narrower airline chair to be able to navigate to his seat.

In Melbourne, the tournament organiser had arranged transport to the hotel for the players and their entourage. A big word for Asha. It sometimes surprised him what words he used.

It took around forty minutes to get to the hotel in a suburb called Albert Park. Robert told Asha that Albert Park is where the Australian leg of the Formula 1 Grand Prix circuit takes place, usually in late March. So, they are about two months too early!

Andrew had a room with Elisa while Robert and Asha had their own rooms in the hotel booked for the tournament. It was very well organised with sponsored cars taking the players and their entourage (that word again) to and from Melbourne Park where the tournament was taking place.

After they had checked in and dropped their luggage off, they took a taxi into the city, where they had dinner in an Italian restaurant. Asha really enjoyed the food. He had some pasta to begin with and then some fish.

The following day was a practice day. Robert, Elisa and Asha went with Andrew to the tennis centre. Andrew introduced them to some of the players before getting changed and making his way onto one of the outside courts with his long-time doubles partner Billy Wong.

The Melbourne tennis venue was much bigger than the one in Sydney in all respects, with greater crowd capacity and more courts.

Being at Melbourne Park brought back memories for Robert of the time he took Yung-Su there to play in this particular tournament. He remembered it being a very hot day.

Yung-Su had won his first-round match in the morning. It had rained a little in the morning. So, his match had been played indoors. But the weather had cleared up and Robert wanted him to get acclimatised to the Melbourne heat. So, he suggested that Yung-Su practise outdoors in the afternoon. His answer was "thinking about it". Robert was not amused. But he did not put any pressure on Yung-Su. Later, Yung-Su came back and reluctantly agreed to practise outdoors.

The hour arrived. It was three p.m. and thirty-five degrees Celsius. Yung-Su was not happy. But they practised for one hour.

Robert then went back to the hotel while Yung-Su watched some Koreans playing doubles.

When Yung-Su got back to the hotel, Robert let him into the room. Once in the room, Yung-Su moved towards Robert and pointed at him, saying, "All you do is push, push, push." Robert said that, if Yung-Su wanted to be a top tennis player, he needed to be pushed and to push himself hard.

Yung-Su ended up being runner-up in his Division of both singles and doubles.

That night was the draw for this Melbourne tournament. All the players and their guests assembled in one of the large meeting rooms, where there were snacks and drinks on offer. Andrew seemed happy with the draw.

The competition started the next day. Andrew's match was scheduled for eleven a.m. and he won it fairly comfortably.

As Asha watched some of the games, he looked around at the Melbourne skyline sitting under a cloudless blue sky with a large orange ball beaming down on them in thirty-plus degree Celsius temperatures. This could have been India!

Asha also had the opportunity to do some sightseeing, including riding a tram to St Kilda and visiting the National Gallery of Victoria as well as dining in some first-class restaurants. This had been a great experience and a very enjoyable week.

One night they went to Crown casino. This was the first time that Asha had ever been inside a casino. They entered the complex through a retail arcade, mainly clothes and restaurants. As they approached the casino itself, they were asked for identification. They passed the test as they were all over the age of eighteen. It was overwhelming at first. It looked like a huge cavern with many tables and lots of poker machines as Asha learned they were called. It was also pretty noisy.

Robert led them to one of the bars. He had been there many times and knew his way around. They collected their drinks and strolled through the casino until Andrew decided he wanted to play at one of the tables.

"Asha, this game is called blackjack," explained Andrew. "The object is to get the cards you are dealt closer to twenty-one than the dealer. Better still receive the first two cards as an Ace and a King, Queen, Jack or Ten. This is called blackjack. Watch and you will see."

Andrew found a spare chair and hopped up onto it. Robert took the seat next to him. Asha was excited for them. There were eight players around the table plus the croupier. Elisa explained to Asha this is the name given to the dealer. Bets were placed, cards dealt, winners and losers and on it went. After about thirty minutes, Andrew and Robert decided to call it quits. They still had chips, the token used instead of money, for the bets.

"How did you go?" inquired Asha.

"Fortunately, we both came out ahead and that is not what usually happens," Robert responded. This is called gaming, a euphemism for gambling. Or you can be even more positive and call it investing. Mind you, not all investments are successful either. Let's get another drink and then we can play the machines."

They found a poker machine that was not being used. Asha sat on the chair and Andrew pulled up his wheelchair beside him, with Robert and Elisa standing behind them. Andrew fed the machine a twenty-dollar note, pushed a few buttons and told Asha to hit the "start" button. He did and the wheels spun, apparently without success. They took it in turns to play. Then Elisa won fifteen free games. It was a great run building up their balance, even going well beyond Andrew's initial investment. Andrew said they would stop at fifty dollars, which they did. A good return for Andrew. But Asha had not really understood the game.

"Asha, what did you think about that?" Andrew asked.

"It was a good win for you. But it did not do much for me. Perhaps, I'm not a gambler!"

Then it was off back to the hotel.

Asha had very positive thoughts about Melbourne. Different to Sydney, being on the 'upside down' Yarra River as opposed to Sydney being on the harbour. But it seemed more together and organised, if that makes sense, with a number of parallel streets running up from the Yarra, crossed by a number of intersecting lanes and streets. Such an easy grid to understand.

Once again Andrew retained his singles' title. This time winning in straight sets. As in Sydney, he also won the men's doubles with Billy.

On the final night, there was a dinner for the players and guests in the hotel. Everyone was chatting away in a very friendly manner. The players had left their fighting spirits on the courts.

Asha asked Andrew why he was so good at wheelchair tennis. He said he was not really sure. But after some time reflecting, he said that, as a kid, he used to sit on the ground throwing balls at the garage door and trying to catch them. That probably helped with hand-eye coordination.

"Because I could not run like others my age, I would race them in my wheelchair. I would practise my quick push starts and then push as hard as I could to the finish line. So, that has helped with my speed across the court. Since the days I first started playing tennis, I have trained hard and practised and practised."

"Well, all that hard work has certainly paid off. Well done. You told me that you are ranked pretty high in singles. Do you think you can make it to number one?"

"No. I have been ranked in the top ten for some time now. But I will not make it to number one, partly because I do not play in enough tournaments. I play only in six or so tournaments because of my commitments at university."

"Andrew, that's a pity because you have the ability to be number one."

Robert then asked Asha what he thought of Melbourne.

"What I saw of it, I really liked. The wide streets, lots of trees, the trams. I had never seen trams before and I think it is a great way to travel around the city." The weather was great. It was warm and there had been no rain."

"We were lucky. Melbourne has a reputation for having four seasons in the one day," Robert commented.

"But it has been too short. Overall, I have thoroughly enjoyed my visit. Not to forget the tennis. Watching it has really confirmed my desire to play the game and play it well.

Andrew, congratulations on your successes."

They all raised their glasses, Andrew included, and toasted him.

"Thank you all for your support. It has been tremendous to have you all here. I don't always have my fan club touring with me."

Andrew was smiling as he said that. And they were all very happy.

Asha had been in Australia for around three weeks and he pinched myself to make sure that what he was experiencing was real. And it was. Asha was living his dream.

Chapter 10
Initiation

Asha was back in Sydney for the 26th of January, which coincidentally happens to be not only Australia Day but also India's Republic Day marking the date the Constitution of India came into force in 1950.

He watched the ferries racing up the harbour and back to the bridge with Andrew, Elisa and Robert from one of the apartment's balconies. The ferries were full of people and strewn with colourful banners and bunting.

Then Robert suggested they go down to Hyde Park to see some old cars on display. Asha was pretty impressed by the number and range of makes. It was a lovely sunny day, not too hot, just fine for wandering around.

At night, Robert took the three of them to an Indian restaurant overlooking Darling Harbour, a location near the city centre with shops, many restaurants and the end of the journey for the harbour's water. Home away from home for Asha, Indian food in a different Sydney restaurant.

Robert had booked this some time ago and they had a table on the balcony with a front row view.

As it got dark, a barge and some tall ships entered the area through the gap created by opening the swing bridge. They circled around giving all the spectators a good view.

"Look over there — the monorail," Andrew pointed out. "It does a small loop, taking in the edge of the city. It is a tourist attraction rather than a mode of transport from A to B."

Andrew and Elisa had been on the monorail but not Robert.

Robert ordered a bottle of wine and they all ordered the dishes they wanted from the set menu, which had a good selection of veg and non-veg dishes. Asha went for seafood as his main dish.

Just before nine o'clock the fireworks started. Initially, Asha was startled with the fireworks being so close, literally rising above their heads. Lots of colour and lots of noise. But then as soon as Asha got used to the spectacle, it was all over. The show had lasted for twenty minutes. But the smoke lingered much longer with no wind to blow it away.

"What an experience," Asha exclaimed, "It was mind blowing. And the food was great. Is all this really happening to me?"

"Yes, it is all real," Robert responded. "We do not do things in half measures in Sydney. Just wait until New Year's Eve. Time to go."

Robert had arranged for Andrew and Asha to rent a two-bedroom ground floor flat near the university. He had generously said that he would pay the rent. This was on top of the monthly allowance that he was giving to Andrew and Asha. Another huge help that was much appreciated.

They moved into the flat in the middle of February. It had a kitchen, a dining/living area, a good-sized bathroom with bath/shower, a toilet and laundry. At the back, there was a small patio and a garden. They were independent.

There was a small shopping centre nearby, with a pub and a couple of restaurants.

What more could two bachelor guys want? Girls, at least, for Asha. Once he had his calliper, he had gone out with a couple of girls in India but nothing too serious.

"Andrew, this is great. Such a comfortable apartment and a convenient location."

"I am happy with this as well."

Now that the start date for university was close, Asha was a little apprehensive about starting university. "How is a disabled Indian going to get on and be accepted?" Asha thought out loud.

Andrew assured Asha that he would be fine. "I did not have any problems and have built up a broad circle of friends. The university caters well for those with disabilities. It is also a multicultural campus. You will fit in well. It is normal to be uneasy about new things. Just relax and enjoy the experience".

The university term started with Orientation or 'O' Week in the last week of February. This turned out to be a fun week.

On the first night, there was an icebreaker where Asha was able to meet people from many parts of the world over some drinks and finger food. Andrew was right. The campus is very multicultural.

The next day, they went on a tour of the university. The university campus was huge. It had every service that a village would offer: post office, medical centre, library, banking facilities and a sports centre that included a swimming pool. There were retail shops as well as food and beverage outlets. And there were accommodation blocks. But no tennis courts. Asha got a map for future reference so he would be able to find his way around.

Then they were introduced to some of the teachers, who went through the programme for the term. Asha had four lectures and four tutorials scattered well across the week. Concepts would be introduced in lecture format and expanded in more detail during the tutorials. That left plenty of time to study.

In the middle of the week, they went surfing at a beach not too far from the campus. At first, Asha was not sure about going. But a couple of his new-found friends encouraged him and told him they would help if necessary. They suggested that Asha could just surf lying on a body board. Sounded interesting to Asha.

So, off they went by coach to the beach. Near the water, they got ready. Asha took off his calliper and then Scott, one of his friends, piggy-backed him and dropped him off in the water. Asha had never been piggy-backed before by anyone other than his family. Mind you, at forty-five kilograms, Asha was not very heavy. Another friend, Philippe, brought his and Asha's body boards along and they swam out from shore. He then helped Asha onto the board and they paddled and tried to catch a wave back to shore. Asha fell off a couple of times but finally got used to it. It was very refreshing, but tiring. Yet something Asha thought that he would like to do again.

"Hi, Asha. How was your day?" inquired Andrew when Asha arrived home.

"Great. I'm going to have a shower to get rid of the sand and saltwater. I'll tell you about it when I get back."

"Good. I'll look forward to that."

A short time later, Asha returned with his wet locks. "That feels better. I feel so refreshed."

They then sat around the table drinking beer while Asha told Andrew about his surfing adventure.

At the end of the week, there was the Welcoming Ceremony Cocktail party. This was another opportunity to get to know people better, talk about the week just gone and what they were looking forward to. In Asha's case, he just wanted to get stuck into learning and studying.

Asha also joined the Social Club, which was charged with organising various functions during the year.

As Andrew had suggested, there were no problems with him fitting in.

Asha developed a plan for the whole week under Andrew's guidance to schedule his classes and study periods as well as down time. While doing that, Asha thought about all the things he needed to do, the main one being study, and all the things he wanted to do: exercise, sport and socialising. On top of all that there was the diary that he wanted to keep a note of his activities and feelings. He had been pretty good at keeping it up to date so far.

Andrew had decided to stop the gym activities during term and only do lap swimming. Asha went the opposite way, deciding on the gym to, hopefully, build up his body.

When they had similar class times, Andrew and Asha would go to university together, Asha walking and Andrew pushing his wheelchair. It was only about 400 metres from their place to the front gate and the terrain was flat. Andrew preferred using his wheelchair to crutches. It meant that he did not have to wear his leg braces and use crutches. Also, using his wheelchair was good upper body "exercise" for tennis. Fortunately, the university was wheelchair friendly.

"Well, Asha, how was your first week?" Andrew asked.

It was Friday night and they had met up in one of the campus bars with some of Andrew's and Asha's classmates.

"I can't lie. It was pretty tough. The teachers have been very helpful and I have found some interesting classmates from various parts of the world. Hopefully, it will get a little easier as I get used to the routine."

And, as time wore on, it did get a little easier. Asha got involved in some strong teams to work on the assignments. And he developed a good balance between study and socialising.

Asha got on very well with one of the girls from the Social Club. Her name was Amy, who was in her first year of a five-year Economics/Law double degree. After a few months they started going out together for dinner or to movies. Occasionally, they would make up as a foursome with Elisa and Andrew. Elisa was studying Music and Music Education at the Sydney Conservatorium of Music.

Asha had also built up a healthy collection of acquaintances in addition to Scott from Toronto in Canada and Philippe from Copenhagen in Denmark, male and female. Some were from Asian countries, including a couple from India. He had made a pact with himself that he did not want to have just a clique of acquaintances from India.

These acquaintances had different things in common with him. Some liked spicy food. Some liked wine. Some liked movies but different styles: comedy, adventure and romantic. And some liked different kinds of sport. Of course, the Indians were mad about cricket.

One Friday night Asha went out drinking with some university friends.

"Good morning, Asha, or should I say, good afternoon. How do you feel?" Andrew belted out.

"Not good. I am very hung over. What happened last night?"

"Well, around ten o'clock last night, there was a knock at the door. Scott was carrying you. Apparently, you kind of passed out in the pub. Scott had bundled you into a taxi, brought you home, took off your clothes and calliper and tucked you into bed."

"I sort of remember bits of that but not too well."

"Aw well, we have all been in similar situations. Take it easy next time."

Andrew and Asha did little cooking in the flat. They would have breakfast at home. Lunch was whatever, wherever. And dinner was takeaway, delivery or down the pub. Then the treat was when they went over to Robert's for a proper dinner, which happened about once a week.

Andrew and Asha had settled into their flat. Because of the different class times, they did not really get in each other's way. However, it did become a bit of a traffic jam when they were both in and using their wheelchairs.

They were well set up with a television and music system, which occasionally led to discussions about what to watch and what to listen to. But most of the time they were in sync, some documentaries, sport and crime (that is watching it) on television and contemporary pop and rock music.

They were really comfortable in their place and together.

One Saturday morning, Andrew was lying on his bed doing his leg exercises.

"Asha, are you awake?"

"Yes, Andrew, come in. Good timing. Can you help me with one of my exercises by lifting up the bottom part of my right leg until it is vertical?"

"Sure. Let's get going then."

After Asha's usual struggle to control his leg while it wobbled in its upright position a few times, he said enough.

"Well done. Good effort. Dad suggested the same exercise to me as well as the other ones, but I am too lazy to bother. But don't let me deter you.

I've had my shower and am going down to the bakery to get croissants for breakfast. Is that fine? Also, let me know any time you want help with this exercise."

"Great. I'll shower now and get the coffee going in time for your return."

"OK. See you in fifteen minutes. You'll better get a move on."

Asha did get a move on. The coffee was brewing and the table set just before Andrew returned.

"Good, you are ready and coffee is on the go. Here are the croissants, lovely and crispy on the outside."

It got a bit more crowded when Elisa and/or Amy came round. Separate rooms or areas of the flat per couple when they were not all chatting away together, watching television or dining. Yet, somehow it usually worked out well.

Both Andrew and Elisa were very strong-minded characters and very confident. Whereas Amy and Asha were more mellow but would still stand their ground when it was important.

One night, Amy and Asha were watching television when Andrew and Elisa returned from a movie. Immediately, Elisa started telling them about the film and what they had missed, oblivious to their interest in the programme they were watching. Then, when Andrew came back from the toilet, he did the same, raving about how good the movie had been. By this time, Asha was getting somewhat annoyed and asked them to be quiet, telling them how involved they were in this drama series. That was it. Wheelchairs and handbags at ten paces.

"Don't talk to us like that," Andrew roared at Asha. "We were just being sociable and sharing our enjoyment."

"That's fine. We were enjoying this programme before we were rudely interrupted."

"If that's how you feel, I'm going to bed. Come on, Elisa. Goodnight."

By that time their interest in the programme had waned. Distractedly, they watched the programme through to the end and then Amy and Asha talked about what had happened. Had they behaved wrongly? Anyway, it did not matter, at least for the time being. Amy went back to her apartment and Asha went to bed.

Asha always felt that Andrew was a little selfish. He generally wanted to get his own way. Was that a product of being an only child, brought up in comfortable surroundings?

Andrew was the planner, the main decision maker, which made life easy for Asha as long as that was the path that he wanted to follow. Whether at home or travelling, they occasionally argued about where to go and what to do. Asha would only dig his toes in if he was totally against the idea and his priority was elsewhere. But they never got physical with each other, just verbal.

On the occasional Friday nights, Philippe, Scott and Asha would go out for a drink and some dinner. They were both interesting people, thought Asha.

Scott was studying for a Bachelor of Business degree. He said that there are a lot of similarities between Sydney and Toronto, big metropolitan cities centred on the arts and sport. But, one huge difference was that Toronto got extremely cold in winter.

Philippe was studying for a Bachelor of Arts degree. He liked being near the sea in Sydney just like Copenhagen. But he did not like being isolated from the rest of the world as he described it. Copenhagen is close to many countries in continental Europe, whereas Sydney is so much more remote.

They were both intent on making the most of their time in Australia.

Saturday was the day for chores around the flat, food shopping and tennis.

Andrew had already joined a tennis club, which was not far from the flat. So, Asha joined as well.

Andrew had an old tennis wheelchair that, fortunately, was a good fit for Asha. He also gave Asha one of his tennis racquets. Andrew had a number of racquets through a sponsorship deal with a sports manufacturer. So, Asha was well set up to try his hand at the sport.

Initially, Andrew showed Asha the basics of the game. How to move around, how to prepare to hit the ball and then how to place the ball. At the end of each session, they would do hit ups, with Andrew taking it very easy. Asha got good practice that way. But it did not do much for Andrew's game. He got his challenges through playing with able-bodied players.

They practised twice a week. Sometimes they played doubles against able-bodied players. It was hard but good fun at the same time.

They were both well accepted by the club. The clubhouse facilities were good and wheelchair accessible. They had a good dining room and bar as well. A good place to socialise.

The first term was finished and Asha was very happy with how it had gone.

Asha's tennis was improving and now it was time to put all that tennis practice to good use in tournaments. First cab off the rank was a trip to Japan and South Korea with Andrew for two weeks.

Just before they left, Asha spent time with Robert on his balcony talking about a bunch of things. How were things going with Andrew? How was Asha's tennis game? Spending much time with Amy? It was like twenty questions. But the main topic was university.

"Well Asha, the first term is out of the way. How did it go?"

"Robert, as I told you before, initially it was a bit of a challenge. But I put my head down and, with some help and encouragement from Andrew, it seems to have worked out. All the assignments went well. And I am confident that I will get good results from the end of term exams."

"That's good news. Now for your next challenge, tennis. Fortunately, Andrew is a very experienced traveller. So, you are in very good hands. Enjoy the trip and do your best."

"Thank you. I know Andrew will take care of me. I am really looking forward to experiencing two more countries."

Asha could understand where Robert was coming from. He just wanted to make sure that everything was fine with Asha and that, if he needed advice, be sure to call on him.

"Asha, before you go overseas, don't you think you need a haircut?" Robert suggested.

"I think you are right. It is getting pretty long and untidy."

"I'll take you downstairs to the hair salon where I get my hair cut."

"I have never been to a hair salon before."

"It is also referred to as a barber's shop."

"I've never been to one of them either. My father always cut my hair as well as my brother's."

"I used to take Yung-Su to the same place. He was always interesting with his hair. I never knew what colour it would be when he came to Sydney. One time, his hair was electric blue. But he decided he wanted to get rid of that colour and return to his more normal black.

When I took him downstairs and told Ernie what Yung-Su wanted to do, he was a bit dubious if it would work. Anyway, Yung-Su and Ernie agreed to give it a go and see what happened. Well, the hair colour did change, not to black but yellow. Yung-Su was certainly going to stand out for some time. Eventually, all the product washed out and his natural colour was restored. But not for too long. He continued to experiment with different colouring and styling."

"Robert, what colour do you think would suit me?"

"I think you ought to stick with black."

Chapter 11
Asia

Robert drove Andrew and Asha to the airport. He parked the car, unloaded the pile of luggage, with him carrying the bags and Andrew and Asha pushing their tennis wheelchairs.

At check-in, Andrew and Asha had to take their tennis wheelchairs to the oversized luggage chute. It was Asha's turn to get used to the process.
Robert said goodbye to them.

"Safe travels. Enjoy the trip and see you in a couple of weeks. As I said before, I'll pick you up on your return."

"Bye," Asha replied.

"See you later, Dad."

Normal procedure going through security and then they made their way to the airline lounge. Andrew, being a frequent flyer, had the right status to get them both into the lounge.

They had some time to wait before boarding, early boarding for Andrew. They had some snacks and sat around chatting.

"Asha, another adventure coming up for you. I am sure you are looking forward to it. Your first tennis tournament."

"Yes, definitely. I've decided that I really like travelling. New places and new people. And, I am very keen to see how I perform in the tournaments."

"I have travelled so much with my parents and for tennis that I have become a little blasé about the whole thing. But I still enjoy it. It is not so much about sitting in a plane. It can be a bit boring and a lot of the sameness, particularly in economy. I try to pass the time watching a movie or just reading."

The flights from Mumbai to Sydney were all new experiences for Asha and the time seemed to pass quickly, particularly as he had slept for some time after Singapore. This might be a little different as it is no longer a novelty. If there is a movie Asha liked the look of, he thought he would watch it.

Surprisingly the first leg seemed to pass quickly. Then they had to change planes in Tokyo with a transit time of over two hours. That was when it started to become a little boring. They did some window shopping in the terminal concourse to kill time. Finally, they boarded their plane bound for Fukuoka another two hours away.

In the hotel at Fukuoka, while they were waiting for the draws for the tournament to start, a young man wheeled up to Andrew and Asha.

"Hi, my name is Lee, Yung-Su. Andrew, I recognised you from photographs your father showed me. How are you?"

"I am fine. Excuse me. I need to get a drink."

Then Andrew wheeled away, leaving Asha with Yung-Su.

Yung-Su and Asha chatted while the draws were taking place. Yung-Su's English was not the best but they were able to understand each other, albeit with some difficulty.

Yung-Su asked about Robert and how he was doing. He did not seem to show any bitterness about the fall out with Robert.

Yung-Su was a little older than Asha and was studying Education at Daegu University. Apparently, he was also a very good wheelchair basketball player and had already represented Korea in both tennis and basketball.

Once the draws were finished, Asha said good night to Yung-Su and went off in search of Andrew.

"What happened back there with Yung-Su?"

"I was surprised to see him and I felt a little uncomfortable. I'll be fine with him the next time we meet."

Yung-Su got through to the semi-finals of the main draw singles before losing to another Korean, whom Andrew beat in the final. Asha played "B" grade, which is two levels below the main draw, in what was his first tournament and was pleased with his performance as well as surprised at getting to the semi-finals.

They had one day to spare between the end of the tournament and their travel to Daegu in South Korea. So, Andrew, Yung-Su and Asha went sightseeing. Their timing was impeccable as it coincided with the cherry blossom season. One of the Japanese organisers offered to drive the three of them to one of the parks renowned for cherry blossoms.

What a wondrous sight of a forest of trees coated in pinkish flowers. They wandered down paths through tunnels covered in the fresh blossoms. It was a lovely sunny day, making the experience that much more memorable.

Then off to Daegu.

The Daegu tournament organisers had arranged a coach to pick them up from the Busan ferry terminal with a number of other players.

So, they all boarded the fast ferry for their three-hour journey. It was comfortable and relaxing. A good alternative to flying. Then another hour of road travel and they were at their hotel.

"Andrew, we have travelled by car, plane and ferry," Asha pointed out. "What about going to Seoul by train? Only joking."

Yung-Su had overheard Asha's comment.

"There is a bullet train between Daegu and Seoul. I have been on it a couple of times and it is accessible for wheelchair users."

"Sounds like a good idea. But, with all our luggage, it would be a bit of a hassle as we would then need to get out to Incheon airport," Andrew said.

"Good thinking."

They spent a lot of time with Yung-Su. Andrew was now fine in Yung-Su's company.

Yung-Su took a taxi to his home on campus and drove his car back to pick Andrew and Asha up. He had changed out of his wheelchair and into his leg braces plus crutches. This made it easier for them all to fit into his car, with plenty of room for Andrew's wheelchair. Asha understood the logic but was surprised that Yung-Su had ditched his wheelchair, based on what Robert had told him about Yung-Su's mobility preference.

Yung-Su took them for a drive around the city and the nearby hilly and green countryside out to the main Geongsan Campus of Daegu University, which was less that a one-hour drive from the city centre. Andrew and Asha enjoyed the scenery and voiced their appreciation to Yung-Su for the tour.

The first night they were in Daegu, Yung-Su introduced them to Korean food. The main dish was barbequed eel with various accompaniments. Very tasty. They also sampled the local liquor, *soju*, distilled from rice and quite similar to vodka. At first, Asha thought it was a little strong. But he got used to it and ended up liking it.

Yung-Su did better in the main draw singles, losing to Andrew in the final. Miraculously, Asha won the B-grade competition. The coaching and encouragement by Andrew had paid off. Or was it the extra kick from the *soju*?

Asha's first trip to North Asia had been most enjoyable, helped by the tennis success in Daegu. However, meeting Yung-Su was particularly good and he got on so well with him.

Andrew and Asha took the coach, which the tournament organisers had arranged, to the airport. Before leaving, they said their goodbyes to Yung-Su and Asha vowed to stay in touch.

They caught a flight to Seoul and then a connecting direct flight to Sydney.

"Well, Asha, you did very well in the tournaments you played. You are making good progress. When we get back to Sydney, we will keep practising and training together. Watching you, I noticed a couple of areas that need improving. So, we will work on them."

"Thank you, Andrew. I thoroughly enjoyed both competitions, particularly the second one. And, I do want to get better. I will work hard under your guidance."

"Another two victories for you. What's next?"

"There are tournaments in England and France during the next term break and I'll aim to play in both of them. Are you going to come along as well?"

"That would be great. Are you pleased that you met Yung-Su and spent time with him?"

"Very much so. Although I was apprehensive initially because of his falling-out with my father. I got a chance to see how he is first hand. So, no regrets for me. What happened is between him and my father."

When they got back to Sydney, they told Robert that they had met Yung-Su who was asking how he was. Robert also asked how Yung-Su was. And that was about it in terms of the conversation about Yung-Su. Asha thought that Robert probably realised that they would come across Yung-Su. So, he was not surprised but did not feel like discussing it further.

However, later on, during one of Asha's times together with Robert on his balcony, Robert opened up about Yung-Su. Robert had been so intent on helping someone with polio to aspire to their potential whether that related to education, sport or life in general. But Robert felt it had not quite worked out with Yung-Su. There was the language difficulty and the tyranny of distance. Robert had felt that, if he had been able to be closer to Yung-Su and spend more time with him, things might have turned out for the better. These days they stayed in touch by telephone but did not see much of each other.

Chapter 12
Yung-Su

Robert began describing to Asha the background on Yung-Su and how their time together evolved. "As I told you and your family previously, in my last year of high school, there was a fellow classmate who had polio. I think his name was Paul. However, his arrogant and negative attitude did not endear him to me nor to his other classmates. Perhaps, he was crying out for help but nobody was willing to listen. Least of all me.

"There was another experience that I did not tell you about. A teenager played football (soccer) with us, wearing one below the knee calliper and one full-length calliper. He tried very hard to run and kick the ball. Great effort. But and there is always a but, his brother and he were bullies and people avoided them whenever possible. I never really thought about these situations until much later in life.

"In early 1998, I decided I wanted to give something back to the world. This may seem odd as I was already caring for my disabled son. But, somehow, that was not enough to assuage my guilt.

"I chose to help young men with polio. Pretty altruistic. But, at the same time a little selfish. In particular, I was feeling guilty that I had shown no empathy to people with polio over thirty years previously and had done nothing to help Paul. I wonder what happened to him. In some way, it was also an effort to recognise all the support that had been given to Andrew by many other people.

"So, off I went searching the Web, trying to find a teenager with polio whom I could help by providing some financial support and encouragement to do his best scholastically and in sport.

"It turned out to be more difficult than I thought it would be, coming up empty search after search. And then I stumbled on a rehabilitation centre outside Seoul in South Korea. I telephoned the centre and spoke to one of their directors. He said that they only had one teenage boy with polio, whose name was Yung-Su. Everyone else suffered from cerebral palsy.

"Yung-Su was seventeen years old and had contracted polio at the age of seven years. Yung-Su came from a poor farming family. He had a mother, father and three older brothers.

"About one year after he contracted polio, Yung-Su was moved to the rehabilitation centre in Seoul because his family could not look after him properly. From time to time, his family visited him and they also had him spend time at the farm with them.

"However, to all intents and purposes, he was raised by the people at the centre. This ensured he was treated properly for polio. But it did not give him the true family surroundings.

"Both his legs as well as his stomach muscles were affected. He could walk wearing leg braces and using crutches. But he preferred to ride his wheelchair. Mind you, later on, his favourite mode of transport became a car. Sitting behind the wheel masked his disability.

"I started communicating with Yung-Su by fax and telephone through an interpreter at the centre as his English was not very good and my Korean (Hangul) was non-existent.

"A couple of months later, I found out about a junior wheelchair tennis camp in San Diego. Yung-Su's profile stated that he played wheelchair tennis (and wheelchair basketball). I asked him if he wanted to go to the tennis camp and he said yes. This was either extreme naivety or unbounded trust on his part.

"There was one hiccough that almost caused the trip to be cancelled. When Yung-Su applied for a visa, one of his answers suggested that he did not plan to return to Korea. As a result, his application was declined. I got in touch with one of the organisers who got an influential senator in the USA involved. His interjection managed to turn things around and Yung-Su was granted a visa. Whew!

"I met Yung-Su for the first time the day before we flew out of Seoul bound for San Diego. The Director and a social worker from the centre met me in the hotel lobby and we sat down to wait for Yung-Su. It was not too long before he wheeled himself up to our table, looking very nervous and shy. One of his teachers was with him. Yung-Su was encouraged to sit with me, which he did with some reluctance.

"The director, teacher and social worker took Yung-Su and me to a Korean restaurant. When we got to the restaurant, we were confronted with a long flight of stairs. Yung-Su was wearing his leg braces and using crutches. Even after allowing Andrew to do as much on his own as he could, allowing him his independence, for some reason, I wanted to help Yung-Su. I offered to carry him up the stairs. Yung-Su ignored my pleas as he climbed the stairs step by step, putting two crutches up onto the next step and then jumping up. It looked so much like hard work.

"When we got to the private room, we had to take off our shoes (Korean tradition). Yung-Su was not excluded from that. After taking off his shoes, he slid on his bottom over to the low table where we all sat on mats and had a delicious lunch.

"When we got to the top of the stairs to leave, I obviously had not learned from my earlier experience and wanted to carry Yung-Su down. Off he went on his own, with the only concession being him giving me one crutch so he could hold onto the handrail with one hand, put the crutch in the other hand on the next step and jump.

"Meanwhile the other three were just going along on their own way and allowing Yung-Su his independence.

"Back in the hotel room, Yung-Su took off his leg braces. But he hid his legs under the bed covers. He seemed to be ashamed of his legs because they were small. I told him that his legs were fine by me and he took them out from under the covers.

"This concern about the size of his legs continued for a long time. On other occasions, when room service was delivered in our hotel, Yung-Su, sitting on the sofa in shorts, would cover up his legs so that the delivery person could not see them. And yet, he would play tennis (and basketball) in shorts.

"The same behaviour applied when swimming. He was not comfortable going swimming with me in public. He felt that he stood out and people looked at him as an item of curiosity. He did not like people looking at his small legs. Yet, when he went swimming with the other (disabled) tennis players, he lapped it up. He felt at ease among his peers and was just part of the crowd.

"Quite a conundrum.

"To me, this just demonstrated that it did not matter when other disabled people were around. Yet, if it was just him and me, he was exposed and his lack of self-esteem took over.

"I do not think that Andrew was ever self-conscious about his legs and his disability.

"Asha, what about you?"

"Robert, when I was pole-hopping I was very self-conscious. That was one of the reasons I kept looking down because I did not want to see people staring at me. But now I do not have a problem. I am proud to be able to walk wearing a calliper. And I do not mind showing off my polio leg. Anyway, I now realise that it does not matter what other people think as long as I feel good about myself, which I do."

"That's great, Asha. OK. Let's get back to Yung-Su."

"The following day, we took off on a long journey: Seoul, Vancouver, Los Angeles and San Diego.

"As I knew from my experiences with Andrew, it is different travelling with someone with a disability. At times, special courtesies are offered and at other times not.

"Going through immigration at Seoul airport, there was a special gate for diplomats and the disabled. Does that put diplomats in their place!? Anyway, that saved long queues.

"Once, when I used that special gate with another disabled person in tow, the official said to me, "Why are you here? You are a manager." I then pointed to the person, sitting in his wheelchair, and we were processed. Perhaps managers are not allowed to be disabled!

"Yung-Su and I settled down on the plane in business class. Yung-Su did not eat much. He was more interested in the movies, music and electronic games. When he wanted to go to the toilet, he locked his leg braces in place and walked, holding onto my hands that I placed behind my back.

"When Yung-Su and myself got to Vancouver, the airline personnel ushered us through the corridors to a special baggage carousel and then to our connecting gate for the flight to Los Angeles. Great service.

"In Los Angeles, the service from a different airline was not as good. When we checked in, we were not seated together and they were too busy to change it. However, we did get escorted separately to the tarmac and our aircraft. On board, we sat together and nobody asked me to move.

"When we boarded, I had to give Yung-Su's wheelchair and crutches to the staff to put in the commuter airline's hold. In San Diego, they would not let Yung-Su have the wheelchair at the bottom of the stairs of the aircraft. He had to walk to the terminal entrance to get it. How bureaucratic and thoughtless?

"Sometimes people are helpful, sometimes not.

"We were met by Mitch the co-organiser of the camp and a lady and we made our way into his van for the drive to the hotel. This was my first experience of being in a vehicle driven by a disabled person using hand controls. Mitch had been injured in a car accident. By the way he was driving this time, it appeared to me that he had not learned to drive more carefully.

"Through Andrew playing, I knew about wheelchair tennis and knew how to recognise talent. Even with that background, I was not prepared for what was going to happen with Yung-Su. From the time Yung-Su hit the first tennis ball, it was clear he could play tennis well. My impressions got better day by day, supported by very positive feedback from the instructors about his ability and speed.

"He was also a bit of a celebrity, having travelled so far.

"On the last day of the camp, Yung-Su teamed up with an able-bodied player in a doubles match against one of the instructors (highly ranked wheelchair tennis player) and another able-bodied player. Yung-Su's team won. More star status for him.

"The only problem I had with Yung-Su was that he was not eating very well, missing Korean food. I spoke to the director from the centre about this and he told Yung-Su if you don't eat you will die. Perhaps a bit dramatic. But it worked. Things improved a little after that.

"I asked Yung-Su if he wanted to make a career out of playing wheelchair tennis and he said yes. I am not sure if he really understood me.

"Next stop was Disneyland. We flew up to Los Angeles and took a fairly lengthy and expensive taxi journey to our motel in Anaheim.

"When we got inside Disneyland, Yung-Su did not seem too enthused, showing little interest in the rides.

Having been there before, I had thought that some of the simple rides would have been good for Yung-Su. Unfortunately, not. I tried and tried to encourage him to go on a ride. But there was no change in his mood.

"As the morning wore on and the park became more crowded, it was clear that this was not to Yung-Su's liking. I guess that when you are in a wheelchair, sitting at bum level in a crowd of people, it is not the most comfortable place to be. So, back to the motel.

"There were things for us to do at the motel, including playing tennis and pool. Yung-Su turned out to be not a bad pool player.

"One night when we got back to the room, Yung-Su went to the bathroom and spent a fair amount of time there, giving me some cause for concern. Nothing to worry about. Yung-Su was merely preparing my birthday present, which consisted of a card and T-shirt. What a wonderful surprise. I wore that T-shirt, on and off, for many years and never wanted to discard it. However, when there were more holes than material, it was time for it to go.

"Yung-Su was still suffering withdrawal symptoms, not having had any Korean food for a few days. I promised him that I would find a Korean restaurant in San Francisco, our next port of call.

"When we checked into our hotel on Union Square, our room was not ready. So, I decided we would take a cable car down to Fisherman's Wharf. We had a wander around enjoying the atmosphere, before making our way back to the hotel and then out to dinner at a Korean restaurant. The food was great, making Yung-Su very happy.

"The following day we went shopping, buying, amongst other things, a tennis racquet. As we left the store, the security alarm went off. We were assured that we were fine and allowed to go on our way. When we got back to the hotel, we found that the security tag was still attached to the racquet. It was a very difficult job to separate the two but perseverance won out.

"That night we went to China Town and had a most enjoyable dinner in a Chinese restaurant where I had eaten previously. A creature of habit.

"Our last stop was north of the border in Vancouver. I had arranged for a stretch limo to pick us up at the airport. Yung-Su liked that.

"Then our trip was nearing an end as we flew back to Seoul.

"This had been a good time together for us. Two relative strangers growing more comfortable in each other's company and becoming friends.

So, Asha," Robert ended, "that was my initial introduction to Yung-Su."

The story fascinated Asha. Different ages, different abilities, different languages, different cultures. In many ways, it was a similar to the relationship between Robert and himself.

"With my background with Andrew," Robert added, "I thought I was conditioned to spending time with a disabled person like Yung-Su. Before I left, Andrew and I had discussed what to expect, particularly around tennis.

"Language apart, the hardest thing for me to accept was his discomfort with the size of his legs (and his overall disability) in public away from other disabled people. That had never been a problem with Andrew. And they are both in very similar situations. I guess everyone deals with what they have in their own way."

Asha asked Robert what had changed with him and Yung-Su.

"I am neither a psychologist nor psychiatrist. But this is my interpretation.

"Yung-Su spent most of his time growing up with other people who had a disability and had to use a wheelchair or crutches. This became Yung-Su's comfort zone, particularly riding in a wheelchair.

"Then I came along and tried to get him to do more walking and to feel good about doing this in public. This was not me being bloody-minded.

"Before he left the centre, he was given details of the exercises he had to do to prevent him developing sclerosis. The main points were to stretch his back and spine. Asha, some of the exercises I showed you came from trying to help Yung-Su. There were others that specifically related to manipulating the spine. Walking was another way of stimulating the spine, instead of sitting down all day.

"In the end, Yung-Su chose the wheelchair over walking — no compromise. As for the exercises, I suspect they also went by the wayside. Although I remember one time when we were talking on the phone and I asked him about exercising. His response was yes. I crawled from the bed to my wheelchair this morning.

"Of course, Yung-Su had every right to choose. After all, Andrew had made the same choice but the circumstances were different. There was no medical requirement for Andrew to work on his back.

"This was one of the factors that led to us going our own ways. I felt I could no longer help him. I had set out to improve the quality of Yung-Su's life: education, sport and general welfare. I had a plan but Yung-Su had a different plan or maybe no plan at all.

"Perhaps, Yung-Su was right. All I did was push, push, push. Push what I wanted Yung-Su to do.

In the end, it did not work. Just two stubborn fools!

I am back again but only at the end of a telephone, that may not be enough."

"Well, I think you tried your best," Asha summed up. "At least you are still in touch."

Chapter 13
Europe

Up until this year, Asha had never been outside India, not even outside Maharashtra. Now he had moved to Australia, had been to Japan and South Korea and now more international experience ahead. Am I still dreaming, questioned Asha?

By the time they got to England a couple of months later, for the British Open, Asha's ranking allowed him to play in the second draw, one down from the main draw that Andrew would play in. This would be a little more difficult for Asha. However, he progressed through to the semi-finals, losing in three tight sets. Yet he was happy with his performance. Importantly, Andrew won the main draw singles.

Andrew had been a huge help in the development of Asha's tennis, spending time coaching him while he continued to work on his own game. The investment seemed to be paying off.

"Asha, well done. Your game is developing in the right direction."

"Thank you. I enjoyed it. Another winning tournament for you out of the way. Well done. Now for some sightseeing in London. I'm looking forward to it."

"Me too. I've never been to London before. Mum and Dad lived there for a while before moving to Australia. They told me a lot about the city. But they have not been back for a number of years and things will have changed. So, another new set of experiences for both of us."

The tournament had been in Nottingham about 200 kilometres north of London. They had hired a car at London Heathrow airport after the flight from Sydney and were now driving back to London to spend a couple of days there. They dropped the car off at the rental place and took a cab to their hotel in Chelsea, an affluent suburb which is less than five kilometres to the west of Central London.

Travelling, for Andrew in particular, had its challenges. He had a large bag for his clothes and other things he needed, his tennis bag and tennis wheelchair as well as his day wheelchair. He did not travel with his crutches and had stopped using his walking stick. But he was used to all that, being a very experienced traveller. Nothing seemed to faze him.

Asha did not travel with his day wheelchair, just his suitcase, tennis bag and tennis wheelchair. But still enough to bother about. Asha would hop to and from the bathroom in the hotel and to and from the showers at the tennis or use his tennis wheelchair.

So, there was a lot to fit into the cab, in this case a maxi taxi that was wheelchair accessible.

Robert had told Asha a lot about Chelsea, the football team he supported. When he lived in London, he had gone to many of their games and had continued to follow them from afar. Football had not really been one of Asha's sports nor that of Andrew. So, they did not bother about making a trip to see Chelsea's Stamford Bridge stadium.

Their hotel was near a tube station with wheelchair access that they could use to get to suitably accessible stations in Central London. On the first afternoon, they took a tube from Fulham Broadway to Westminster, made their way up to Trafalgar Square and Nelson's Column back to 10 Downing Street, through Horse Guards Parade down The Mall to Buckingham Palace and back to Westminster Abbey, the Houses of Parliament and Big Ben before making their way along the Thames Embankment back to their hotel. Now that was a good work out for both of us, Asha thought to himself with Asha walking and Andrew pushing. Walking distances did not seem to bother Asha. All that hopping around over the years had strengthened his left leg. But the occasional rest was still necessary.

On the second day, they took the same tube ride and went down to the Thames Embankment to take a boat trip to Greenwich. It was a different way to see the city, another view of the Houses of Parliament, The London Eye, Somerset House, St Paul's Cathedral, the Tate Modern, the Monument and the Tower of London to name a few.

Greenwich is the domain of Greenwich Mean Time and the Meridian Line as well as landmarks such as the Cutty Sark, the National Maritime Museum and the Royal Observatory. Greenwich is the place where all time zones are measured from.

They had lunch and then wandered around the various sites, which were very interesting.

For the return journey, they took the Docklands Light Railway to Bank station. This gave another perspective of the city from a more elevated level, including views over Canary Wharf which is one of London's major business districts. At Bank, they changed onto the District Line to go back to their hotel.

"That was a whistle-stop tour," Andrew commented. "We did a lot in the two days. I thought it was such an easy city to get around, particularly the public transport. Now I feel like I need a rest to recover. But that is unlikely to happen."

"I really enjoyed it," Asha remarked. "Perhaps, we did pack too much into the available time. But it was worth it. I would definitely like to come back. There are so many other things I would like to do and see. Unfortunately, we did not manage to go to any cricket matches nor to the theatre. What about you?"

"I would have liked to have gone on the Eye to get another different view of the city and to have spent time in Westminster Abbey."

The next day they travelled to Paris on Eurostar, which offered a special fare for a wheelchair user and companion. It really impressed Asha how considerate they were about those differently able.

They boarded the train at Waterloo Station with some assistance from one of the stewards with their luggage and were shown to their area, which comprised of one space for the wheelchair user and one seat for the companion of the wheelchair user.

They had a brief stop at Ashford in Kent and then through the Channel Tunnel and into France.

They enjoyed a light meal and a glass of wine served at their table as they watched the countryside, first of Kent, the Garden of England, and then the rolling hills of France.

"This is a great way to travel," Andrew proclaimed. "So comfortable and relaxing."

"I am enjoying this immensely," Asha noted. "I was not sure about being in the Tunnel for so long. It felt a bit eerie. Didn't you feel a little frightened?"

"No. It was fine, Asha. Anyhow, I had my eyes closed for most of the travel through the Tunnel, enjoying a brief siesta."

"What's a siesta?"

"It's a tradition in some parts of Europe to have a siesta, which is a short nap taken after the midday meal. But I just use the word as meaning any short nap. Now we are about to arrive in Europe, we ought to abide by that custom."

"I don't think so. I want to spend as much time as possible awake and enjoying Paris."

Upon arrival at Gare du Nord station, they took a taxi to their hotel just off the Avenue des Champs-Élysées where all the players would be staying. But they had two days of leisure before the practice sessions were due to begin at Roland-Garros, the venue for the French Open.

After checking in and off-loading their luggage, they decided to go for a stroll, first along the Avenue to the Arc de Triomphe. Unfortunately, the Arc is not very accessible by wheelchair. So, they just admired it from the roadside as traffic raced around it entering and exiting at one of its ten access roads.

They made their way back down the Avenue, stopping at a cafe for a beer. It was fascinating sitting outside on the Avenue watching the traffic and the bustle of people going, wherever, on business, shopping or merely having an afternoon walk.

Then it was off to see the Eiffel Tower about two and a half kilometres away. But this time by taxi. The first two levels of the Tower were accessible. This gave them a good 360-degree panorama of the city allowing views across the Seine to the Arc de Triomphe, the Basilica of Sacre-Coeur in the distance, The Louvre as well as Notre-Dame Cathedral.

They made their way back towards their hotel and found a little French restaurant to have dinner.

"Andrew, what a great first day in Paris! Pity we could not get up to the top of the Tower. However, it was good to be able to get up part of it and look out over

Paris, such a beautiful-looking city. Trying something new for dinner has been a superb experience. I was a little worried about the snails and frog legs, which fortunately turned out to be very tasty. It was also good to try new wines."

"Asha, I did not really enjoy the snails. Too chewy for me. And I kept picturing the poor creatures that I used to find in my garden. But the frog legs were good, a bit like chicken. The tourist part was also interesting, particularly when we looked out from the Tower. That is the kind of experience I thought I could have got from the Eye in London. OK. Let's go. I'm feeling a little tired."

"Even after your siesta?"

Then it was off to bed with a packed agenda planned for the next day. Asha was also really exhausted by the long day, with, perhaps, too much walking.

This was their last day of leisure before the tennis commitments, at least for Andrew as Asha was not playing since the tournament was limited to the top eight men and women in the world rankings. They made a reasonably early start, first with breakfast and then off to the Louvre museum.

As they approached the museum, the glass Pyramid immediately caught their attention. They did not need to queue for a long time as the line moved quickly. Their bags were searched and then they made their way to the lower ground floor lobby to purchase their tickets.

First stop was to see the *Mona Lisa*. Naturally, there were many people around the masterpiece, looking at the painting and taking a photograph of it. They got close enough to get a good view of it to see her eyes "moving around".

They also saw the marble statue of the Winged Victory of Samothrace and the marble sculpture of Venus de Milo, both very famous pieces.

But Asha's favourite work of art was *The Lacemaker* by Vermeer. *The Lacemaker* was a relatively small oil on canvas painting but so delicately done with wonderful detail of the woman doing work with her threads.

After the Louvre, they made their way to Notre-Dame Cathedral, stopping on the way at a little bistro for a light lunch of a filled baguette, ham and salad for Andrew and chicken and salad for Asha and a glass of white wine for both of them.

Although not the largest cathedral in the world, the Notre-Dame might be the most famous of all cathedrals. The gothic masterpiece was located on the Ile de la Cité, a small island in the heart of Paris. It impressed Asha as a magnificent building with its several large rose windows standing out. The west side featured three wide portals, the gallery of Kings and the famous gargoyles. All in all, very interesting.

Then it was onto the Rodin museum. They had an afternoon snack and a drink in a café near the museum first and that set them up nicely.

After paying the entrance fee, they entered the museum gardens and, on the left, stood Rodin's monumental masterpiece, called *The Gates of Hell*. This was inspired by Dante's *The Divine Comedy*. Then off to the left behind some bushes and shrubs was the statue Asha had come to see, titled *The Thinker*. Of all the works by Rodin, *The Thinker* is by far the most famous one. It was originally modelled for *The Gates of Hell* and then enlarged into this form. Asha was amazed that such a famous statue was outside, open to all the elements. He was stunned by its size (71.5 cms high) and beauty. Asha sat on a bench beside Andrew for some time and just looked at it. He was in awe and could hardly discuss its beauty with Andrew, who was also fascinated by its immense presence. Such a wonderful piece of bronze artistry. No picture could do it justice.

Back towards the entrance was another extremely impressive bronze statue of *The Monument to The Burghers of Calais*. This honours six leading citizens of Calais who volunteered themselves as hostages to the English King Edward III in exchange for his lifting an eleven-month siege on their city in 1347. This was one of the versions of the statue. While the original statue still stands in Calais, other versions stand in Victoria Tower Gardens in the shadow of the Houses of Parliament in London, in the Rodin Museum in Philadelphia, at Stanford University in California and in the sculpture garden of the Hirshhorn Museum in Washington, DC.

"Andrew, I remember seeing a small-scale version of this in the NSW Art Gallery in Sydney when we went there during my first week in Sydney. Even although it was quite small, I was impressed with it. That was the beginning of my interest in Rodin."

"Asha, I remember. I am also a great fan of Rodin's work. Such a wonderful opportunity to see the various works first hand."

They wandered around the gardens and through the museum. But there was nothing to compare with the three exhibits mentioned above.

If they had more leisure time in Paris, they would have gone on a cruise along the Seine to get a different perspective of the city, the way they did in London. Perhaps another time.

So, back to the hotel and then, after a shower, they went out to an Italian restaurant for dinner.

"What a brilliant day that was, nicely rounded off by another great meal washed down with some fine wines. Asha, what was your favourite part of the sightseeing?"

"I liked everything. But, if I had to pick one, it would have to be the Rodin Museum. I still cannot get over how impressive seeing *The Thinker* in person was. And the meals have been delicious."

"My favourite was the Louvre. I was so fascinated by the *Mona Lisa* painting. I know it is very well known and I have seen it many times in print and on television. But being in the actual room was a little weird, watching the eyes follow me around. I need a good sleep. We did so much today."

Sightseeing over and off to serious tennis. Andrew again won the main draw. A day after the tournament finished, they journeyed back to Sydney via London and Singapore and then they returned to their university.

Both Andrew and Asha had enjoyed such a great time together. They had got to know each other really well.

And Asha was able to tick off visiting two other major cities in the world: London and Paris. Is this really happening to me, Asha continued to muse?

Chapter 14
End of Asha's First Year in Australia

It was good to return to see Amy, Elisa and Robert again, as well as his other friends, contemplated Asha.

Soon afterwards Andrew and Asha invited Robert and the girls over to their place for dinner. It was not going to be anything elaborate. Just beer and pizzas while they showed them the masses of snaps from their trip.

Robert asked them if he could bring a friend along. He just said that he had met Alice recently and thought that this was a good time for them to meet her.

Robert met Alice at a function at the NSW Art Gallery and had been out with her a couple of times while Andrew and Asha were away. Nothing serious. Just good friends.

Alice had lost her husband about the same time that Pauline had passed away. Alice and her husband had migrated to Australia from Vietnam about fifteen years previously. She had two children: Annie and John. Annie had finished university over a year ago and was working as a cadet reporter in Canberra. John was in his third year at university. She had not talked in detail about her background and her family. Robert was much the same introducing Andrew and Asha briefly, again without much detail. They spoke more about their jobs, in particular Annie's work as a psychologist. They also talked about the interests they shared in the arts.

Alice told Robert that they had Anglicised their names when they came to Australia. Their family name was Nguyen, which they changed to Newman. And they had chosen "simple" first names.

Amy and Elisa had only just arrived when there was another knock at the door. Asha opened the door to be greeted by Robert and this petite woman of Asian origin. He was not expecting this.

"Guys, this is Alice," introduced Robert. "Alice, meet Andrew, Asha, Elisa, Andrew's girlfriend and Amy, Asha's girlfriend."

After the initial shock, at least for Asha, they all had a drink, with a slice of pizza, as they chatted. Alice did not say too much. She talked a little about her children and said that Andrew and Asha had something in common with her son, John, as he also went to the University of New South Wales.

Then they settled down as Asha beamed each photograph onto the wall, with expert commentary by Andrew, starting in Nottingham with the tennis.

"Well done, Andrew," enthused Robert. "I am so proud of your tennis achievements. What started out as a way for you to get exercise has blossomed into a sporting career.

Alice, Andrew is an all-round sportsman: a good swimmer, a good basketball player and a brilliant tennis player."

As Robert spoke, his face was beaming, which was in contrast to Andrew's rather embarrassed look.

Then they moved on to London and Paris.

Everyone seemed to enjoy the reminiscing in words and vision. Asha certainly did. It brought back some delightful memories.

Asha also sent a selection of photographs by email to his family. Then he had a very long conversation with them talking them through London and Paris. His mother seemed so happy that he had been able to have such an experience. But, as usual, when the call finished Asha felt flat. Here Asha was getting all these benefits, while his family was struggling.

Amy and Asha were now spending a lot more time together when they had down time from uni and study. They enjoyed having a night out together about once a week for dinner or a movie.

Asha had not told his family about Amy. They had not asked if he had a girlfriend and it was too soon to tell them. At least, that was how he felt. Asha was not being secretive just being cautious.

Term end arrived in December with exams which would be followed by a two-month break. Time had passed so quickly and a lot had happened. Asha had a good year studying, made new friends and did a lot of travelling. He was very satisfied with how the year had gone and very appreciative of the opportunity that Robert had given him. He was also very happy for the way that Andrew had accepted him and how he had helped Asha in many ways.

After the exams were out of the way, it was a fun time leading up to Christmas. Amy and Asha exchanged small gifts before she departed for her home town of Perth to spend the holiday season with her family.

Asha felt somewhat lonely after Amy had gone. Andrew had Elisa and Robert was busy closing the calendar year at his business. Robert also had a heavy social calendar with a number of invitations to Christmas parties.

So, Asha turned to uni friends, particularly Scott and Philippe, who were also miles away from their families. They went to the beach a couple of times, Asha board surfing with their help as well as just lounging in the sun. At other times, they would have a long lunch, chatting about how different it was to be in Australia at this time of year away from their families.

Then Christmas was upon them. A small family gathering consisting of Andrew, Elisa and Asha congregated at Robert's place.

On Christmas Eve, Asha went with Robert, Elisa and Andrew to evening service at the nearby Anglican Church. It was very calming, listening to the sermon and the hymns that were sung by the congregation. Another interesting experience for Asha. However, during the service, a noise came from the back of the church. It was a drunk, perhaps a homeless person, mumbling to nobody in particular. He took a seat in front of them and sat quietly taking in the solemnity.

As they left the church, Asha felt so much at peace with everything.

On Christmas morning, Andrew, Elisa and Asha went down to the pool while Robert prepared the food for lunch. Nothing hot. Just cold prawns, meats and salad.

Lunch was most enjoyable: great food, beer, wine and company. Asha had never experienced a Christmas like this before. In India, they did not really celebrate Christmas, at least not in the same way. It was usually a quiet time.

Everyone was in great spirits, not just because of the alcohol. They had all experienced a very busy year and it was time to relax.

A week later, it was New Year's Eve and Asha's first New Year's Eve outside India. In India, they did not do much to celebrate the New Year. But Asha gathered that, in Australia, it was much different. This was a time to really celebrate and let your hair down.

Robert, being of a Scottish background, always celebrated this time of year and had invited a few of his friends, Andrew, Elisa, Asha, a couple of Andrew's friends as well as Alice and her children to his apartment to bring in the New Year. It was to be a very informal gathering with a lot of finger food washed down with your beverage of choice.

Alice and her children were the last to arrive and what an entrance. Robert let them into the apartment, with Alice leading the way followed by her children, Annie and John. Robert and Alice got the introductions out of the way quickly and they moved back into the apartment to mingle with the other guests. Andrew went to be with his friends, leaving Asha with Annie and John. They talked and talked and before they knew it midnight was upon them.

Asha had been told so much about how incredible the midnight fireworks were over Sydney Harbour and was really looking forward to them. And Asha was not to be disappointed. "Ten, nine, eight, seven, six, five, four, three, two, one… H-A-P-P-Y N-E-W Y-E-A-R!" The dark sky above the Harbour burst into light, with large plumes generated from the fireworks set off from barges along the Harbour on both sides of the Bridge. The Bridge, itself, turned into a surging waterfall of colour as fireworks continued to create different symbols in a co-ordinated fashion. WOW! What a truly magnificent display, the likes of which Asha had never seen before.

A new year and the end of Asha's first year in Sydney. The dream continues.

Chapter 15
First Anniversary

Go confidently in the direction of your dreams. Live the life you've imagined.

Henry David Thoreau

Robert decided to have a small dinner party to celebrate the anniversary of Asha's first year in Sydney with Andrew, Elisa, Asha and Amy. The discussions around the table reminisced about the past year and, in particular their time at university or, in Elisa's case, at the Conservatorium. The quartet had become close friends, albeit Andrew and Elisa had known each other a little longer.

Robert was really surprised at how easily Asha had settled into Sydney. This had been a huge step for him from the rural and suburban life of India to a Western city life.

Biased or otherwise, Robert gave a lot of credit for this to Andrew. From day one, Andrew had taken Asha under his wing, not to smother him and to do everything for him but to encourage and guide him. They had done a lot together from sharing a flat to going to the same university to wheelchair tennis and travelling. But they had also led their separate lives, particularly Andrew with Elisa.

Asha came round to visit Robert at least once every two weeks, sometimes with Andrew and Elisa, but mainly on his own.

Asha was a deep thinker and they would have intense conversations over dinner or with a glass of something on Robert's balcony.

Asha would talk about his concerns for India: the high levels of poverty, the corruption, poor infrastructure and communication systems. He felt really frustrated and helpless about the plight of a large part of the population in India, particularly in his native state. This included the ongoing challenges of his family in their efforts to keep their heads above water. Someone had given him a chance and hope for a brighter future. Who was going to help the other Indians in desperate need!?

India was a nation divided into three: the very wealthy, the growing middle class and those struggling just to survive. Possibly a fourth — those who would not make it through. As far as Asha could see, the government did not have any answers. And there did not seem to be much of a move by those with money to use it for the betterment of their fellow citizens. What would happen if someone else like Robert adopted someone like Asha (and his family or, for that matter, their village) and looked after their welfare? Robert thought that was a very interesting idea. But how practical?

Asha did not talk much about politics. He had not cared about politics in India and was not showing much interest in Australian politics. Being on a student visa and unable to vote in any election, he felt that he did not have the opportunity to contribute to the outcomes in Australia.

They talked a little about horse racing. After their experience in Mumbai, Robert had taken Asha to the races a couple of times in Sydney to give him more exposure. Just the public area even although Robert was a member of the race club. Asha's appetite for racing continued to grow. So much so, Robert bought him a membership. Andrew had not shown much interest in racing. So, it was good for Robert to have someone close to share his enthusiasm for the sport.

Encouraged by Amy, Asha was actively involved in the social club at university. This gave him an outlet to meet people from different backgrounds and to grow his network.

Robert and Asha talked about the events that the club organised, such as movie nights and specific fundraising activities for children with disabilities.

Asha enjoyed going to the movies. Whenever the opportunity arose, he would go to see a Bollywood film. He also liked going to Western films, particular dramas.

But it was the fundraising that was so close to Asha's heart. He knew, first hand, the importance of less able children being given the opportunity to make the most of their lives through rehabilitation as well as integration with society. He focused on raising funds to provide children with sports wheelchairs. He felt that playing sport was good for the mind, the body and socially. One time, he took Andrew along to a wheelchair tennis camp. The kids were so excited to have such a star in their midst, and, apparently, took great benefit from Andrew's instructions and demonstrations.

Asha always had his future on his mind. He wanted to succeed academically to repay Robert's endeavours. But, most importantly, he wanted to be able to support his family in India and enrich their lives.

Still a long way to go. But Asha had certainly made an excellent start. Long may it continue.

Asha had to pinch himself. He had been in Sydney for one year. Time had flown so fast. Asha had never really thought about the future. He had felt destined to a life of difficulty. Now he had been given a wonderful opportunity by Robert and needed to make the most of it. So, what did the future hold for him? First cab off the rank was his degree. Then what? Marriage, job, children… and friendships.

Andrew and Asha had grown very close together, almost like siblings. Asha looked upon Andrew as his big brother and mentor. When he needed a push or some advice, Andrew was there to help. Otherwise, Asha just got on about his business.

Andrew and Asha had their little fights, mainly about doing their share around the flat. But, in the main, they got on extremely well.

Asha had some interesting thoughts comparing Andrew to himself. Andrew had a greater level of disability than him, with both legs affected compared to his one. Yet that did not seem to faze Andrew. He just got on with life and was accepted by his friends for the person he was and for his abilities that were many. He was handsome, very smart and an accomplished sportsman. Andrew was an inspiration to Asha, who just wanted to follow in his footsteps. Andrew had become his role model.

It had been a very busy year, moving into the flat, going to university, learning the ropes of wheelchair tennis, travelling and meeting new people, particularly Amy. Fortunately, Asha was able to balance things out and make sure that he studied hard. That had to be the number-one priority and it was.

Looking back over the previous twelve months, any apprehensions or concerns Asha had about approaching his new life had not materialised. He had been accepted by most people he met. There had been a couple of negative instances.

One was in university. Asha had been wandering around the gardens of the campus, taking some time out to relax and think. As another student, who Asha did not know, walked past him, he mumbled something along the lines of "Go back to where you came from. We do not need your type here." Asha was a little taken aback. When Asha got home, he relayed his encounter to Andrew. Andrew told Asha not to worry about it. Unfortunately, Andrew said that there were still some pockets of racism around and it would probably not be the last time that Asha would encounter such attitudes.

The other was when Andrew and Asha were sitting having a quiet drink in their local pub. A drunk came up to them and started making fun of them, calling them "cripples". Before the situation got more heated, his mates pulled him away. The odd thing was that the next time he saw them in the pub he came over and apologised for his behaviour.

Everyone is different in their own way. Why can't people just accept that and not get wrapped up in their prejudices?

Initially, Asha had been a little homesick. But, once university started and he had become very busy, that dissipated. He stayed in touch with his family with regular phone calls. They were always keen to find out what was happening with him.

Robert was still seeing Alice occasionally and Andrew and Elisa were always doing things together.

One day, Asha contacted John and arranged to meet up for a coffee in the city. When Asha arrived, John was already at a table. He stood up to greet Asha. It was then that Asha noticed his prosthetic legs protruding below his shorts.

"I did not realise that you were disabled. I know that is not very polite. I'm sorry. I did not mean to say that. I was surprised because neither you nor your mother mentioned that you were an amputee."

This family is full of surprises, Asha said to himself.

"Alice had only said that Andrew and I had something in common with you, John."

John did not seem perturbed by Asha's outburst.

"I am used to wearing prosthetics and never thought anything about it."

"John, I was surprised because when I saw you before, you seemed to walk normally. So, seeing your prosthetics was a bit of a shock."

Having gathered his composure, Asha and John sat down, ordered drinks and started talking about their backgrounds, John in Vietnam and Asha in India. Asha also told him the story of how he had met Robert and what had followed. John commented about how fortunate Asha had been. Then John told Asha about growing up in Vietnam.

John had stepped on a landmine as a young boy and had both legs blown off below the knees. He spent several months in hospital recuperating while the ends of his legs healed. Then he was fitted with prosthetics and learned to walk unaided. His sister was also very supportive of him and, as he said, a little protective.

His father was a lawyer and his mother a psychologist. They both encouraged Annie and John to work hard at school. But it was still a tough environment politically. As a result, his parents decided to uproot the family and move to Sydney where his father had managed to get a job in a legal firm. John was eight years old and Annie was twelve.

The family had settled into the Australian way of life very easily. Alice set up her own psychology practice and Annie and John progressed through the school years. Then, just as John was about to start university, there was a bombshell. His father was killed in a car crash. As he told the story, there were tears running down his cheeks. He said he missed his father so much. He had been his inspiration. Asha consoled John as much as a relative stranger could.

After that meeting, John and Asha got together regularly. John did not play any sports. But he enjoyed swimming. His main interest was in electronic games. Something that Asha had never bothered about. They both liked movies, eating and good wine. And, very importantly, they enjoyed each other's company.

John invited Asha to drive to Canberra with Alice. They were going to spend a few days with Annie. But Asha could not go as he was playing in the Sydney and Melbourne wheelchair tennis tournaments again. That was a pity as Asha would have liked to see Canberra and the scenery along the way. Maybe some other day.

Asha played in the main draw in both tournaments, getting knocked out in the quarter-finals each time. Andrew just kept on winning, retaining both main draw singles titles once more as well as the doubles. He had now gone two years without losing a singles match.

When Alice and John got back from Canberra, the quartet met up with them at Robert's for Sunday lunch. Prior to lunch, they all went down to the pool. Alice and Robert did not bother getting into the water. But the rest did, mixing throwing a ball around, swimming and generally horsing around, particularly Amy and Asha. It was a lovely warm sunny day, making the pool an ideal place to be.

John was very mobile out of the water, very balanced walking on his stumps. In the water he was even more impressive, easily beating Andrew and Asha in a race along the length of the pool.

They finished up spending a little time in the spa, just relaxing and chatting away. Then it was back up to the apartment for one of Robert's seafood barbeques, washed down with lashings of beer and wine.

What a most pleasant afternoon! Awesome!

Chapter 16
More Travel

After the Melbourne tennis Asha went back to Nagpur for a holiday to see his family. Andrew went with him.

Andrew had never been to India before and his eyes and mind were truly opened by the experiences. Firstly, just the sweet smell of the air as they left the aircraft in Mumbai. Then the crowds as they exited the international terminal to get a taxi to the domestic terminal. They had one suitcase that they were sharing and Andrew was in his wheelchair, with his crutches, which all had to be piled into the taxi.

The travel between the terminals seemed to take ages for such a relatively short journey. This was caused by the density of the traffic. Vehicles were constantly honking. This caught Andrew's attention and he also commented on what seemed to be no road rules, with vehicles taking up whatever part of the road they could.

The flight from Mumbai to Nagpur was uneventful. Ranjiv picked them up for the 150- kilometre drive to the farm.

Again, Andrew was fascinated by what he saw as they left Nagpur, the poverty of people living by the roadside and in nearby slums and the poor and disabled begging. He vowed there and then to return to India to live, to practise medicine and to help those in need. This was a very bold statement, coming from someone who used a wheelchair or crutches. Perhaps this decision was that of a son following in the footsteps of his philanthropic father.

India was not renowned for its positive approach to the less able and, in many parts of the country, it is not easy for wheelchair pushing. So, it would be very challenging for Andrew.

"Andrew, a very worthy idea. Perhaps, you are just reacting to the immediate situation?"

"Perhaps, Asha. Anyway, I'm looking forward to more experiences during our holiday."

And Asha left it at that.

After about three hours, they arrived at the rambling farmhouse. Andrew was immediately taken by it and its situation, deep in the countryside and away from the city.

Andrew had Asha's old room with its en suite bathroom complete with its Western toilet. Ranjiv had changed all the toilets in the house from a squatting to a Western arrangement because of Asha's condition. Asha shared with Bishu.

They had a very relaxing time with Asha's family as well as spending time with some of his friends. Occasionally they would go into the main part of the city to do some sightseeing or shopping. Dinner was mostly at home, cooked by Anji and Visha. It was always a sumptuous smorgasbord of chicken, vegetables and accompanying chutneys.

On the way back to Mumbai, they spent some time with Asha's aunt and uncle in Powai. Asha showed Andrew where his father and he had met. They also went to the hotel where Robert used to stay. The staff remembered Asha and asked how he was and what Robert was doing. It was a Sunday, so they had dinner, bringing back wonderful memories of Asha's time with Robert that really transformed his life.

Yet their holiday was not quite over. They had a stopover in Singapore for two days on the way back to Sydney. Another different experience for Asha. Very clean compared to Mumbai. Very humid and it seemed to rain at three o'clock each afternoon! But a big city, similar in many ways to Sydney: tall buildings, good shopping malls and great food. Yet another city to add to the growing visit list. Where will the next one be?

Robert picked them up at Sydney airport and dropped them off at their flat. The following day they reacquainted themselves with their girlfriends. Asha was so happy to see Amy again and she seemed very happy to see him.

A couple of days later, they went down to Shelly Beach to catch up with some friends from uni. It was a small secluded cove with lovely white sand. As they arrived, some of their friends were playing football or throwing a frisbee around. When they saw them, they came over to say hello. One of the men picked Andrew up from his wheelchair and carried him over the sand to the area where their towels had been laid out. The rest all followed and got ready to go in the water. This was to be Asha's first swim for a while. Two of his friends, piggy-backed Andrew and him into the water, where they frolicked around, swimming, diving and tossing a ball as well as throwing the frisbee. It was such fun and so refreshing.

After they dried off and relaxed for a little while on the sand, they set off for the barbeque area at the rear of the beach, where they commandeered the nearby table and mingled around the barbeque, chatting and drinking as well as savouring some nibbles. Everyone had brought various foods and drinks to share. It was a great time, back in the company of friends on a glorious summer's day.

Then it was time to return to university for Asha's second year. Both Andrew and Asha had excellent results from their previous year's exams. But it was only going to get tougher. Asha had a very busy life: study, social club, tennis and a girlfriend. So, he had to continue to make sure that he got his priorities right and that there was a balance.

Asha managed to fit in two tennis tournaments in Korea. Andrew had decided not to go as he could not really spare the time. So, Asha shared rooms with Yung-Su in both Seoul and Daegu. It was great seeing him again and being able to spend time with him, just the two of them. Nothing against Andrew.

The first morning they were together, Yung-Su saw Asha lying on the bed exercising his right leg.

"What are you doing?" Yung-Su asked.

"These are the exercises that Robert taught me. The same ones he taught you if I'm not mistaken! Aren't you going to do them?"

Stunned silence. Then, after a while, Yung-Su said no. Asha did not bother pursuing the topic. He had his reasons. So, Asha decided that it was best to let sleeping dogs lie.

When Asha finished exercising, Yung-Su surprised him.

"Sometimes Robert used to hold my hands and walk backwards. I strode forwards wearing my leg braces. I liked doing that. Could you be Robert and help me walk by holding my hands?"

"Of course. I'll put on my calliper."

Yung-Su put his leg braces on. His legs were similar to Andrew's, thin and the same length as each other. His leg braces were a little different to Asha's one. Similar structure with a manual locking system at the knee. But the bottom parts fitted into small leather soles that, in turn, sat inside his shoes.

Yung-Su locked each leg brace and using his hands swung his legs over the side of the bed one by one. Asha helped him into a standing position and then they began to move slowly. It was not easy for Asha moving backwards as it was not easy for Yung-Su to go forwards. But they managed it, step by step.

"You are not doing it properly," complained Yung-Su..

"What do you mean?"

"Well, you are supposed to say — lift, push — as I move each leg."

"OK. Let's go. Lift, push, lift, push…"

Asha could see the intensity in Yung-Su's face, concentrating on the actions. It was easier for him to move his right leg. But there was more strain in propelling the left leg forward.

They went up and down the room twice followed by a rest, two more repetitions and then they were finished. Yung-Su looked exhausted as he lay back on the bed. But soon he perked up.

"Let's go down to breakfast," beckoned Yung-Su.

Then another surprise. Yung-Su kept his leg braces on and they walked down to breakfast.

"Robert had told me that you preferred to ride your wheelchair rather than walk wearing leg braces and using crutches."

"That is true. But with you I feel very comfortable on my feet, walking with you."

Asha had been self-conscious pole-hopping but thought that he could not do anything about it and just accepted it. Asha did not know anyone else with a physical disability like him. So, he had spent all his time with able-bodied people in contrast to Yung-Su's experience. It was only when Asha met Andrew and was introduced to wheelchair tennis that Asha associated with others with disabilities. He felt content with both able-bodied and disabled people.

Ever since Asha's operation and being fitted with the calliper, he had become almost fixated about legs and callipers.

Once his leg had been straightened, he found out that it was four inches shorter than his left leg. Or was it that his left leg was four inches longer than his right leg? Semantics. In any case, Asha was lop-sided. But that had not mattered to him because he was able to walk. Asha guessed that he could have had an operation to lengthen his right leg, which was not really practical because of the size of the gap. Or have his left leg shortened, which Asha thought would be stupid. Another option might have been to take two inches off his left leg and fuse it to his right leg. Asha thought both impractical and nonsensical. In the end, Asha was happy with his lot. Furthermore, it was only his right leg that was affected. Others like Andrew and Yung-Su were doubly affected. They needed to wear callipers and use crutches or push a wheelchair to be mobile other than crawling. At worst Asha could hop around just like he had done for many years. Or when Asha had been travelling with Andrew or Yung-Su, he could borrow their wheelchair. Asha felt very lucky.

On Asha's previous visit to Korea, he had enjoyed the local food as well as *soju*. This experience continued as Yung-Su introduced him to some other Korean cuisines. They were quite spicy but Asha did not mind them. He had a taste for *soju* but managed to control his intake. After all, he was there to play tennis.

Yung-Su beat Asha in the quarter-final of the Seoul tournament.

Yung-Su had driven up to Seoul from Daegu, which he told Asha took him around two and a half hours. This turned out to be very handy.

The day after the tournament finished in Seoul, Yung-Su and Asha went horse racing. Being a member of a Sydney racing club gave Asha reciprocal rights to the course in Seoul. Yung-Su had called the club earlier in the week and made the necessary arrangements. They drove to the course and on the way, Yung-Su called the race club contact he had been given. He was told where to park. As they were getting out of the car, the contact approached them, introduced himself, and led them to the grandstand. Yung-Su was wearing his leg braces and using his crutches as he was not sure how wheelchair friendly the race course would be. They were taken to a private room where refreshments were laid out. They were being treated like VIPs. The races were interesting as they were run on sand as opposed to the turf that Asha was used to. Also, the monitors were showing pony racing from Jeju, an island off the south coast of Korea. Very different. They had a great day out, enjoying the racing from the balcony of the grandstand. They had a little flutter on each race. Yung-Su did all right. Must have been Asha's coaching? Asha ended up a little ahead for the day.

The next day they drove out to the rehabilitation centre where Yung-Su had been brought up. It took about thirty minutes through suburban countryside. The road was very good. Asha commented to Yung-Su on how fast he was driving, not that Asha was frightened. Yung-Su replied, with a huge smile on his face, that he drove just like Robert. Asha just laughed because he knew what Yung-Su meant. They did not do much at the centre as Yung-Su did not know anyone there well. So, they just went to a restaurant near the centre that Yung-Su used to frequent. The owner still remembered him. It was a very small and basic restaurant but the food was delicious. They shared *bulgogi* (barbequed beef) with many accompaniments.

Then it was time for them to head to Daegu for the next tournament. Asha enjoyed the drive, looking out at the countryside, listening to Korean pop music and chatting with Yung-Su.

And Asha managed to get revenge, beating Yung-Su to win his first main draw singles title. I must like playing in Daegu, Asha thought.

Asha had enjoyed his time in Korea and had developed a very strong relationship with Yung-Su. They spent some time talking about Robert and his influences on their lives. They were mostly positive. But Yung-Su still voiced disappointment about Robert and him parting ways and not having time together. He wished that any differences between them could be resolved. Yung-Su, just like Robert, would not explain exactly what the problem had been.

While Asha was away in Korea, he managed to stay in touch with Amy, which made him very happy. Asha was delighted to see her again when she came to the airport to pick him up.

Asha visited Robert a short time after his return and told him about how Yung-Su felt and his desire to mend bridges.

"Asha, if only it could be that easy. I had been very angry with Yung-Su's behaviour and he did not seem willing to change. So, I decided to stop any face-to-face contact, even although we had the occasional brief telephone discussion. As far as I am concerned, it is up to Yung-Su to make the first move."

This saddened Asha because it was clear to him that they both wanted their relationship to be put back on an even keel. But how to do it with both parties apart geographically as well as philosophically? Perhaps, just let sleeping dogs lie. Don't force it and wait for an opportunity.

Asha told Andrew about his conversation with Robert about Yung-Su.

"Yes, Asha. It has been a problem for some time. But there is nothing we can do."

"You may be right."

Chapter 17

Coming of Age

"Andrew, I have a personal question," asked Asha.

"OK. What is it?"

"When did you lose your virginity?" Andrew smiled and chuckled.

"When I was sixteen.

"Sometimes when my father travelled on business, my mother would go with him. Other times they would just go away for a weekend together. They knew I could look after myself.

"Over time, I became friends with a few girls. Girls did not seem to worry about my legs. They enjoyed my company.

"But Elisa is the first long-term girlfriend that I have had. I love her," Andrew said.

"I am twenty years old and still a virgin. When I was using the pole to get around, girls were not interested in me. Then when I had the operation and got the calliper my relationship with girls improved. But there was never anything serious."

"Asha, that's fine. What has brought this on? Are you thinking about having sex with Amy?"

"Yes."

"Do you have condoms?"

"No."

"Well, when we go shopping at the weekend, you'd better get some."

Andrew got his wallet out. "Take this just in case you need one before the weekend."

A few weeks later, Andrew and Elisa went away for the weekend. So, Asha invited Amy to spend the weekend with him at the flat. Asha was very nervous. He had not done anything like this before. Amy said yes.

On the Friday night Amy came over. They went out to dinner at an Italian restaurant within walking distance from the flat. They both enjoyed the meal, washed down with some Riesling.

Amy was in very good spirits and they talked exuberantly about university, Asha's time in Korea and their families.

But Asha had a little difficulty concentrating. He was thinking about what would happen when they got into bed.

They strolled, arm in arm, back to the flat. When Asha got inside, he went off to his bedroom to take off his calliper and to get into his wheelchair.

Asha poured some Sauvignon Blanc for them and they sat together on the settee in the lounge listening to some music and chatting.

Amy lifted up Asha's polio leg and placed it on her lap. She pressed into his calf and ran her fingers up and down. Then she massaged the soul of his foot, pushed his toes backwards and forwards before rotating his ankle.

"Amy that was a fabulous feeling. Thank you."

After a little time, Asha's amorous feelings took over and, clearly, Amy felt the same. Then they made their way to the bedroom.

Asha was feeling a little apprehensive and nervous. He had put a couple of condoms under his pillow. Well prepared. Asha had also practised putting a condom on and it had worked out fine. Hope the same happens tonight. Nothing to worry about!

Asha woke up in the morning with Amy by his side. What a great feeling. And Asha was no longer a virgin.

Indian culture seems to frown upon sex before marriage, particularly for the female. And Asha thought that this caused more trouble.

As Asha was lying there, thinking and looking up at the ceiling, Amy moved over and kissed him. So simple but meaningful.

The rest of the weekend was splendid. I think I am in love, Asha thought. No, I know I am in love, Asha said to himself with a very broad smile.

On Sunday the 18th of July, Robert threw a party at his place to celebrate Andrew's twenty-first birthday which had taken place on the 12th. A few friends from university, the tennis club and NSW Wheelchair Tennis attended as did Alice, John, Elisa, Amy and Asha. Annie could not make it.

They had a great night: champagne and a seafood barbeque. Robert gave Andrew a watch, Elisa gave him a gold chain and Amy and Asha gave him a polo shirt. Andrew was quite emotional and thanked everyone for their presence and gifts, particularly his father and his late mother whom he missed very much.

After the guests had gone, Andrew and Elisa went to bed as did Amy, leaving Robert and Asha on the balcony, each with a glass of wine.

They sat in silence.

Robert went into reflection mode. Andrew is twenty-one. Where has the time gone? It only seemed like yesterday that Pauline and I had landed in Australia and then Andrew was born. But so many changes over the past few years.

Asha looked at Robert and remembered the day they met. The day that changed his life.

Robert was still in reverie. Pauline's death was the saddest day of my life. It was not unexpected as she had been battling cancer for some time. But it was still a shock. Andrew also took it very badly. But we have both managed to do what Pauline asked us to do — make the most of the future.

Sitting in calm spirits, Asha and Robert continued down memory lane.

I am still pinching myself. Here I am in Sydney. Can you believe it? thought Asha.

I got back into building my business and Andrew focused on study and tennis. And then meeting Asha.

I have experienced so much. My new family giving me so much support and encouragement. Robert is my father figure and Andrew my big brother.

The business has really developed beyond my imagination. I have put so much sweat and tears into it. There were the highs and not so highs. I'm not that far off being fifty. Perhaps it is time to slow down and seek other interests, even getting someone else to take over running the company on a day-to-day basis, while I stay on as non-executive chairman.

University has been great, meeting new friends, particularly Amy.

Travel has been enormous: Mumbai, Singapore, Sydney, Melbourne, Fukuoka, Daegu, Seoul, Nottingham, London and Paris. Where next I wonder?

And there is now another person in my life, Alice. Yet, I am not sure where it is leading. I do not think I am ready to commit to her.

"Asha, you have been very quiet, "What have you been thinking about?"

"Just reminiscing."

"Me too. Time for bed. Good night. See you in the morning."

"Good night, Robert."

This was a big year for Andrew. He was to represent Australia in wheelchair tennis at the 2004 Paralympics in September in Athens. Elisa and Robert went with him, while Asha stayed in Sydney. He was able to watch highlights of the singles final on television and was ecstatic to see Andrew win the gold medal and then be able to watch the award ceremony. Asha was very proud of his best friend. Andrew also won the doubles gold with Billy.

The year turned out to be very rewarding for Asha. It had been very well balanced in terms of his activities. Good tennis results. Excellent scholastic results again. Great fun organising events at uni during the year, particularly the Valentine's dinner. His relationship with Amy had blossomed. Andrew and Robert had been brilliant with him. Asha had spent quality time with friends like Philippe, Scott and John.

Asha's interest in racing had continued. Robert took Andrew, Elisa, Amy and Asha to the members' restaurants at both the Randwick and Rosehill courses. Randwick was a bit run down, whereas there was ongoing development at Rosehill. This made it feel like a more modern course, with good facilities, particularly The Winning Post restaurant overlooking the course. On their visits to Rosehill, they would stay at a nearby hotel and go to Hooters after the races. This was great fun with Robert even joining in, particularly when the Hooters girls got up to dance.

Time was passing so quickly, helped by being so occupied with a number of activities, study being the most important.

Asha's second year in Sydney and uni was over.

Chapter 18
The Quartet in Bali

Andrew retained all singles and doubles titles again in Sydney and Melbourne. Asha did not do as well as he had hoped. He felt he was losing interest in tennis with so many other things going on in his life.

"Andrew, I was not happy with how I played in both Sydney and Melbourne. The energy did not seem to be there."

"Asha, I noticed that. Although I continued to win the titles, I am also starting to think it is too much. I cannot see me continuing to play in tournaments."

Yung-Su had stopped playing tennis to concentrate on basketball and, therefore, had not travelled to Australia. Pity. Asha was hoping to see him again to have a good talk with him about how Robert felt about their relationship. That will have to wait for another time as this is something that needs to be done face to face.

Looks like we are all losing interest in tennis, viewed Asha.

After the tennis tournaments, Andrew, Elisa, Amy and Asha headed off on holiday together to Bali for a few days. As soon as they got off the plane at Denpasar,

Asha could see and smell the fragrance of flowers such as frangipani. They collected their luggage and made their way to the hotel cars that would transport them to their hotel apartment in Sanur.

It was late afternoon, so, after unpacking, they made their way to the bar for a snack and drink. Then, over dinner in the hotel that night, they discussed the plans for the following day. They had organised an all-day tour.

"Well, here we are, the first full day of our holiday," Asha commented. "Let's make the most of it."

After breakfast, they set off with their driver/guide, with the first stop being Celuk, which is famous for gold and silver crafting. They watched some of the craftsmen at work and then they were enticed into the shop. Both Andrew and Asha bought a small piece of jewellery for their girlfriends, Asha's a bangle and Andrew's earrings.

Onto Ubud, a major arts centre. They wandered from gallery to gallery, viewing the displays of paintings and sculptures. Although tempted, nobody purchased anything. They continued on their tour of the island, ending up at a restaurant for dinner that featured Balinese dancing, with great movement, vision and sounds of the gamelan musicians. It had been a long day but a most enjoyable day.

Asha was in a happy mood. "Well, the end of our first day. What a great start to our holiday."

Andrew agreed. "Everything has been most enjoyable, sightseeing, bargaining and the food. Let it continue. See you in the morning."

The following day was Asha's twenty-first birthday and the quartet had decided to stay around the hotel and relax.

The four of them went down to breakfast and there was the first surprise for Asha. The other three had organised a Champagne breakfast.

"Happy birthday, Asha," chorused the others. "Welcome to the twenty-first club."

"Thank you. Very pleased to be part of it."

They then sat around the pool for the rest of the morning, reading, swimming, playing ball in the pool, mixed with the occasional drink at the pool bar, where they also had a light lunch. After lunch, they had a rest in their rooms. Mid-afternoon, they were back by the pool (bar). Then it was time to dress for dinner sitting outside in the main restaurant overlooking the pool. Such a beautiful evening. The presents were handed over to Asha. There was a gold bracelet from Andrew and Elisa that they had sneakily bought in Celuk and a watch from Amy. Asha was very happy, being in such a beautiful place with wonderful friends. They had a mixture of Indonesian and French dishes, naturally washed down with some excellent wines. What a fantastic way to celebrate Asha's twenty-first birthday.

"Thank you, guys, for organising such a memorable day for me and my appreciation for all the presents."

"Our pleasure," the others responded in harmony.

The following morning, they started off slowly with a late breakfast followed by some time by the pool and then a light lunch before heading off to Kuta by taxi. Kuta's only about twenty minutes away.

The primary reason for going to Kuta was to do souvenir shopping. They meandered from shop to shop along the main street, all wanting to buy for their families. There were T-shirts everywhere, local craft, bags and a lot of jewellery.

Amy and Asha had decided to move in together as Elisa had already moved in with Andrew and they were going to keep the flat. So, Asha also wanted to buy something for Amy's and his new abode. It turned out to be a Buddha carving.

After a couple of hours of shopping they were loaded up with carry bags and were feeling thirsty.

They found a very good-looking garden cafe/bar overlooking the beach, by the name of Poppies, ordered some drinks and snacks and talked excitedly about their stay in Bali. Everyone had thoroughly enjoyed their time in Bali. The girls liked the shopping. Andrew's favourite was the pool bar: swimming, drinking, playing and eating. Clearly, Asha thought the highlight was the day of his twenty-first birthday. Above all, they had all experienced a memorable time together.

And then the sunset. What a magnificent sight as the giant red ball, slowly sank out of sight.

This reminded Asha of a time that Robert's driver took Robert and him to downtown Mumbai. Asha had never been there before and he remembered being quite excited. It was a long drive, well over an hour because of all the traffic.

The first stop was to visit the Gandhi Museum. The three-storey house belonged to one of Gandhi's friends. Gandhi stayed there over a number of years between 1917 and 1934. The Museum contains a display of photographs, posters and other items relating to Gandhi's life. This was a very educational visit for Asha. Asha had heard of Gandhi but had not been aware of his important contribution to events that led to India's independence from British rule.

Asha and Robert did some shopping for some clothes for Asha: underpants, socks, trousers and shirts. Then they went down to the Gateway of India located on the waterfront. Asha thought it was a most imposing structure, with its impressive stone triumphal arch. But what Asha did not like was the number of beggars pestering the visitors. They did not bother him, a brown-skinned cripple. But little children kept putting their hands out in front of Robert as they made their way to the Taj Mahal Palace Hotel, which is older than the Gateway and steeped in history.

As they entered the hotel, Asha was particularly taken by a huge display of flowers in the middle of the lobby. They made their way to one of the restaurants overlooking the Gateway. Robert and Asha talked about their day while sipping drinks, Asha's a fruit cocktail and Robert's a glass of white wine.

Asha could still see the children begging at the Gateway and asked Robert about his impressions. He said he was saddened by all the poverty in India that resulted in such begging. And he felt helpless. If you give to one, do you need to give to everyone? Impossible. This is something that the Indian Government needs to deal with, a huge task albeit. But they need to make a start. Robert also thought that the Indian billionaires had a part to play by contributing to proper housing.

Then the glorious sunset. This huge red ball dipped into the Arabian Sea and then suddenly it was gone. Just like what has just happened in Bali.

Then it was time to go back to the hotel in Sanur, have a light supper and go to bed for the last time in Bali.

That was a wonderful holiday and another place to add to the geographic list, Asha thought to himself. So far so good, every new place that I have been to has been memorable.

Chapter 19
Horse Owner

When Asha and Amy got back to Sydney, they went flat hunting and found one in Kingsford not too far from the University.

Understandably, Robert told Andrew and Asha that he would no longer be paying their rent. He would still give them allowances. There were two people in each flat earning money from part-time jobs and that was enough to cover expenses and leave some over.

Amy and Asha had both taken up part-time jobs at the beginning of the year. Asha's was in a solicitor's office doing admin work eight hours a week and Amy was working as a waitress in a restaurant, also doing eight hours a week. Just more activities to add to their already busy schedule.

Robert gave Asha a share in a racehorse as a belated present for his twenty-first birthday. This was a big surprise and such an awesome gift. Asha's interest in horse racing had continued to develop since his first race-track experience in Mumbai. Asha followed the horse racing articles in the newspapers and had the odd bet at weekends, with mixed fortunes. Amy and Asha even went to the track at Randwick in the public enclosures occasionally.

Robert also had a 10% share in the same horse. The horse was a two-year-old colt and was about to start its racing career. Its name was "Invincible". A bit presumptuous Asha thought. He knew nothing about horse breeding. But Robert told him that the horse had very good pedigree and ought to be able to do well over both the sprint and middle-distance races. Let's hope, Asha wished.

Invincible's first race was midweek at a provincial track in New South Wales. Robert and Asha did not travel to see it. And they were not able to watch it on television as Asha was at uni and Robert was away travelling in Asia. But it won at reasonable odds and Asha had a good return from his smallish bet. Its second race was at Randwick on a Wednesday. Again, Robert and Asha could not make it to see him race. But another win. However, the odds were not very enticing. But a win is a win. Invincible then stepped up to Saturday class at one of the autumn carnival two-year-old races in Sydney.

The quartet and Robert went along to Rosehill where they had a table in one of the bars in the members' area. As race time approached, Asha got more and more nervous, but excited at the same time. The adrenalin was certainly flowing.

And they are off, the race caller announced as the group watched the start on the racecourse television monitors. It was a field of twelve and Asha could see Invincible in the jockey's blue and yellow colours take up a prominent position just behind the leaders. Into the straight and they sprinted for the finishing post. Invincible came to the outside and moved up to the leaders, running them down on the line for a magnificent win. Asha shouted with joy and hugged Robert as Amy and Elisa were jumping up and down. Andrew had a huge smile ear to ear. He was very happy for Robert and Asha and congratulated them, not for one moment being jealous of their success. That was the type of person he is. Robert and Asha then went down to meet up with the other owners for the presentation. What a thrill!

"Asha, three wins now," Robert beamed. "How do you feel?"

"I cannot believe it. Beyond my wildest dreams. First to have a share in a horse was exciting enough. But, to see Invincible win today in the flesh was magnificent."

That was the end of his first campaign and Invincible went off to the paddock for a well-earned rest to return to racing in the Spring of 2006 as a three-year-old.

Because of Asha's interest in horses, Amy suggested they go horse riding in Centennial Park. Asha was not sure. But Amy was very keen. So, never one to step back from a challenge, they visited stables near the Park and made enquiries. Asha explained his polio leg situation. But the stable person said that they had experience with disabled riders before and did not think there would be any problem, so they made a booking for the next day.

When Asha and Amy got to the stables, Amy was excited, but Asha was a little apprehensive. Asha had never been on a horse before whereas Amy had ridden a number of times.

"You'll be fine," Amy told Asha.

Asha was helped onto the back of the horse with some degree of difficulty. Feet into the stirrups and the rein in his hands. It was time to set off. Amy and Asha each had a handler with them leading the horses. Across the road and into the Park and Asha was almost shitting himself. However, once inside the park, his nerves settled as they continued with the ride. By the time they had finished one circuit, which Asha found out was around four kilometres, Asha felt like a professional.

Asha told Amy that it was a great experience and thanked her for encouraging him to have a go. Amy said that she was pleased that Asha had enjoyed it. Then she asked Asha what their next adventure ought to be. Before Asha could respond, she suggested climbing the Sydney Harbour Bridge. Apparently, this had been on her bucket list ever since she had arrived in Sydney. Amy had a long list of things she wanted to accomplish and this was at the top of the list.

Asha then remembered the conversation he had with Robert while they were on the Manly Ferry. Robert had pointed out the people climbing the Bridge. Asha had thought it looked a bit frightening. But probably something he would do. So, it was agreed that it would be Amy's and Asha's next adventure.

The following weekend, the quartet was at Robert's apartment. Asha regaled all concerned about his riding experiences, telling them that it had been so easy and that he had not been at all afraid. Amy looked at him with a smirk on her face.

"OK, I was terrified. But, in the end, I did enjoy it after a nervous beginning."

The others laughed in a good-natured way.

Elisa had done some riding but nothing serious. And, as a young boy, Robert had taken Andrew riding. Asha then suggested that, perhaps, they could all go riding.

"Thank you, but no thank you. Once was enough for me," Andrew declined. "But by all means the four of you can go if you want."

Elisa and Robert did not seem interested. So, that was the end of that discussion.

Asha then told them that Amy and he had booked a bridge climb. Well done was the chorus, followed by, when?

"About two months away," was Asha's response.

They sat around and continued to chat and drink well into the afternoon. They had enjoyed a very tasty barbecue of chicken accompanied by baked potatoes and onions, "cooked by Robert's fair hand," was Asha's addition to the conversation.

Another most enjoyable get-together in Robert's apartment.

"Amy, I think we need to buy a barbecue for the balcony in our new apartment as it is a tremendous way to cook, particularly on warmer days."

Chapter 20
More Challenges

Andrew had been teaching Asha in his car how to drive using hand controls. Initially, Asha found it a bit confusing. He was supposed to use both hands for the accelerator and brake as well as indicating and using the handbrake. Did he push the control to accelerate and pull to brake or vice versa? Asha had to get it right or there could be dire consequences. With Andrew's encouragement and perseverance, Asha did get used to all the controls. Fortunately, he was able to pass the test first time.

With some financial help from Robert, Asha bought a car, which was a Honda Civic. He had a disabled parking spot at the University, which made it easy to drive to and from there.

Asha found that, even if he wanted just to use his wheelchair, while driving, he had to wear his calliper to anchor his leg to the floor, otherwise it just moved around as Asha had little control over it. This was in contrast to Andrew, whose legs were more stable.

After Asha moved out of the flat that he had been sharing with Andrew, they still managed to stay in touch, in addition to the driving lessons.

Andrew and Asha had given up competitive tennis because of time and financial pressures. So, this gave them more freedom in organising their activities. They still played tennis together once a week, more for exercise than anything else. When Andrew retired from tennis, he had not lost a singles match in over three years. What a remarkable achievement!

They also joined a fitness club that had great weightlifting facilities as well as a swimming pool. Initially, it was a little daunting in the gym. Asha always felt the eyes staring at two guys in wheelchairs. But that soon passed as Asha concentrated on the various machines. Andrew was a great help, acting as a coach for Asha just as he had done in Robert's apartment gym. Andrew had a great upper body, developed through years of pushing, playing wheelchair tennis as well as weights. Asha's body was pretty wiry. The only exercise he had done apart from some work with weights from time to time was pole-hopping, if you could call it that, and wheelchair tennis, for which Asha had not really trained hard. Perhaps he could have become a pole vaulter!? After the weights session, they would do a number of laps in the pool. Then a shower and off down the pub for a couple of drinks. A bit of a contrast.

Every couple of weeks they would also get together for a couple of drinks and a meal, just the two of them or with friends. Always good fun nights out, just relaxing and chatting away.

The date of the Bridge climb for Amy and Asha had arrived. It was a lovely spring day and they had booked a twilight climb, going up in daylight and back down in the dark.

When they arrived at the climb office, Asha had to talk with one of the staff to convince them that he was capable of doing the climb, which he did. Then they were given grey and blue all-in-one suits to change into. Finally, the pre-check preparation, going through some of the procedures, including how to latch onto the rail. And then it was time to set out onto the catwalk below the road deck.

Then the initial test, climbing the first of what turned out to be four ladders that took them to the upper arch and into the open air. So far so good. They were at the end of the group, staying in touch, as they made the steady climb, while looking out towards the Sydney Opera House and beyond to the heads. At the summit, the group halted to take in the breathtaking views as the sunset. This was also the opportunity for the guide to take photographs of the group. Then they crossed the spine of the bridge to descend in the dark, illuminated by a torch on their heads. It felt like being miners down the pit. As they descended, they could see and hear the trains roll past. Finally, the experience was over. Asha and Amy changed back into their own clothes and visited the shop to view the pictures the guide had taken. They ended up buying a photograph of the group at the summit, waving and smiling and, perhaps, shouting in ecstasy.

"Well Amy, that was splendid," Asha gushed. Amy agreed. All the gym work and swimming had paid off and Asha had conquered the climb quite easily. All in all, they had managed well over one thousand steps spanning more than three hours.

They sauntered to the Shangri-La Hotel to go up to the thirty-sixth floor to take in a different perspective of the bridge and to relax with a glass of wine and a snack. Their luck was in. There was a place available right by the long floor-to-ceiling window looking straight down the Bridge's roadway. Such a magnificent view of the structure that they had just climbed. They sat there, talking about the climb, something they agreed they would never forget.

But then it was back to earth.

Amy and Asha had been busy making their flat as homely as possible. It had been unfurnished. Over time, they had gradually built up the furniture content, put a few pictures on the walls and scattered plants in the living area and on the balcony. They had also bought a barbecue that was positioned on the balcony.

It had only one bedroom with a small study area, lounge/dining, bathroom, toilet and a good-sized kitchen. There were different areas in which they could study separately or do their own thing, such as watching television or listening to music.

The balcony, although not as well positioned as at Robert's place, was still fine for them to eat out or merely sit in the open air, reflecting.

Asha was comfortable with the freedom the two of them had, being on their own and not needing to worry about Andrew or Elisa. There was less congestion as well as greater flexibility in terms of what they wanted to do.

It was another very busy but rewarding year. Where had the time gone? Uni, study, work and socialising. That was where the time had gone.

Yet another fabulous year.

Chapter 21
A Gathering in India

After the university year finished, Asha took Amy to India, initially to meet his parents. In addition to introducing Amy to his family, they were going to attend Visha's wedding. Andrew, Elisa and Robert would join them later.

Amy had similar responses as Andrew had about the experiences in India. She thought about the noise, the crowds, inadequate sanitation and abundant poverty.

But she thoroughly enjoyed her time in India, got on with Asha's family, particularly Visha, who is two years older than Asha. They would go shopping together, mainly for clothes, or take in a movie or just go out for lunch.

While staying at Asha's parents, Amy and he had separate rooms. Amy had Asha's old room, same as when Andrew was there. Asha shared with Bishu again. Asha had not told his parents that Amy and he had moved in together.

After a couple of family days, Amy and Asha moved to Robert's normal hotel in Powai to join the rest of the gang and prepare for the wedding.

When Asha and Amy entered the hotel, there were some staff members who recognised Asha again, starting with Sandeep at the concierge desk and then the assistant manager. They both seemed very pleased to see him and asked how he was.

"I am very well. This is my girlfriend, Amy. We are both studying at the same university in Sydney."

Still the same staff as when Asha had taken Andrew there.

They checked in and went up to their room. To Asha's surprise, they had been given a suite. How did this happen? As Asha found out later, because of the amount of time Robert had stayed there, they had all been upgraded. Just brilliant. They would be very comfortable for the five days of their stay.

Asha telephoned Robert to let him know that they had checked in. Robert said that they were all to meet in the lobby in about thirty minutes.

They had to go shopping for appropriate Indian-style clothes for the wedding festivities, loose-fitting *kurta* (shirt) and *shalwar* (pants) for the men and bright saris for the ladies.

As they left the lobby and turned left towards the shopping centre, Asha told Amy that this was where Robert and he had met. But this time Asha was walking and not using a pole.

They were all very fortunate to get what they wanted in the first fashion shop they visited.

Asha and Amy hung up their purchases in their room and then returned to the lobby and to the adjacent bar. It was homecoming time for Robert. The two barmen immediately recognised Robert and shook hands vigorously. Robert introduced the rest of the group to Abijeet and Aniket before they sat down at one of the tables. Time to relax with refreshments and some snacks. A little later they moved into the restaurant area so they could avail themselves of the buffet for dinner.

"It is great to be back in my old stomping ground," Robert smiled.

Visha, the rest of the family and Arun, Visha's fiancé, and his family had moved into a hotel in Vashi where the wedding and various celebrations would take place.

On the day before the wedding, there was the henna ceremony when Visha had her arms and feet decorated by a paste or dye from the henna plant. While this was going on, a number of women were dancing and singing, making this a very festive occasion.

The wedding ceremony was very moving as well as being very spiritual. Visha looked beautiful, festooned in colour with gold literally dripping from head to toe. Arun looked handsome and very regal in his tunic and breeches, just like a military uniform from days gone by, topped with a turban. They stared into each other's eyes as they made their vows. Asha was very happy for Visha and very pleased to welcome Arun into the family.

The day after the wedding, Robert took the quartet to one of his favourite restaurants for lunch. On entering, he was recognised by one of the senior waiters and greeted warmly. Asha had been there once before and he remembered Asha as well.

"On just about every visit to Mumbai, I would come here at least once. Always to enjoy my favourite dishes of Bombay duck and fried prawns," Robert explained.

Andrew, Elisa and Amy looked at Robert strangely.

"What is Bombay duck?" Andrew inquired.

"Well, it is actually a fish."

The waiter brought some fresh produce to show them. There was a whole fish and a large crab. Robert decided to go with a recipe using the whole fish as well as his tried and tested Bombay duck and fried prawns. Everyone thoroughly enjoyed the Bombay duck as well as all the other dishes. What a great lunch.

Robert had planned other activities during the stay in India.

There was the trip to the vineyards. None of them had visited any of the Indian vineyards previously. They had tried some of the Indian wines and liked them. So, here was a chance to do some tasting on-site.

Robert had hired a car for the next day for the five of them. The driver picked them up and they set off a little after two thirty p.m. On the way, they stopped for fuel and some refreshments.

As they left suburbia, the countryside was flat and green. But further on, a range of undulating brown hills appeared and stayed with them through to the outskirts of Nashik.

They headed for their first vineyard, called Sandon. The roads out of Nashik to the vineyard were rough. They were too late for the tasting tour. So, they went up to the bar area, sat on the veranda, ordered some wine, Sauvignon Blanc to start with, and some snacks. This was a great location, overlooking the vines and dam as the sun set. Three or four more wines and then time for dinner, which offered a choice between Indian and Italian. The consensus was the former.

The food was just OK. But they enjoyed their best red wine.

Then they headed off to the hotel and, after a couple of missed turns, they got there and checked in.

They sat for a while in Robert's room, drinking a Merlot from the vineyard with some French fries.

"That was a very good start to our tasting journey," offered Robert. "What did you guys think?"
Andrew and Asha responded while the girls sat back nodding in agreement.

"A great location and very enjoyable wines, like the Merlot we are drinking."

"I liked the Sauvignon Blanc very much. I am looking forward to some more wine tasting tomorrow," Asha viewed.
Then off to sleep for everyone.

The plan had been to get down to breakfast around eight a.m. — wishful thinking. With the travel and late night, everyone had slept in and only made it down for ten.

After breakfast, on the road again in search of the next winery, Yanda, which was close to the one they had visited the previous day. They got there around eleven thirty a.m. but it did not open until twelve noon. So, back to Sandon. Very handy that it was so close by.

There, they were faced with disappointment after disappointment. The tour was not available. So, they went up to where they had been the night before. They chose the five wines they wanted in the tasting package only to be told that they could not make their own selection and were limited to the winery's option. Having tried a number of the wines the night before, they wanted to try something different. But Andrew's choice of a Zinfandel red was not available by the glass. Enough was enough and decided against the wine tasting. Robert and Asha bought some wines from the cellar door before returning to Yanda.

Yanda was a much different experience, more flexible. They tried seven wines. Asha's favourites were the Sauvignon Blanc and the Merlot. They then did the tour, followed by sitting outdoors overlooking the dam, sipping on a glass of wine. Some snacks were enjoyed while relaxing and enjoying the view. On their way out they bought some wine, including a bottle of Merlot for Asha.

Then off in search of the Grampians vineyard. And a search it was because it was very poorly signposted. Eventually getting there along rough roads.

They had the tour and then the tasting. They were the only people there and had some good interaction with the host, who showed them a few of their wines, even their top red. Part of the conversation included the marketing of their wines and the price points for the wines. Robert suggested that they were leaving some money on the table as he thought their wines were under-priced, compared to some of the others they had tasted.

Asha had difficulty understanding how busy Sandon had been but there had been few people at Yanda and even less at Grampians. And, yet, to his palate, the wines from the three vineyards were comparable in quality. Perhaps Sandon is older and better known, with Yanda quite new and Grampians so far out of the way, Asha posed to himself?

With the winery experiences over, they headed back to Powai, making good time for most of the journey until a few kilometres from their hotel when they ran into a traffic jam. Anyway, there was no rush for them.

Asha summed up. "It has been a great couple of days. Thank you for suggesting the winery tour, Robert. Although I have tried a number of Indian wines before, I was pleasantly surprised by the consistently good quality of all the wines we tasted."

"I agree about the quality," confirmed Robert.

"The only thing I did not like was how spread out the vineyards were, particularly out to Grampians. Take a look at the vineyards in the Hunter Valley and Orange in New South Wales as well as the vineyard areas in other parts of Australia. There are many in close proximity to one another. Also, the Nashik vineyards did not seem to be well promoted and badly signposted."

Keeping up the hectic schedule, they had another event organised for the day after returning from Nashik.

Weeks previously, when in Sydney, Asha and Robert had decided to go to the horse racing at Mahalaxmi race course in Mumbai, the same racecourse they had gone to before. Robert had contacted the secretary of the Royal Western India Turf Club Limited who had agreed to make tickets available free of charge. Robert had also booked a table at one of the restaurants within the racecourse.

Robert organised a hotel seven-seater SUV car to take them to and from the race course.

Near the airport, they hit a significant traffic snarl. It was not clear what the cause was until a bit further on when it became apparent that part of the road had been closed for roadworks. By that time, they were running late for the booking at the restaurant. So, Robert asked Asha to call ahead and let them know about the hold up. Robert also asked him to call the secretary to find out where to pick up the tickets. The driver dropped them off in one of the racecourse carparks and they found their way to the gate where the tickets were.

Where to now? Robert asked someone for directions to the restaurant. They were not too clear and the first effort took them to the wrong place. But they got back on the right track and soon reached the restaurant. Robert had asked for a window table. But there was not one available and they were seated at a round table near the window. This did not really matter as they had to go out to put their bets on and to see the races in any case.

The rest of the afternoon went very well, good food, drinks and some winners.

Elisa had the winner of the last race, her first for the day. She was so excited. Robert pushed her to pick up her winnings at the tote window. She came away with the money in her hand shouting to Andrew about her win.

Back in the car Robert told the driver where to go. All he would tell the group was that "they would end on a high note".

Arriving at the towering five-star hotel, the group was still not sure what their destiny was. Once inside the hotel, Robert led them to the lift to go up to the thirty-fourth floor.

Up they went and out into the open air. While standing and wondering where to sit, a lady, who turned out to be Australian, suggested they go through to the other side. Great advice. There they had a view overlooking the Arabian Sea. Although they had just missed the sunset, it was still a wonderful place to be.

Robert asked one of the staff if they could sit in one of the booths. His reply was that it was for members. Robert suggested that they would move if any members turned up, which was fine with him.

Robert had already decided that Veuve Clicquot French champagne was going to be the order of the day. Even better, it was happy hour and the champagne was half price. Drinks and snacks ordered, everyone relaxed imbibing the ambience while photographs were taken.

Later on, when an area became available at the edge, they moved over there. A DJ was playing some "quiet" music. Robert asked if he could play some dance music. Disappointingly, he said that Robert would have to wait until the later scheduled time for dance music. Nevertheless, Robert asked Amy for a dance first and then Elisa, invitations both accepted and they waltzed around for a short time.

A wonderful end to the day.

"So, what is your verdict on the day?" Robert posed.

"It was one of the best of best days: betting on horse races, wining and dining and finally, sitting in the thirty-fourth floor open lounge with a cool breeze, facing the sea and sipping champagne. And as you said Dad… 'we would end on a high note'."

"This the final instalment in our Indian travels. We have packed so much in. So many fabulous memories, shared by friends," Robert concluded.

"I'll drink to that" Asha enthused.

"Me too," was Andrew's view.

Robert's experience with the accommodation and dining on his previous visits had proved to be very beneficial, adding to the enjoyment of being together in India.

Asha was very happy to show Amy aspects of Indian life. Amy thoroughly relished the fabulous and varied experiences.

And Andrew confirmed that he wanted to return to India to work. Elisa thought that would be a good adventure. However, Robert was a little ambivalent about that. Asha did not say anything.

Chapter 22
Perth

Shortly after Amy and Asha got back to Australia, they travelled to Perth to spend the Christmas/New Year holidays with Amy's parents and the rest of her family. Amy has an older brother and older sister, both married and living away from her parents in Perth.

There had been little time spent at home between trips, merely unpacking bags, washing clothes and repacking.

Amy had told her parents, Ella and Roger, about Asha's polio leg and wearing a calliper as well as the occasional use of a wheelchair. So, this prepared them for the first meeting with Asha.

Ella and Roger met Amy and Asha at the airport and drove them to their dwelling in the beachside suburb of Cottesloe. It was a large bungalow with an in-ground pool right on the beach - very impressive thought Asha.

Ella and Roger knew that Amy and Asha were living together so there was no issue about putting them in the one room, which also had an en suite.

On Christmas Eve, they went to a Presbyterian church. Amy's parents are regular churchgoers but not

Amy. Asha had been in an Anglican church once before, so he was interested to find out if this was different. As it turned out the service was more down to earth and family oriented.

On Christmas morning, a champagne breakfast was savoured by the pool.

Afterwards the presents were opened. Amy and Asha had brought some gifts from India for Amy's parents and other family members. Asha gave Amy a gold bracelet (from India) and she gave him a mobile phone. Her parents gave them both casual shirts.

The weather was beautiful. It was sunny and very warm. This was Asha's third Christmas away from India and the first away from Sydney. But he still felt very much at ease in this new environment. Ella and Roger had made him very welcome from the outset.

Amy's brother and sister with their spouses and children, one each, arrived around noon. The two children, one three and the other four years old, were fascinated with Asha's calliper and even more so when he took it off to go in the pool with them.

After a brief swim, it was time for a big lunch with all the trimmings: prawns, turkey, Christmas pudding. All washed down with champagne and white and red wine. What a great day.

On Boxing Day, Amy and Asha travelled down to Margaret River with Ella and Roger, just under 300 kilometres away, for a few days. They stayed in a two-bedroom apartment in the middle of Margaret River.

Being the holiday season, the township was bustling. But that did not stop them wandering up and down the main drag exploring what was on offer.

On their first night there, they visited one of the pubs which was having a sausage sizzle. Asha's sausage sandwich was eased down with some beer. Everyone else was having wine. Asha was of a mind that he was in a pub and able to sample some of the produce from the local boutique breweries. Plenty of time for wine tasting later.

Since Asha's arrival in Australia, he had developed a palate for wines. So, he was looking forward to visiting some wineries.

For the remainder of their stay, they explored the superb scenery of the countryside mainly south of Margaret River.

One day they drove down to the Cape Leeuwin Lighthouse. This is situated at the most south-westerly tip of Australia, where the Indian and Southern Oceans meet. The Lighthouse is thirty-nine metres high and the top can be reached via a narrow winding staircase. The climb is definitely worthwhile to be able to watch the two oceans crash against each other with such powerful force.

This was a beautiful sunny day with little wind, making the views from the top of the Lighthouse most enjoyable. But what must it have been like for the Lighthouse keepers many years ago in the worst days of winter, which would have been bleak and wet with gale-force winds?

On the way back to Margaret River, they took a self-guided tour of one of the caves with its dazzling formations of stalactites and stalagmites.

Back at the apartment, being exhausted from the exercise and time spent in the fresh air, they rested up with a glass of wine before heading off for dinner.

Ella and Roger have a favourite restaurant in Perth that has a sister eatery in Margaret River. The restaurant was very busy. Fortunately, Ella had booked a table. A sumptuous meal accompanied by local wines went down very well as they talked about the abundance of vineyards around the Margaret River region, all in beautiful settings.

Asha felt very comfortable in the Margaret River area and thought he would not mind living down there. So different from city life. Nothing like India. And so many things to do. Would he get bored? Not if he could find an interest, such as wine making. One can only dream!

The next day and last day in the area was spent on a coach tour of wineries, cheese and chocolate factories and a boutique brewery. They were the only ones on the coach which gave some flexibility in how long they could stay at the various places. Just a great way to sample some more of the local produce.

They were back in Cottesloe for New Year's Eve. This time bringing in the New Year with Ella's and

Roger's family and friends enjoying finger food, a barbeque of prawns and some fine wines brought back from Margaret River. There were no fireworks displays in the Perth area. However, with the time difference between Sydney and Perth, they were able to watch the Sydney fireworks on television. Although not the same as watching from Robert's balcony, they still saw a splendid display.

One more city and region visited and a fabulous time.

The end of another incredibly busy year. Then it was back to Sydney for the start of another scholastic year.

Chapter 23
Dubai

In March 2006, Robert had planned another business trip to Mumbai. This time he wanted to tie it in with a holiday away from Mumbai.

He had looked into travelling on the Palace on Wheels, particularly because of the stops at Jaipur, the Pink City with many wonderful palaces and other buildings and Agra to see the Taj Mahal. But the timing did not work out for his planned visit to India. He also considered taking a boat trip on the Kerala waters but the season was wrong.

However, one day he had been reading a horse-racing magazine in his lounge room and there was an advertisement for the Dubai World Cup Horse Racing Tour. Because of Asha's interest in horse racing, Robert asked him if he would like to spend a few days in Dubai with him before his business meetings in Mumbai.

Of course Asha said yes. Asha's interest in horse racing had grown and this would be a great experience to be at one of the greatest racing meetings in the world. Furthermore, Asha had never been to Dubai before. It meant a week away from uni. But he felt he could manage that.

"Robert, why did you invite me?"

"Asha, I wanted some company. You are interested in horse racing and Andrew is not."

After John had finished his degree the previous year, Alice had decided to return to Vietnam and John would go with her, leaving Annie behind in Canberra. Alice felt she had something to offer her old country. In John's case, there were good work opportunities in Vietnam for him in the field of computing.

Robert had been surprised by Alice's decision and disappointed to see her leave. They had been more friends than anything else. But that still left a gap in Robert's life.

So, that left Asha as Robert's travelling partner option.

Because of Robert's airline status, they were travelling first class and able to use the first-class lounge. On the way to the airport, Robert told Asha about the lounge set up with its meals and day spa and suggested they have a massage. Asha had never had a massage before and agreed that it would be a good thing to try. Robert had already predicted Asha's response and had booked them into the day spa for a massage.

When they got to the day spa, two tables were ready for them. They undressed down to boxer shorts, in Asha's case, wrapped a towel around their waists and hopped onto the tables. Asha was not entirely sure what to expect. Initially, he asked the masseur if he could massage his polio foot first, which he did. Asha then rolled onto his stomach and the masseur proceeded to caress, stroke and pummel his body from head to toe. Some of the lads at university had told him about massage happy endings. But not here in such a legitimate and classy place.

Massage over and dressed, they made their way to the restaurant for a light meal before the flight.

"That was brilliant, Robert. I feel so energised."

"I think it is a good way to relax before a long flight."

The flight to Dubai was uneventful. On arrival, an airline car whisked them from Dubai airport to their hotel.

When they checked in, they were assigned smoking rooms when non-smoking rooms had been requested. *Do rooms smoke?* After a much persuasive discussion on Robert's part, non-smoking rooms were found for them.

"Asha, sorry about that. There were two points to address. Firstly, I do not like smoke-infested rooms. Secondly, I had made a point about reserving a non-smoking room and that was what the hotel needed to honour."

"Robert, I understand and well done arguing your case."

The following morning was a very early start. Asha and Robert met the rest of the tour group in the lobby before getting on a bus for the ride out to the track for Breakfast with the Stars. There was a very impressive set up with many tables set out by the track with a number of food stations scattered amongst the tables. The food stations offered a wonderful array of breakfast delights with the chefs willing to cook your eggs in the style of your choice. They enjoyed a lavish buffet breakfast, listened to guest interviews from the stage and watched some track work.

They had a walk around the lawn area and then into the Godolphin Gallery where they were able to witness the unveiling of the statue of Dubai Millennium, the greatest horse ever to race for the Godolphin stable, a renowned global racing giant. The statue, with jockey Frankie Dettori on board, was modelled by Madame Tussauds, well known for its waxworks of famous people. The owner of the Godolphin enterprise, His Excellency Sheikh Hamdan bin Mohammed Al Maktoum, did the honours with Dettori also in attendance.

"What a magnificent-looking horse! And the likeness of Dettori is very good."

"Very lifelike," Asha added.

The statue was a gift to His Highness Sheikh Mohammed bin Rashid Al Maktoum, Godolphin's founder and driving force. It recreates the moment when Dubai Millennium, with Frankie Dettori in the saddle, passed the winning post for his greatest victory in the Dubai World Cup at Nad Al Sheba in 2000. According to the literature, he put up a devastating performance, leading all the way to win in a record time of 1 minute

59.50 seconds which still stood at that time, for the ten furlongs on dirt at the Dubai course. Dubai Millennium had won nine of his ten starts when injury ended his racing days in August, 2000. Tragically he died from grass sickness on April 29, 2001, during his first season as a stallion at Sheikh Mohammed's Dalham Hall Stud in Newmarket, England.

That afternoon, they went on a safari, setting off in a cavalcade of four-wheel drives, not really knowing what to expect. Then when they reached the sand dunes, it was like being on a roller coaster, up and down the dunes, twisting and turning. Towards the end Asha became carsick and they had to stop briefly. Then they continued to an area set up with a Bedouin tent, the location for their Arabian barbeque dinner complete with entertainment including a belly dancer. There were camels that you could ride and sandboards to slide down the dunes. Too energetic for Robert and Asha.

It was a most enjoyable evening set in the desert sandscape under the stars.

"What a brilliant way to end our first full day in Dubai!" was Robert's description.

The following day was a bus tour away from Dubai. They had a couple of sightseeing stops before lunch. A most remarkable thing happened in the restaurant. They did not charge for Asha. Robert asked why and they would not tell him. Asha's guess was that it was out of respect for a disabled person.

That night Robert and Asha had dinner in the Al Mahara restaurant at the Burj Al-Arab Hotel, a luxury hotel, at that time named as the world's only seven-star hotel.

Robert had made the reservation by email from Sydney. As they approached the hotel by taxi, they were stopped by security to make sure they had a hotel or restaurant reservation. They entered the splendid hotel and made their way to the Skyview bar for a drink before going to the restaurant. They had a glass of champagne each.

"I am blown away," blurted Asha. "I am going to telephone my family. I cannot believe this and I do not think they will be able to comprehend what I am doing."

"Just relax and enjoy the experience."

The restaurant was accessible by a three-minute virtual submarine voyage. Unfortunately, it was under maintenance and they had to use the common lift. They were seated next to the aquarium. In some ways, it felt strange eating seafood and watching the fish swim around.

"Wow! What a location! I hope the tank does not burst," Asha observed.

As they were leaving Robert remarked to Asha "A delicious meal and a wonderful experience. "Two great days so far. And the race meeting is still to come. Really looking forward to that."

"Me too."

On race day morning they went to one of the souk markets, which had a tremendous array of shops selling mainly items of gold. They wandered from shop to shop, ending up not buying anything. As they were leaving, they bumped into someone from their tour and shared a taxi back to the hotel. They were so engrossed in chat, not realising for quite some time that they were not heading for their hotel. The driver had misunderstood the name of the hotel they wanted to go to and was driving off in the direction of another hotel in the same chain, well away from their hotel. A fair — or is that fare? — price was negotiated when they eventually reached their destination.

Then it was off to the races.

The air was alive with chatter as they drove to the course in the coach. Once inside, they made their way up to their seats in the Millennium Terrace on the second floor of one of the stands.

Having settled into their seats, the first task was to select the winners of the six thoroughbred races. Betting was not allowed in Dubai. But you could enter this competition where there was prize money for the person or persons picking all winners.

"Asha, great seats. Such a superb view across the whole track and down past the winning post."

"The atmosphere seems odd to me, with a mixture of calm and the buzz of anticipation. I am very excited."

Next off to the bar just behind their seats for a glass of wine for Robert and a beer for Asha. On his way there, Asha noticed all the tables of food that had been set up. The spread looked enticing.

As the races unfolded, they were able to sample the wares, with the "menu" changing from entree to main and onto dessert. There were a number of stations set up serving hot, delicious food, in different styles from many parts of the world.

"I never expected the catering to be so impressive," Asha commented.

"We ought to have known from the experience at Breakfast with the Stars."

Part way through the meeting, there was a different type of entertainment with acrobats and hot-air balloons.

But even although neither of them was lucky in choosing the six winners, they had a great time at the races.

"What an experience! Robert, it was a great idea to make the trip here, not just for the races but also for all the other interesting activities as well."

The next day was their last day in Dubai. After breakfast, they headed back to the souk market. Being a bit more decisive this time, they actually bought a couple of items. They then took a taxi to the Mall of the Emirates, which was only six months old at that time. Just like many things in Dubai, this was extraordinary. There was a vast array of shops, food outlets and a cinema complex. But the most intriguing item in this desert city was an indoor snow ski slope. Robert tried to organise for Asha to do some snowboarding but time did not permit, so they went to see a movie. They finished their visit with some shopping before heading back to the hotel to get ready for their departure.

There is a saying that you only ask a question if you know the answer. After checkout, Robert and Asha were waiting in the lobby for their transport to the airport, when the concierge approached them. He engaged in conversation and asked Robert if he had enjoyed the stay. Bad mistake. Robert then outlined the trials and tribulations of the stay. Not only had there been the problems at check-in, there seemed to be reluctance by the housekeeping staff to clean their rooms and respond to any requests. On two days, the rooms were not cleaned until Robert asked for them to be cleaned. One day, before going out, Robert requested housekeeping to provide clean towels and to pick up the iron and ironing board from his room. When they got back late in the evening, nothing had been done. So, Robert had to make the request again, this time with a successful outcome.

The tour leader had overheard the conversation with the concierge and told Asha and Robert that they were not the only ones in the group unhappy with the service. As they found out later, the tour group no longer uses that hotel.

"Well, Asha, we have ended our stay the way we began it, embroiled in discussion with the hotel staff."

"Robert, you gave honest feedback. I hope they have taken it on board and will change their ways."

They went to the airport together in a taxi. Then Robert would fly to Mumbai and Asha back to Sydney.

On the way, Robert and Asha had a good reminisce about their time in Dubai. Asha asked Robert if he had enjoyed the tour and if he thought it was worthwhile.

"I think it was great value for money and time well spent relishing such experiences. Every single one was brilliant with the race meeting itself being the highlight. I will remember this for a very long time. Here's to the next time. Perhaps, Invincible will become good enough to race in Dubai?"

"Let's hope so. Robert, thank you for the opportunity. It was way beyond my imagination. Such an incredible city."

The travel list continues to grow: another city and another fantastic experience.

Chapter 24
A Mixture of a Year

Invincible was back in training and due to make his return to racing after nearly a year away from the track. He had experienced a number of minor setbacks while he was in the paddock having a break from racing. He had also gone through some growing pains.

His first race after the spell was very disappointing. He did not seem to put in enough effort and tailed off last. Everyone was puzzled by this. After another very poor effort two weeks later, he pulled up with a torn tendon. The decision was then made to retire him and prepare him for stud duties. End of the dream! And no Dubai, at least for him. Such a pity, with an early end to what seemed to be a promising career.

Asha was now in his fourth year at uni and things were going well. Amy was also doing well in her studies. Their part-time jobs were giving them other interests and they were pretty busy socially.

It was June 2006 and time for Asha to get a new calliper. The company that made his original one in Mumbai had a branch in Sydney to which he had been a number of times to get some maintenance done on his first calliper. But it was now beyond that, well-worn and not fitting as well as it ought to. Also, his boots were showing signs of wear and tear.

Asha's leg was measured. But there was no need to measure his feet for new boots as he would be wearing normal ones on both feet with a build-up on the bottom of the right one. This was because the new calliper would fit inside his footwear.

The measuring reminded Asha of one occasion when the orthotist used a handheld device to try to detect muscle movement in his polio leg. But just like sending missions to Mars to look for life there, no sign of muscle movement was found in his leg.

Three weeks later, Asha went back to try on the new calliper. As he walked into the orthotist's room with a feeling of excitement, he could see a calliper standing next to a chair. It was his. It looked very delicate. It was much different to the old one. It was newer technology. It was made of moulded plastic "buckets" that would fit around his thigh and calf areas as well as a plastic foot component. The metal, attached to the "buckets" from thigh to ankle was a much lighter material. The knee-lock mechanism that linked the top and bottom "buckets" had a bar at the back for semi-automatic locking and unlocking.

Asha sat down and took off the old battered warhorse that had served him so well. He lifted up the new one and it felt very light comparatively, light as a feather. He put his leg inside the calliper and attached all the straps, including the knee pad. There were two differences. No T-strap from his boot to support his ankle as it was held very well within the lower bucket. And no belt around his waist as his hip was held by the upper bucket. He then slid the black boot over his foot and did the bootlace up. As advised by the orthotist, he had bought a pair of new boots, using his left foot for fitting. The right boot was the same length as the left boot to accommodate the calliper fitting inside. And the heel and sole had been built up by the mandatory four inches. Looked good. For the first time, Asha had flexibility in terms of the type of footwear he wanted, not being restricted to custom-made boots with a slot for the calliper to fit into.

Asha stood up and bent down to lock the calliper manually, forgetting that all he had to do was straighten his leg and the calliper would lock into position. Asha took the first tentative step. A couple of more steps and then he was striding around the room. The calliper felt comfortable, providing great support and, indeed, it was quite light. A huge difference. The old calliper would now be relegated to the position of reserve.

Such impressive technical skills to get the calliper fitting so well.

The specialist watched Asha walk around and asked him how his left leg, his so-called good leg, felt.

"My left leg is fine, although it does get a little tired at times as it is the one that usually takes most of my weight."

He then surprised Asha by suggesting that he ought to use his wheelchair more often, just to give his left leg some respite. After all, it had been doing most of the heavy lifting for over twenty years. Nevertheless, Asha was not sure about using the wheelchair more. He liked the freedom of walking. He decided to keep that suggestion in the back of his mind.

There were other advantages of the new calliper. Asha did not need a zip up the inside of his trouser leg as the footwear was separate from the calliper. And he could try trousers on before he bought them and have any alterations made.

When Asha got home, Amy could not wait to see the new Asha. Asha was also excited, like a kid in a toy shop, to show Amy the different him. Asha was already very happy with the new calliper.

It was halfway through the year. Hadn't time flown?

Amy and Asha had been in the habit of having the occasional weekend lunch or dinner party at their flat. Amy was a very accomplished cook and really enjoyed creating different menus for various occasions, particularly birthdays.

For Andrew's birthday, Amy produced a Christmas (in July) feast with all the trimmings. The highlight of the meal was a turducken, which is a de-boned chicken stuffed into a de-boned duck, which was in turn stuffed into a de-boned turkey. It took a lot of effort on Amy's part. But, based on the responses from the assembled feasters, it was well worthwhile. Absolutely delicious, Asha thought and he was very proud of Amy.

"That was such a delicious meal, Amy," proclaimed the diners.

It had been a great night, not only for the food and drink. They had made it into an occasion by dressing formally, the men in tuxedos and the ladies in their best party dresses. That is, except for Robert, who had really excelled by donning his kilt with the rest of the traditional Highland outfit.

"Robert, you look very handsome and very impressive in your Highland outfit. Perhaps, we ought to have a night when we all dress in our native costumes?" commented Asha

"Great idea. But what would the Aussies wear?"

"Dad, we'll find something. Perhaps, shorts and sandals, such as thongs!"

As usual, the focus for the rest of the year was study. But Amy and Asha still made time to do the things they liked such as going racing, dinner parties and watching movies. Once they did manage to do something different, at least for them. They went off on a wine-tasting weekend to the Hunter Valley with Andrew and Elisa and four other friends.

They drove off early on the Saturday morning for the 150-plus kilometre trip in a convoy of four cars.

They stopped briefly at Wollombi to take in some refreshments they had brought with them before continuing onto the motel where they had booked rooms for the night.

Then it was off to their first tastings, in two cars, with designated drivers. That was followed by a light lunch at one of the vineyards.

They had booked a tour for the afternoon to enable all of them to enjoy the wines. This was a very sensible and enjoyable way to do it. They took in four wineries and were able to sample a range of whites and reds. Asha's favourites were a Semillon and a Cabernet Sauvignon. He stocked up on both varieties to add to the wine collection.

The day finished with a brilliant dinner with first class local produce and wines. What a way to celebrate the region! Unfortunately, all good things need to end and they headed back to Sydney the following morning after a hearty country breakfast.

John returned to Australia in October, leaving his mother behind in Vietnam. He had been missing Australia, particularly not being with his girlfriend, Eve.

He stayed with Amy and Asha for around a month while he went looking for a job and reacquainted himself with Eve. He managed to get a job as a business analyst with a bank. Eve and John also decided to move into an apartment together.

John had been an easy-going guest, causing no hassles. The only issue was being a little tight for space when John and Asha were both using their wheelchairs around the flat. But they got by.

Amy and Asha also got to know Eve a lot more. She seemed to be a good match for John, being pretty smart with a positive outlook. She had a job as a librarian. The four of them would go out to dinner together about once a week.

John also had to visit his technician to get new prosthetics. Asha asked him how often he needed to get new "legs".

"When I was young, I would get new prosthetics every two years or so. This was to make sure that the length of my legs was appropriate for my body size. But ever since I stopped growing, I have not had any new ones. The current ones are in a poor state and much better technology has come on the scene. So, time to upgrade. These will be the first new prosthetics in almost eight years. Hopefully, they will last a good length of time."

Asha went along with John when he was getting his new prosthetics. Watching John put them on made Asha compare his calliper to John's prosthetics. Asha's calliper was like scaffolding holding up his leg, a bit clumsy and pretty manual. Whereas John's prosthetics were more robotic, taking over the human form, and very modern and sleek. Prosthetics, at least to Asha, seem to have made more advances over time than orthotics. Asha understood that there are technological advances being made with orthotics. But the newer models are very expensive. Asha was not, for a moment, suggesting that prosthetics are not expensive, particularly the hi-tech models. This is the price people pay for being disabled.

While John was putting on his prosthetics, Asha thought about his friends. In Nagpur, all his friends were able-bodied. Yet, since Asha had come to Australia, a number of his male friends have a disability: Andrew, John and Yung-Su. What does that say about the culture and acceptance of being disabled?

John slid liners, a cushioning material, over his residual stumps. Then he pulled on the sockets at the top of the prosthetics onto his stumps. The technician helped John to his feet and led him to the nearby parallel bars for John to test out the prosthetics.

"They feel fine and are working well. Let me go for a walk around the room. Great! Tremendously comfortable."

John sat down again. No adjustments required. Once dressed, he stood up, ready to go. In turn, Asha got up, locked his calliper and off they went. John was walking very freely while Asha was walking along with one straight leg. John was more disabled than Asha, yet John had easier natural movement in terms of walking, going up and down steps, sitting and standing!

They went to a nearby pub for a drink.

"John, I am really impressed with how well you walk. It must have been difficult to begin with."

"Yes. Very difficult. I fell over a number of times. But no serious damage. Then, as confidence built, the falls disappeared."

"I did not really have any problems wearing the big calliper. Mind you, I remember one time I set out to walk and my right leg collapsed under me. I had not locked the knee properly. A bit silly.

"John, this may seem like a strange question. Do you miss not having legs?"

"Asha, not strange. I think about having legs from time to time. I miss not having legs a little. But I am so used to my situation that it does not matter anymore. After all, I cannot do anything about it.

"Asha, what about you? Do you miss not being able to walk normally?"

"Not really. I have never been able to walk normally. The first time I put my right leg on the ground to walk was when I got my first calliper. And for that, I am very grateful to Robert.

"If Robert had not stopped me in Powai, I do not know what would have happened to me. Perhaps I would have still been using a pole to hop around. And I would not have met Andrew, Elisa, Amy, of course, as well as yourself. And I am sure that I would not have enjoyed the experiences of travel and living in this wonderful country. So, in some ways, contracting polio turned out to be good for me."

"Looks like you landed on your feet, so to speak."

"Anyway, thank you for the drink. I'm off. My shout next time."

"OK. Bye."

That was interesting, thought Asha. At the end of the day, John and I have disabilities but we are both very able because of the ongoing technical developments.

Another very busy year that had been most enjoyable. A great trip to Dubai. Wonderful times with friends. Getting closer to Amy. Another scholastic year under Asha's belt.

To round off the year, the quartet plus John and Eve gathered at Robert's apartment for Christmas lunch. It was a boisterous occasion. Everyone was in high spirits, emotionally and physically. They all made a return visit to Robert's apartment to bring in the New Year.

Another year beckoning, full of promise Asha hoped.

Chapter 25
Bishu's Visit

It was now the final year for Andrew, Amy and Asha.

Elisa had finished her course in 2006 and applied for a number of teaching posts and was successful with a private school in the eastern suburbs of Sydney that was looking for an understudy for their principal music teacher. Asha was very pleased for Elisa. She had worked hard at the Conservatorium as well as developing her piano skills as a tutor and as a performer. She had become an accomplished musician with a broad spectrum of genres from classical to jazz. She had performed on stage a number of times.

Amy thought it was about time that Asha was exposed to some culture by way of opera. Asha had not really listened to much opera and his only real experience was when Robert had taken him to the Sydney Opera House to see *La Traviata*. At the interval, Robert asked Asha what he thought and Asha's only comment related to "these screeching women".

When Amy told Asha that she had bought tickets to see *La Traviata* at the Sydney Opera House, he had to confess that he had seen that opera previously and had not been too impressed.

"Let's see if your opinion has changed," Amy responded.

They dressed up a little for the opera, had a snack and a glass of wine in the foyer before taking their great seats, which were halfway back in the stalls, slap bang in the middle of the row. "Well done Amy."

As it turned out Asha really enjoyed the event, as did Amy. Asha thought it was joyous, dramatic and, of course, sad, with some fantastic arias.

"Well, well, well! Asha, what happened to the screeching women?"

Asha could hardly come down after they left the Opera House, still embroiled in the story and the music. He said to Amy that they needed to do this again. Great entertainment in such a marvellous setting on Sydney Harbour.

La Traviata was not the only music event for them at the start of the year. They also went to see *Il Divo*, such a polished act with great voices and memorable tunes. They really had a great time. This was different to the opera. But it was still first-class entertainment.

To keep the memories and to keep the music going Asha bought CDs of both *La Traviata* and *Il Divo*. He had not bothered much about CDs before. Andrew and Asha had not shown much interest in music. But Amy was different. She loved music. She had built up a small collection from pop to musicals, which she would play, mostly at weekends. So, these two were Asha's contribution. For a couple of weeks, they were the only

CDs they played, one after the other, over and over, never tiring of them.

This year was Bishu's twenty-first birthday and, as a special present, Asha paid for him to visit them in Sydney at a time that coincided with term break.

Amy and Asha had a great time being Bishu's tour guides, showing him around the sights of Sydney and its surrounds. It turned out to be a very busy and tiring time. They tried to link logical activities together, planning alternate driving days with walking days.

One day it was the eastern suburbs and Watson's Bay, another Kirribilli, Bradley's Head, Manly, North Head and Palm Beach. Some of it they did by public transport, mainly bus and ferry. Bus to Watson's Bay, fish and chips on the grass, ferry back to Circular Quay, completing the circuit by bus. So easy. The other travels were by car.

On the way to Manly, they stopped at Kirribilli to give Bishu a chance to look back at the city and then onto Bradley's Head, again a view back towards the city and the Bridge. Stunning sights.

In Manly, they had fish, prawns and chips for lunch on the beach. Surprise, surprise. A creature of habit. Fortunately, Bishu also liked the food very much. He'd never experienced anything like this before. How could you beat fresh seafood under a blue sky beside the ocean? But he thought the seagulls were a bit of a nuisance.

At Palm Beach, they had a swim. Asha's dear younger brother had to carry him into the foam of the surf. Bishu really enjoyed himself in the water, swimming out and trying to catch the waves back to shore, which he did a couple of times. Amy and Asha were more comfortable staying closer to the beach.

Then there was a visit to the NSW Art Gallery that interested Bishu a lot. He was a keen artist, particularly portraiture. Ranjiv had encouraged Bishu by buying him brushes, paints and canvases.

Naturally enough Asha pointed out the Rodin sculpture of *The Burghers of Calais*. Bishu said he liked it. But he preferred some of the more modern paintings, like those by Jeffrey Smart.

After ushering Amy and Bishu through a number of rooms in the gallery, they ventured outside again and made their way into the Royal Botanic Garden, such a relaxing place, apart from some screeching bats. They had a sandwich and a drink at a cafe and then continued down to the Sydney Opera House with its gleaming sails. Bishu was impressed with what he described as "an astonishing piece of architecture". Bishu had seen the Opera House in books and on television. But he had never imagined how beautiful it would be in real life. Amy and Asha could not agree more. Just splendid.

They must have been full of beans as they decided to walk across the Harbour Bridge to Kirribilli. It was quite an easy stroll, taking them around an hour. But Asha did not feel like walking back so he called a water taxi to take them the short distance across the harbour to The Rocks. On the way across the bridge, Asha had noticed the rooftop of a pub down below. So, they headed off in search of it. A short climb and they reached the pub. And yet another climb and they were on the rooftop, offering views from Circular Quay to the Heads. The beer went down very well.

One of the drive days took them out to the Blue Mountains with a stop at a wildlife park on the way. Bishu was fascinated by being able to wander amongst some of the wildlife, particularly the kangaroos and pat them and feed them. He was most happy when he was able to stroke a koala and get his photograph taken with it.

When they reached Katoomba, they had some lunch and then went off to a scenic park where they were able to view different aspects of the mountains, in particular The Three Sisters. They travelled across the gorge in a cable car. They endured the hair-raising experience of going down into the rainforest in old rail cars that just seemed to drop off the mountain. That was followed by a leisurely walk along the boardwalk, looking at all the plants and trees as well as listening out for the sounds of the forest. The return journey in their 'spaceship', at least that was what it looked like to Asha, was very smooth.

Bishu bought some more souvenirs to go with those he had purchased at the wildlife park. He was building up a good collection of memorabilia and presents.

Before heading back to Sydney, they called into a chocolate factory, where they all had hot chocolate. The chocolates looked so tempting that they bought some to take home, that is if they would last the journey.

Bishu's second ferry ride was over to Taronga Park zoo. They took the gondola up from the bottom and then meandered gently back down to the bottom. Great exhibits. Asha's favourite was the giraffe enclosure. They looked so ungainly with their spindly legs. Amy and Bishu both liked the elephants.

Their final drive was the longest. They went to Canberra and then back across country and up the coast to Sydney. The highlight for Bishu was the visit to Parliament House. Although there was security around, he was surprised at how much freedom they had throughout most of the building including being able to sit in the visitor's gallery overlooking the chambers where the politicians sit when Parliament is in session, unfortunately not the day they were there. After an overnight stay in Canberra, they headed for Bowral to visit the Bradman museum. The Museum houses a great collection of Bradman memorabilia as well as detailing the history of cricket. Bishu was a bigger fan of cricket than Asha. He could hardly believe where he was, viewing exhibits of the great man as well as other historical items. Will they build such a "memorial" to Tendulkar in Mumbai, his birthplace?

Naturally, they had a barbeque at Robert's apartment in Bishu's honour. Such a memory for him, standing on the balcony, under a blue sky in bright sunshine, staring in awe at the beautiful harbour, with the glint of the Opera House in front of the Harbour Bridge on one side. Asha pointed out to Bishu some of the places they had been to, from the Bridge at one end up to Manly in the distance. Asha asked Bishu if there was a better sight in the world. He said he did not know the answer. But this must be one of the best.

Some more questions from Asha followed. "Well, Bishu, we have travelled a lot while you have been here, on foot, by bus and ferry as well as by car. Do you have a favourite?"

"Everything" was the reply.

Bishu's visit was over and they went to the airport. After check-in, they sat together in a café having a final drink together and then they said their goodbyes. Bishu said to Asha "My time with you has been beyond my wildest dreams." Tears started rolling down Asha's face as Bishu disappeared into the departure area.

Chapter 26
Andrew and Robert

While Asha was playing host to his brother, Robert had taken Andrew on a trip to New Zealand. They had not spent much time recently together just the two of them for some time.

Robert had been to New Zealand many times on business and for pleasure.

The first time was with his wife in 1972. As they had been driving from Auckland airport to their hotel in the city, it immediately struck him that it felt like they were in the England of thirty years before by the look of the road signs and the uniforms of the policemen.

But there was not much going on in Auckland. It seemed as dead as downtown Sydney was at that time on a Sunday.

In the 90s for a period of time Robert was travelling to Auckland regularly. They were usually one night, one day trips.

For Friday lunch he and a colleague frequented a French restaurant, which did a delicious whitebait fritter. Robert enjoyed other dishes that he chose, mainly because of the potato ingredient. When the restaurant staff found out that Robert was making his last trip, they decided to name a dish after him, calling it chargrilled eye fillet steak with crunchy pickled onions, field mushrooms and "McDonald" potatoes. Sounds absolutely mouth-watering. They sent Robert a copy of the menu with that dish on it. He had it framed and it now hangs on a wall in his study.

It was also on one of these visits that Robert had an interesting and positive hotel experience. His flight arrived late in the evening and by the time he got to the hotel it was getting towards midnight. He checked in and went up to the room. The entrance had twin doors. As Robert opened the door and entered the room, he was taken aback. There before him was a grand piano and a dining table with eight chairs and a sitting area with a sofa and armchairs. And then there were the normal hotel items of bedroom and bathroom. But he had no time to relax and enjoy the spacious surroundings. It was off to bed because he had an early morning meeting. What a waste.

As an aside, Robert encountered a similar situation in Adelaide. He was there on business and Pauline had been able to join him after he had been there for a couple of days. After work, Robert went back to the hotel to meet Pauline. He opened the door and there she was sitting in the bedroom. Why are you crammed into this room? Unbeknown to Pauline, Robert had a suite. This was the separate bedroom and, as Robert opened the adjoining door, the large lounge room part of the suite appeared. At least this time, he was able to enjoy all the comforts for a few days with Pauline.

Robert also went to Auckland on business just before Team New Zealand's 2003 defence of the America's Cup event there and, by that time, it had changed radically. There was much more going on, with more of a big city and touristy atmosphere.

Robert stayed at a hotel on the waterfront. One morning, as he was getting dressed for work, he got the surprise of his life. He noticed out of the window a cargo ship heading straight for his hotel room and not too far away at that, and then it changed course. Phew!

All in the past and now looking forward to a very enjoyable time with Andrew.

The flight over was memorable for the wrong reason. They were flying economy class. The meal trolley came round and Robert got his selection but they were waiting for the chicken dish that Andrew wanted. Robert started on his meal thinking that Andrew's chicken would not be long. Robert kept eating and Andrew kept waiting. When Robert had finished his meal, he asked one of the cabin crew about the chicken. The barked response was — *It is coming!*

On the way back, a similar problem. Robert got his meal and Andrew was told by one of the crew that she would be back with his meal. Time passed and no meal in sight. Robert reminded her and she was all apologetic about forgetting. And, to make matters worse, they had run out of food in economy. So, off she went to business class to put together a plate for Andrew.

In Auckland, they stayed at the hotel on the water where Robert had the cargo ship experience. They went out for a walk and went up the Sky Tower, which was well worth the visit with its views around Auckland as well as the views down through the glass panels in the floor. But they gave SkyJump a miss. Robert explained to Andrew that he is chicken when it comes to extreme things like that. Andrew agreed.

Andrew was really taken by the restaurant in the hotel. But the same could not be said about the French restaurant where they ate that night. Yes, the very same restaurant of "McDonald potatoes" fame. The layout of the restaurant had changed dramatically since Robert was last there. It seemed more modern. But it still looked very good. However, no "McDonald" potatoes on the menu. Andrew's problem was the lobster he had chosen as a main course. He did not like it so Robert changed plates with him.

After an enjoyable stay in Auckland, they flew down to Queenstown. As they were getting close to the town, they could see the snow-clad mountain.

Robert had been to Queenstown once before in 1997 on a management team building exercise. Exercise being the operative word because there was nothing in the way of business meetings. They went on a jet boat that was exhilarating. They went white-water rafting of which Robert is not a big fan. He had done this once before in Portland, Oregon. He did not like it then and the second time around did not change his feelings. Just Robert being chicken again! The third activity was going up in a helicopter. Unfortunately, it did not last long as the cloud cover was too low. But Robert enjoyed his first ride in a helicopter. The final activity was snow skiing. Robert had tried skiing once before at Perisher in the Snowy Mountains area of New South Wales. He could not get his balance right then. So, he gave it a miss this time, content just to walk the slopes in the lovely sunshine. A memory of Pauline skiing into a pool of water on that Perisher trip came to mind. Enough to put anyone off skiing.

After Robert and Andrew checked into their motel just on the outskirts of the town, they drove back into Queenstown and took the gondola up high over the town to the top of Bob's Peak. This gave them a great perspective of Queenstown and its surrounds. The views across Lake Wakatipu were truly magnificent.

During their stay, they drove around a lot, taking in as many sites as possible from the town itself to Coronet Peak, Arrowtown and Wanaka.

One day they went on an all-day "adventure".

First of all, there was an exciting trip up the Dart River by jet boat, experiencing all the thrills of shallow-water jet boating and jet spins.

They then disembarked to begin the next stage of their journey in an inflatable canoe, paddling and drifting downstream. They were in *Lord of the Rings* country with plenty of time to take in the awesome scenery.

They stopped for a buffet lunch, marred only by all the flies that had come to share the experience. It was still enjoyable, relaxing in the wilderness by the water and under the surrounding mountains. Absolutely beautiful.

They then continued downstream to meet the 4WD coach that would take them back to Queenstown.

It had been a great day and a marvellous experience.

It had been a little challenging for Andrew, with Robert having to lift him in and out of the watercraft.

"Dad, I have had a great time being with you in the open air amidst such wonderful scenery. It was also so peaceful and quiet."

The night before they were due to return to Sydney, they were having a most enjoyable dinner in a restaurant when Robert glimpsed snow falling against the backdrop of Bob's Peak.

When they got up the following morning, there was evidence of snow all around. After breakfast they decided to go up Coronet Peak to get up close and personal with the snow. This was Andrew's first experience of snow. On the way they stopped where there was a good covering of snow to throw snowballs at each other. Part way up to the Peak, it was clear that driving was getting more difficult, with the car sliding around. Robert stopped in one of the sidings offering a tremendous view down into the valley, providing picturesque photographic opportunities.

Then off to the airport. When Robert and Andrew got on board, the guy sitting next to Robert asked if he was cold. Robert was in the shorts that he had been wearing all morning. And it was six degrees outside. But he was not cold. No sense, no feeling.

Andrew was very talkative on the journey back, a little unusual for him. He had really enjoyed the holiday, not just the various aspects of the trip itself but the quality time he had spent with his Dad.

That made Robert feel good on the one hand but reflective on the other hand. Robert regretted not being able to spend enough time with Andrew when he was growing up. They had been doing more together in recent years and that was good. But had that made up for missed opportunities earlier in his life? In Robert's working life over the past twenty years, he had travelled a lot. And, even although Pauline had her own job, much of the parenting had been left to her. Cannot change the past, just learn from it.

Pauline, Robert and Andrew did manage to have a family holiday most years.

They went to Bali, Fiji and Honolulu, places where Andrew could swim and play on the beach.

Another time, they went to the Los Angeles area. This was an exciting trip. They had never been there before and the highlight was to be Disneyland.

But they had one kind of scary moment. Late one afternoon, they were coming out of a downtown department store when it was getting dark. They were in a very big city and a lot of people were rushing around. So, Pauline and Robert each took one of this little blonde-haired, blue-eyed boy's hands and held on tightly as they made their way to catch the bus back to the hotel. It was such a spontaneous reaction and Robert was not really sure why they did that.

Andrew was around five years old then and had got his first wheelchair, mainly for when they were walking long distances. Otherwise, he was very mobile with his below-knee leg braces.

The wheelchair turned out to be very handy for exploring the tracts of the Disneyland Park. They spent a whole day there traipsing along Main Street, bumping into some of the Disney characters and diverting into the various "lands" to enjoy the themed rides. Andrew had a ball.

Robert did not think Andrew stopped smiling from the time they entered the Park until they left. There were also the moments of excitement, chuckling and outlandish laughter, particularly when Mickey Mouse came up to Andrew and shook his hand. What joy! What memories.

In quieter moments in New Zealand, Robert asked Andrew what he remembered about their holidays. Disneyland was the first he mentioned. Robert listened and watched as Andrew's eyes lit up recalling that time.

Robert had a great time with Andrew in New Zealand. They had talked a lot about what Andrew was doing and how he saw the future. He intimated that he wanted to marry Elisa and have children. He also wanted to further his career. Although he was not really sure about what the next step would be for him, workwise. That was Andrew, giving clues but keeping his cards close to his chest.

Chapter 27
Times They are A-changing

Andrew, Amy and Asha attended Elisa's graduation in the middle of the year. They were all proud of her but none more so than Andrew. Andrew and Elisa had grown so close together and, although Asha had not discussed this with Andrew, he just wondered if wedding bells were on the horizon for them. If so, perhaps, they were waiting until after Andrew graduated the following year.

Elisa showed them her testamur (degree certificate) before re-joining her classmates for the all-important photographs.

As for Andrew, Amy and Asha, they were half way through their final year. This time next year, they would be celebrating their own graduations.

Andrew and Elisa went to Robert's for Sunday lunch a few days after her graduation. She excitedly showed Robert her certificate. "Congratulations," Robert said. They were on the balcony having a drink before lunch when Andrew piped up. "I have an announcement." That seemed very formal to Robert. "OK. What is it?" Robert pondered.

"Well," Andrew said. "Elisa and I are going to be married."

Robert kissed Elisa and hugged Andrew as he proffered his congratulations and best wishes. Robert was not really surprised as they had been together for so long. "About time" Robert roared with a huge smile on his face. "And when is the wedding?"

"We have not decided yet," Andrew responded.

What would his mother have said, thought Robert? He was sure she would have been elated for Andrew and very pleased that he was going to settle down with someone who seemed so lovely.

In July, Amy and Asha hosted a lunch for Andrew's birthday. This was becoming a ritual. In 2005 it had been a simple finger food and champagne afternoon tea. Last year had been the incredible turducken. This year was a little less elaborate but still fine fare, featuring a sumptuous poached salmon. It was always just the quartet and Robert. Robert's company was keeping him busy and he was still travelling one to two weeks a month. But when he was in Sydney, he always enjoyed having lunch with Andrew, Elisa, Asha and Amy. Two fabulous sons and two gorgeous ladies on their way to becoming daughters-in-law. Being with them gave Robert the impression of staying young, at least mentally if not physically. Always interesting conversations that were positive unlike the troubles that newspapers and television news reports forever wanted to focus on. Robert would talk about his latest trip that generally generated questions and discussions. Asha was particularly interested in Robert's views on India. The others brought everyone else up to date on their studies. Andrew and Elisa talked about a play or musical they had been to see and Amy and Asha critiqued their latest movie outing. Such joyous company to be in. Robert felt so lucky. After a fairly lengthy period, six years for Andrew and five years for Amy and Asha, university was all over, pending the results of the final year exams. It had been a very challenging time but rewarding. Asha had learnt a lot, expanded his network of friends and had grown in confidence. Asha had been well supported through the process by Andrew, in particular. He was always there for Asha as were Robert and Amy. Elisa had also been a source of encouragement. That's what friends are for.

Asha had made friends with other people like Philippe and Scott. They had celebrated the end of university together before they each departed for their home cities. Sad to see them go. They had not lived in one another's pockets, but they had met socially from time to time. Asha looked back on the time they went on the beach together during 'O' week when they had accepted Asha for whom he is, had provided encouragement, and helped him to get into and out of the water. They had bonded.

The three of them vowed to stay in touch.

One day, it would be great to visit them in their countries, thought Asha.

And then, out of the blue, Asha got a text message from Philippe saying Scott and he had been in an accident and were on their way to a hospital in Darlinghurst.

When Asha got to the accident and emergency area of the hospital, he managed to locate Philippe. He was in shock, not too badly hurt, bruised with a broken arm.

Asha then went in search of Scott, only to be told that the A&E staff had not been able to save him and that he had died as a result of his severe injuries. Asha could not believe it.

Just the day before, Philippe, Scott, Amy and Asha were having a drink together. They were all in joyous moods and talking philosophically about the meaning of life and what they planned to do.

Asha went back to Philippe and broke the dreadful news. He was stunned and tears started rolling down his face. Philippe and Scott had been very close, since they met at college five years previously.

Philippe told Asha that they were on their way to the airport in a taxi that was hit head on by a truck.

Philippe was discharged the following day and went to stay with Asha and Amy for two days while he rearranged his flight to Denmark. They were dark days with no reason to celebrate other than Philippe surviving the accident.

Amy and Asha drove Philippe to the airport, this time without any issues. The goodbyes this time were sadder than a few days earlier.

"Philippe, please stay in touch. Bon voyage." These were Asha's parting words.

Scott's body was flown back to his family in Canada.

The taxi driver survived the crash. But Asha never found out what happened to the driver of the truck.

On Christmas Day, Amy cooked lunch for Robert and the quartet. Well, cooked was probably not the correct term. It was a classic cold Australian Christmas lunch of prawns, ham and salads. All done in a very comfortable family environment They were a very close family that had developed over a number of years. Robert had sort of adopted Asha. Andrew was his brother. Amy was his soulmate and Elisa was about to become his 'sister-in-law'.

"Please raise your glasses. Best wishes to you all. Cheers." Enjoy lunch Robert demanded.

Robert went on to sum up the situation. "Things have been happening so quickly. Elisa has graduated. Amy, Asha and Andrew, you have just finished your courses and hopefully passed your exams. Elisa and Andrew have recently become engaged. Next their wedding. What about the two of you, Amy and Asha?"

Asha blushed a little before spurting out: "Nothing planned. All in good time."

"Don't leave it too long," was Robert's retort.

"OK. Let's change the subject," pleaded Asha.

They had stopped exchanging gifts at Christmas as well as for birthdays. They had decided that it was better to give the money to charities that helped those less well off than them, particularly relating to poverty in Third World countries.

That day, there were two exceptions. Amy had bought Asha tickets for three operas in 2008 for the two of them. Asha was most appreciative. Just adding to what seemed to be a very busy year coming up.

Robert gave Andrew and Asha tickets for the first day of the cricket test match at the Sydney Cricket Ground between Australia and India, starting on 2 January 2008. Robert would also be going along. Something else to add to the schedule.

Scott's death had really hit Asha hard and was constantly on his mind. It was the first really sad thing that had intruded into his life since he had arrived in Sydney. This was a reminder that everyone is mortal and that there are negatives as well as positives — Fate.

Chapter 28
Wedding Season

Andrew and Asha met up with Robert at his apartment on the morning of the cricket. Robert had made up some sandwiches for them to take along in his backpack. Andrew and Asha wheeled along, with Robert in tow, the two-plus kilometre journey to the ground. It was relatively flat terrain and, therefore, easy to push along.

Once inside the stadium, they took an elevator to the fifth floor where there were spaces for people in wheelchairs and a carer's seat for Robert. Before them was a great view looking down at the oval and the cricket wicket. The players were out practising and Asha could recognise some of the players from both the Australia and India teams.

Asha had been a fan of cricket, but not a fanatic like Bishu, from his early days in India, like most Indians, and this interest had continued in Australia. Andrew liked the game but was not a real enthusiast. Yet, for some reason, even with a Scottish background, a nation not renowned for its cricketing prowess, Robert was a keen follower. He had made a habit of attending the first day of the Sydney test matches for a number of years, almost a ritual.

Australia won the toss and chose to bat. So, it would be unlikely that they would be able to see the great Tendulkar bat.

The players came out and lined up for the national anthems. Asha joined in singing both anthems. He felt very emotional, his birth country playing his adopted country. But he was supporting India.

It was a wonderful day out and Asha really enjoyed the cricket, even although India did not fare as well as he would have liked. And he did not get to see Tendulkar bat.

On the way back, they called in at an Indian restaurant near Robert's apartment for dinner. A fitting way to end the day. They shared a range of dishes from entrees to mains with some breads, starting with pappadums. This gave them (Robert and Asha, in particular) an opportunity to dissect the day's play. Robert had been impressed with 'Symonds's hundred, with which Asha agreed. Harbhajan's six-wicket haul was the most positive aspect of India's performance. The food was delicious as was the wine and they left the restaurant in very high spirits.

Amy, Andrew and Asha got their final results towards the end of January. Fortunately, they had all passed with flying colours. All their studies were now well and truly behind them.

With the end of study, Asha's student visa expired. He needed to get a work visa. The law firm that he was joining, the same one where he had been doing part-time work, had agreed to sponsor him.

The external agency that was helping with processing the new visa told Asha that he needed to leave the country pending approval of the new 457 visa. They suggested it would only take two weeks and it might be worthwhile going to a nearby country like New Zealand. Anyhow, Asha decided to go back to India to spend time with his family.

Well, two weeks turned into four and more. There was a bureaucratic hold-up. Asha's agency was getting frustrated, but not as frustrated as he was.

It was good to spend time with his family and old friends. But Asha wanted to get on with work. He was also missing Amy, even although they talked every day.

With much perseverance and persuasion, the agency managed to get Asha's application approved and he returned to Australia.

With great relief, Asha began work, specialising in forensic fraud. Amy had already started her internship with a legal practice in the city, doing family law. And Andrew was working as a junior general practitioner where he had done some work experience. So, the whole quartet was gainfully employed. Fortunately, none of them had any difficulty in procuring work in the area they wanted.

This was a different experience for all of them, transiting from study and part-time work to full-time employment, with its different challenges and expectations.

At night, after a day in the office, Amy and Asha would chat endlessly, over dinner at the dining table, talk about what they had been doing during the day. But, at weekends, it was time out, no office talk.

Asha had really grown to appreciate the opportunity that Robert had given him. This truly was the land of plenty, plenty of opportunities. Asha had been to university. He had developed many interests, such as horse racing, opera, wine and travel in addition to cricket. These interests were all shared by Amy. So, Amy and Asha decided that they ought to plan to spend more time on these interests now that university life was behind them. Not that they had ignored them while at university. With both of them having healthy steady incomes, they agreed to make the most of every moment without going overboard.

In April, the quartet organised a weekend away in Orange, about a four hour drive west of Sydney. It was a lovely drive up and over the Blue Mountains on a beautiful autumnal day.

On the afternoon that they reached Orange, they did a little wine tasting, including a one-on-one — or should that be one-on-four? — with a winemaker. It was really interesting how she explained the characteristics of each wine and how they matched with particular foods. The other vineyard that they visited provided them with what was to become a favourite red wine, one that the vineyard only made when the fruits were of the required very high standard. As a result, there was not a release every year. They picked up some of the 2005.

That night they went to a wine bar where they were able to "taste" other wines, with Asha's favourite being a local Sauvignon Blanc. There was also some delicious food on offer, tapas style, that they shared.

The following day they drove around the district and then made their way back to Sydney. A great weekend and a further education on wines, in this case cool-climate wines.

Then it was the turn of Andrew, Amy and Asha to graduate. They had all achieved very good results and were proud of the outcome of their hard endeavours. Robert and Elisa attended the ceremonies. Andrew's was at a different time to that of Amy and Asha. So, the four were able to celebrate Andrew receiving his award and Andrew joined Robert and Elisa to acknowledge Amy and Asha as they accepted their certificates. A great day for all three and their classmates, some of whom they would never see again.

A few weeks later Amy and Asha hosted Andrew's birthday lunch in their home.

Unbeknown to the others, this would be a double celebration. A couple of days after the graduation, Asha had called Amy's father, Roger, and, as was the old tradition, had asked him for Amy's hand in marriage. There was a silent pause. A shiver went down Asha's spine. What was going on? And then, Asha heard Roger and Amy's mother, Ella, excitedly say, in unison, "YES". What a relief. Asha told them that he had not officially proposed to Amy but would do that after this call had finished.

Asha went to his desk drawer and retrieved the engagement ring that he had bought secretly. Asha marched into the kitchen and readied two champagne glasses. The champagne bottle was already chilling in the wine fridge.

Asha called Amy into the lounge. She looked at him. "Amy, I have something to say to you. Will you marry me?" Tears started running down her face as she mouthed the word that Asha had been hoping for. Asha poured the champagne and they called Amy's parents to give them confirmation. They then called Asha's family. Just like Amy's parents, they were overjoyed. Anji was in tears. But everyone was happy.

Lunch went well, a good sturdy winter roast beef, with Yorkshire pudding and roast potatoes. After that had settled down, Amy brought out a chocolate cake that she had made, ostensibly for Andrew's birthday. Then Asha confessed, holding out Amy's ring finger, that they were engaged. Smiles all round as they savoured the birthday come engagement cake and sipped some champagne.

Elisa and Andrew got married in October 2008 in a small church in the seaside town of Manly, where Elisa was from and where her family still lived.

Asha was best man.

A couple of months before the wedding, Andrew and Asha went along to a tailor to get their wedding outfits made to measure. Andrew was to wear a tuxedo and Asha would have a white jacket with black pants.

As they entered the tailor's premises, Asha could see a look of wonderment on the faces of the two assistants as Andrew crutch-walked in and Asha hobbled in. You could almost hear them say, "What do we have here?"

Anyway, once they got over the surprise, they got down to business.

Measurements were pretty straightforward for Asha but a little more challenging for Andrew as he had to move from balancing on one crutch in either hand to holding onto a table. But, in the end all the measurements were taken.

Then, it was onto choosing the materials. Andrew ended up with a navy-blue tuxedo jacket with black satin piping, the same piping running down the side of his pants. They both then chose shirts, white for Andrew and black for Asha and the opposite colours for their bow ties.

Andrew also chose some blue pants and a yellow semi-casual shirt as his going away outfit.

They went back to try on the clothes three weeks later and all fitted very well.

A couple of days before the wedding, Asha had arranged Andrew's stag night. Friends of Andrew's from his school days, University, tennis and work joined them for a short pub crawl followed by dinner. There were about twenty of them. They had a great night without anything or anyone getting out of control.

Andrew and Asha went back to the apartment that they were renting for a couple of days. They sat up and talked well into the early hours of the morning, reminiscing about their past years together and Andrew talking spiritedly about his future with Elisa. He seemed to be so excited.

The next day they just hung out. Then it was the big day.

Asha moved into a hotel with Amy, the same place where Robert was also staying as were a number of other wedding guests.

After getting dressed Asha went to Andrew's apartment and Amy to Elisa's family house.

The car picked Andrew and Asha up from the apartment and transported them to the church, where they made their way towards the altar to be seated on the right of the aisle. Robert was sitting behind them and Elisa's family across the aisle.

Andrew was a little nervous and impatient while waiting for the arrival of Elisa and her father. His hands were sweating and he could not stop fidgeting.

As the minister came to the front of the altar, the choir, accompanied by the organ, started to sing *Ave Maria*. Andrew and Asha rose and Andrew sidled towards the minister. He was wearing his leg braces and using crutches instead of his wheelchair as he said that would put him at the same height as Elisa.

Elisa and her father arrived with her two young bridesmaids and Amy as her maid of honour. Elisa was wearing an ivory dress with veil. When they reached Andrew, Elisa's father stepped back, leaving Elisa and Andrew to look into each other's eyes. They both smiled.

After the service, the bridal party plus Elisa's parents and Robert made their way to a room to the side of the altar to sign the registry. While that was being done, the choir sang *Jesu Joy of Man's Desiring*, followed by the Hallelujah chorus as everyone, including the bridal party, walked back down the aisle. Asha was walking beside Amy, dreaming about when they would be doing this.

Congratulations Mr and Mrs McDonald, thought Asha.

They all exited the church to bright blue skies, ideal for the photographs. Andrew and Elisa lined up and Asha took Andrew's crutches away as he held onto Elisa lightly for some support. Numerous photographs were taken with family members and friends before the couple turned to each other and kissed.

Confetti was thrown over the couple and then Andrew and Elisa got into the back of the wedding car, which was a Bentley decked out with white ribbons. The rest of the gathering dispersed to reconvene for the reception at a nearby hotel garden setting overlooking the beach.

Andrew and Elisa were there to greet them and welcome them to the party. Everyone mingled as they had finger food and drinks of their choice. This was to be an informal celebration with the speeches kept to a minimum, with one given by Andrew thanking the bridesmaids and maid of honour, one by Asha telling stories about Andrew, some good and some not so good and finally Elisa's father wishing the bride and groom health, wealth, and, above all, happiness.

The bridal couple escaped to a room they had hired in the hotel. When they returned, Andrew had changed into his going-away clothes and Elisa was wearing a summery yellow dress. They looked a handsome pair. Andrew was also using his wheelchair.

Andrew and Elisa then left in the wedding car to a destination unknown, at least to Asha, for their first night as a married couple. More confetti and then the traditional throwing of the bride's bouquet.

Tin cans had been attached to the rear bumper of their car and it made such a clatter as it went down the road.

What a great day it had been from start to finish. Both the bride and groom looked resplendent in their outfits and neither had stopped smiling since they set eyes upon each other in the church.

This was the second wedding that Amy and Asha had attended during the year. In August, they had flown to Seoul for Yung-Su's wedding.

Yung-Su and Asha had stayed in touch over the years, even catching up once when Yung-Su had come to Sydney for a basketball tournament. Asha went to see him play and was very impressed by his athleticism and skills.

The wedding took place in a hall in a Seoul hotel, which also provided another room where the guests could partake of the buffet. When Amy and Asha arrived, as per tradition, they placed their envelope with the cash gift on the table at the entrance with the other envelopes. They watched the ceremony from the back of the room. It was over in a flash. Then the couple and the wedding party made their way to a private room for an exclusive ceremony. As the married couple passed, Asha managed to say goodbye to Yung-Su and wished him well. Short as it was and not being able to spend time with Yung-Su and his wife, Amy and Asha still enjoyed the experience.

Amy and Asha spent a few days sightseeing in Seoul after the wedding before returning to Sydney. This time, Asha was the one teaching Amy about Korean food and the joys of *soju*. Asha's enjoyment of Korean food had not vanished and Amy developed a taste for some of the dishes but was not too keen on the *soju*. Asha wondered why he have never bothered about Korean food in Australia. "We must seek out a Korean restaurant in Sydney when we get back," Asha remarked to Amy. "Sounds good."

Unfortunately, Robert, Elisa and Andrew could not make it to the wedding. Pity. Asha thought the differences from Western culture would have interested them.

Other highlights for the year were the three operas. Amy and Asha were enraptured by each of them, which were all love stories. They were all memorable in their own ways. The first act of *La Bohème* Asha found to be funny and serious at the same time, but, in the end, romantic, with a run of superb arias. The Mad Scene from *Lucia di Lammermoor* was most tense and dramatic. And the aria, *In the Depths of the Temple*, from *The Pearl Fishers*, was most melodic, moving and unforgettable.

Yet another busy and eventful year was ending. Amy's parents came over to spend Christmas with Amy and Asha. They had not been able to make it over for their graduations. And it was the first time they had seen them since they got engaged. So, they had a lot to talk about, including the plans for their wedding.

Robert, Andrew and Elisa joined Asha, Amy and her parents for Christmas Day lunch. Amy put on a superb spread of food, a mixture of cold seafood and meats, followed by a traditional trifle. Most tasty. And the champagne and wine flowed.

Amy and Asha had not seen much of Andrew and Elisa since their wedding. So, it was good to see them as well and catch up. A most enjoyable day.

The quartet plus Amy's parents, this time, all gathered, as usual, on Robert's balcony on New Year's Eve, never getting bored with a fine barbeque and the firework displays.

Isn't life great!

Chapter 29
Not What Asha Had Planned

On a sunny summer Sunday in February, the quartet met up with old friends from University at Shelly Beach as they had done a number of times in the past. When they arrived, the lads were playing football and throwing the frisbee around as had been their habit. Asha joined in the frisbee throwing as Andrew was helped to the area where the girls were sitting on the sand. A real Australian male-chauvinist setting.

Asha was hobbling after a frisbee when his left leg gave way and he fell flat on his face. Asha was non-plussed as he sat up wondering what had happened. There was no pain. A couple of the guys rushed over and helped him to his feet. Asha tried to walk a little but his left leg was not responding too well. Asha was carried to the barbeque area and placed in his wheelchair. By this time, Amy and a couple of the girls had come over to see what had happened.

Asha told them all to go and have a swim and he would sit and rest. This they did. Asha still could not feel any pain in his left leg.

After the barbeque, Amy and Asha set off, leaving everyone else to continue enjoying the afternoon. It was a good job that Asha had travelled by wheelchair.

When Amy and Asha got home, Asha tried walking again. But the same result as at the beach. His left leg was just not cooperating. Asha told Amy that it was probably best that he goes to the hospital to find out what the problem is.

Asha and Amy sat in casualty for about an hour before an intern took Asha into a cubicle. He examined Asha's leg and was not sure what to do. He made a telephone call and then asked Asha to stand up. This he did with some difficulty, locking his calliper and levering himself against the bed to be able to stand straight. The intern then asked Asha to push on the toes of his left leg and lift his heel. Asha could not get his heel off the floor. The intern then told Asha that he thought he had ruptured his Achilles tendon. Asha was then admitted to hospital and placed in a ward to await a visit from an orthopaedic specialist in the morning.

The specialist arrived around eight thirty a.m. He asked Asha to turn onto his stomach. He then ran his hands up and down the lower part of Asha's left leg before confirming to Asha that, indeed, he had ruptured his Achilles tendon. The specialist scheduled the operation for that afternoon.

About lunch time, a nurse arrived to prepare Asha for the operation. His mind went back to the operation he had on his polio leg and now a similar process took place with Asha's leg being shaved below the knee, followed by an anaesthetic, a cap on his head and then off to the operating theatre.

After the operation, Asha felt very woozy and hardly recognised a couple of people who came to visit him in the ward that evening.

The following morning Asha felt much better. He had some breakfast before the specialist came to see him. He said that the operation had gone very well. As Asha had already seen, he said Asha's leg had been bandaged and there was a tube that was providing a drain from the wound into a plastic bag. The drain would come out in a few days and then after a similar period, Asha's leg would be put in plaster for about six weeks.

What to do? Asha just relaxed and accepted the pampering provided by the nursing staff. Asha also received many visitors. Although it was good to see people, particularly Amy, Asha always thought it was a waste of time for them. Asha was sure they had better things to do. And, he was enjoying the time on his own, indulging in reading, listening to music and watching television.

Amy came to visit Asha every day and Andrew and Robert rotated their visits.

"Well, Asha, another stint in hospital. How are they treating you?"

"Very well, Robert. The staff can't do enough for me."

"Asha, seems like we have something in common. In my twenties and thirties, I played squash regularly. During one game, as I lunged forward to reach the ball, the ceiling fell in on top of me. At least so I thought. But there was no debris around me. Just me sitting on the floor, wondering what had happened. I got up to continue with the game. However, my left leg did not feel good. So, I decided to take a break and let someone else play. I watched the next match from upstairs, waiting for my leg to improve. No signs of that. As I did not think I could play any more that night, I decided to walk the 400 metres or so to my home. During the walk home, it became clearer to me that there was something seriously wrong with my leg.

I opened the front door and shouted to Pauline that I needed her to take me to hospital, explaining what the problem was.

Being anal, I had to have a shower first. Upstairs, I hobbled, showered, dressed and then into the car with Pauline.

On the way, my thoughtful wife wondered out loud why she was driving and not me. After all, it was my left leg that was affected and we had an automatic car. Good logic.

It turned out that I had ruptured my Achilles tendon.

So, instead of going home to a dinner of asparagus spears with hollandaise sauce followed by strawberries, washed down with a lovely wine, I was being admitted to hospital."

On the occasions when Robert visited, they always had good conversations, particularly about what was happening in the world. With Andrew, they talked about his work. He was very involved as a GP in a large medical practice. Amy and Asha just liked holding hands and sitting together. Amy could not wait to get Asha out of hospital. The visits usually lasted about half an hour, Amy's maybe a little longer.

Each morning, Asha was woken with a cup of tea, then breakfast, followed by ablutions, consisting of brushing teeth and a bed bath. Asha was not that keen on using a bed pan. However, once the drain was taken out, he was able to get out of bed and wheel himself to the toilet.

Every other day, a physio came to see Asha to massage his polio leg, stretch his ankle and toes and help him with some of his exercises, at least the ones lying on his back.

Importantly, the food was varied and very edible.

After about a week, a blue plaster cast was wrapped around his leg from toe to just below his knee. Once the plaster had set, one of the wardsmen came to see him and told him that he had to get out of bed and hop around on crutches so that he could see that Asha could manage. Easier said than done. Nobody had told the wardsman about Asha's polio leg and the need to wear a calliper for walking.

Asha explained the situation. Asha strapped on his calliper, eased his right leg and then his left leg out of bed, turned his body towards the bed, put both hands on the side and stood up on his right leg. So far so good. Asha turned around and the wardsman gave him two crutches. Asha was well used to crutches but only with a good left leg. Asha pushed the crutches forward and jumped a little tentatively. Then another jump, with the wardsman in close proximity. Then more jumps. Asha got more confident but then nearly fell. This was very difficult.

Asha discussed how he was faring with the wardsman and they decided that Asha would abandon using crutches while in plaster and just use his wheelchair.

Asha got dressed and waited for Amy to come to collect him. He did not bother putting on the calliper. Asha would not need that for some time except as a stabiliser when driving. The wardsman lifted Asha into his wheelchair. Asha sorted out his legs and then they were off home.

Asha had been using his wheelchair more often since the orthotist had told him to do so to give his left leg some respite. Was this Asha's left leg's turn for revenge? It had carried him all those years while he pole-hopped and then took the pressure when Asha wore his calliper. Anyway, thank you left leg. You have done very well and can now take a well-deserved rest.

With Asha using only his wheelchair to get around, he got so used to it and became much better at pushing himself around. It now felt normal to him. Lifting the wheelchair into and out of the back seat of the car was just something that had to be done.

People at work also got used to Asha pushing himself around and did not seem to think they had to make any allowances for his change in mobility. There was a wheelchair accessible toilet at work, which was obviously helpful. Asha already had a disabled parking spot so he could manoeuvre his wheelchair in and out of the car with relative ease. What more could a man want?

There were upsides and downsides. Showering was a little different. Asha had to tape a plastic bag over the cast to stop it getting wet. Then, after easing himself out of the chair and onto the side of the bath, he had two legs to take care of, lifting the right leg and then the left leg over before sitting in the bath. On the other hand, Asha did not need to spend time putting on his calliper while getting dressed. Asha knew what he preferred!

There was another interesting situation that Asha eventually discussed with Andrew. What did he do at a petrol station when he went to fill up his tank? Did he grab his wheelchair from the back seat and fill up himself? Andrew told Asha that locally he had found a petrol station where an attendant would come out and fill up for him. Andrew just had to give him a call when he arrived at the pump. Great service! What happened to the good old days of full-service forecourts?

Elsewhere, he said he just found out the telephone number of the petrol station and let them know he needed help. If they would not help, he just went elsewhere. If the worst came to the worst, plan B, which meant getting into the wheelchair and doing it yourself.

After two weeks, Asha went back to the hospital for a check-up. The cast was taken off and the specialist said that the Achilles tendon was healing well. Then time for a new plaster. Asha was asked if he wanted a walking heel attached to the bottom of the cast. Asha had to think about it for a little while before deciding to give it a go. If it turned out that he could not walk, there was nothing lost.

Back in the flat, Asha put on his calliper, got into the standing position with his crutches and took a step forward, then another. It was a bit awkward to begin with. But Asha got used to it and thought it was a good way to move around occasionally. At least he would be off his backside.

When the plaster came off a few weeks later, his left leg had lost a lot of condition and was quite weak. Weeks of physiotherapy followed. During that time, Asha wore his calliper and used the crutches, one step at a time. Asha progressed from two crutches to two walking sticks to one walking stick before discarding all walking aids, except his calliper. As back to normal as it was going to get. But the time spent walking became more balanced with pushing his wheelchair. Yet, Asha had to make sure that he would be able to WALK down the aisle.

Asha's calliper was three years old and in need of some maintenance. He went to see the orthotist, who checked out the calliper and determined what adjustments needed to be done. He said that, in the main, it was still in good order. Asha told him about what had happened to his left leg and he said that he noticed that when Asha was walking, he was limping a little on the left side. He had a look at Asha's left ankle and suggested that he get a below-knee calliper to support the ankle. Asha sat on the bed while the orthotist put plaster around Asha's leg, toe to knee, just like when Asha got plastered in hospital. But this time, it came off straight away to act as the mould for the calliper.

Based on the orthotist's comments, Asha decided to get a new wheelchair and have the current one available in the office.

Two weeks later, Asha went back to the orthotist to get both devices. The below-knee calliper did the trick supporting his left ankle and eliminating the limping, at least from the left side. And the big calliper was just like brand new. Asha was happy. But the orthotist warned him to take care and not overdo the walking.

The past three months had provided its interruptions to normal life as well as some challenges.

Asha had not been able to go to a couple of operas. Elisa accompanied Amy just to be sociable. Then Elisa found out that opera, at least the two she saw, were great experiences.

Asha had to have some time off work, which was inconvenient. However, when he got back to work, he was able to pick up the cases that he had been working on. The firm was very supportive and the clients were understanding.

Mind you Asha had to do some interstate air travel to meet clients. He had never done this before with both legs "disabled". He had travelled with Andrew in his wheelchair and kind of knew what to expect and do. However, watching and helping someone else who is wheelchair bound is different to being in that situation yourself. Fortunately, it all worked out fine for Asha. The airport and airline staff were all very helpful.

Asha had missed work. He had just celebrated his first anniversary at the firm and was really enjoying the investigative challenges. His speciality was forensic intelligence, in particular related to corporate fraud. The interest was not so much in solving a crime but the process associated with it, gathering the facts and sifting through the information, looking for clues and eventually the solution.

Amy and Asha had to give racing a miss, from an attendance point of view. Although, Asha was still having the occasional bet.

Even while he was recuperating, the focus was on planning the wedding and the honeymoon. Amy, in particular, was in constant touch with her parents, booking the church for 15 August, selecting and then booking the reception venue. Collectively, Amy and Asha put together the guest list of fifty. Amy's mother, Ella, sent the invitations out.

Andrew was to be Asha's best man, reversing the roles from Andrew's wedding. Asha and Andrew went back to the same tailor they had used for Andrew's wedding. They double checked all the measurements. But there were no material differences. They both had decided on black tuxedos with white shirts and black bow ties. Very conservative. Asha also had navy blue pants and a pink shirt made as his going-away outfit. Finally, Asha needed to buy new shoes and have the build-up done on the right one.

Andrew arranged Asha's stag party in Sydney. They started off at the pub that used to be their local when they were attending uni. Then a couple more nearby before a lovely meal, finally ending up in the Cross. A burly bodyguard carried Andrew down the dim stairs into one of the strip clubs. They had a few drinks and enjoyed the floorshow of gyrating bodies. It was a very interesting but uneventful night spent in the company of friends, eating, drinking and having a few laughs. Just a harmless fun night out on the town. That night they stayed at Robert's apartment.

The following morning, a little worse for wear, Andrew and Asha went shopping in the city. They took a train from Kings Cross. When they passed through the ticket barrier, an attendant said something to them that they did not hear properly and just moved on. As the train was arriving at the platform, another attendant came towards them with a ramp and placed it between the platform and carriage so that Andrew could roll onto the train. When they arrived at Town Hall station, an attendant brought a ramp to the carriage that they were in to help Andrew off the train. Great service.

How different to the experiences on trains in Mumbai. On the positive side, in Mumbai, they do have carriages dedicated to people with disabilities. However, they are usually packed and abused by people without disabilities. So, a very uncomfortable way to travel.

Chapter 30
Following in Andrew's Footsteps

The quartet, minus Amy, plus Robert, flew to Perth together three days before the wedding. Amy had travelled the previous weekend.

When they reached Perth, many of the other guests were already there. Asha was very happy to see his parents and brother again. Unfortunately, his sister could not make it as she was close to giving birth. Yung-Su and his wife, Mi-Hyun, had also come to Perth for the wedding. Mi-Hyun had not been to Australia before. In fact, it was her first trip abroad. So, they planned to visit Sydney and Melbourne after Perth.

This was the first time that Robert and Yung-Su had met for many years. They both seemed pleased to see each other again and spent much time deep in conversation, catching up on lost time.

"Good to see you again and lovely to meet your wife," Robert greeted Yung-Su.

"I am pleased to see you again after such a long time."

"I need to ask you what happened. You were supposed to meet me at the hotel in Seoul to go to Sydney with me."

"I was confused and my mother was ill. I did not know what to do."

"But why did you not telephone me?"

"I did not know what to say. As you know my English was not very good. It has improved since then. But, perhaps, the easiest thing for me was just to ignore the situation. That was wrong. And as time passed, it became even more difficult for me to contact you. I am very sorry."

"I think I understand. Let's enjoy the wedding. We can talk more later."

Andrew and Asha sat in the front pew waiting for the fanfare announcing Amy's arrival on the arm of her father, Roger. The trumpets sounded, Andrew and Asha got to their feet and turned their eyes to the pair walking down the aisle, followed by Elisa, the matron of honour, and two of Amy's nieces as bridesmaids. Asha could not take his eyes off Amy, her slim figure, topped with perky breasts accentuated by the cut of her dress. Asha could not see her face properly through the veil but he could see her face in his mind's eye. Her beautiful face and stunning figure were what had attracted her to him all these years ago.

As they arrived at the altar, Asha moved beside Amy followed by Andrew. Asha looked at her and mouthed "You are gorgeous." Her eyes shone through the veil and her mouth lengthened into a shy smile.

The service passed without a hitch, the paperwork was duly signed and witnessed. Then Amy and Asha led the procession, walking back down the aisle. This time Andrew and Elisa were behind them. Asha was so overjoyed.

The reception blurred past in a flash. Amy and Asha danced the bridal waltz. This ended with an impromptu demonstration of wheelchair dancing by Andrew that had the audience in a spin, clapping wildly.

Amy and Asha changed into their going-away gear, said goodbye to the guests and made their way to the airport to catch their flight to Singapore.

Once on board, they relaxed with a glass of champagne, reflecting on the previous twelve hours.

It had been six years since Andrew and Asha had spent a few days in Singapore on their way back from Europe. This time, Amy and Asha were doing the journey in reverse. Singapore had changed a lot in the intervening years. So, there were many new things for them to explore as well as shopping, which was of particular interest to Amy. They had one full day on Sentosa Island and very full it was. There were so many attractions to discover and enjoy. All too short a stay. But they had Paris to look forward to.

Amy and Asha were on a late-night non-stop flight of around thirteen and a half hours to Paris. They had a pre-take-off glass of champagne and then sat back in their business class seats as Singapore was left behind. Then a post-take-off drink followed by dinner that was very palatable. That set Asha up for the rest of the flight. So, time for a sleep.

Asha slept very well and woke up in time for breakfast and to get ready for the landing. It had been a great flight.

Amy and Asha stayed in the same hotel that Andrew and Asha had used. That meant everything would be familiar to Asha in terms of finding their way around. This time, they were a little more flexible, not needing to cater all the time for someone reliant on a wheelchair as was the case with Andrew. Depending on what they were doing and where they were going, Asha would either walk or use his wheelchair. They explored Paris from sunrise to sunset, visiting all the major tourist sites. They ate well and drank very good French wines. What a wonderful time they experienced for a week. They thoroughly enjoyed the boat ride on the Seine, something that Asha had not been able to do with Andrew. This provided a very different perspective to their walks along the banks.

Then it was back to Sydney and life as a married couple. Happy days.

Now that Asha was married to an Australian citizen, he was able to apply for Permanent Residency. This process was much easier than the 457-visa fiasco. PR was granted and Asha was on his way to becoming an Australian Citizen. But one downside was that Asha would need to relinquish his Indian citizenship as India does not allow dual citizenship.

Chapter 31
Yung-Su and Robert

When Amy and Asha returned from their honeymoon, Yung-Su and Mi-Hyun were still in Sydney and Robert organised a barbeque for the four of them plus Andrew and Elisa.

Amy and Asha regaled the audience with conversations about their honeymoon, running the risk of hogging the party. But nobody seemed to care. With Andrew, Asha was able to compare their times in Singapore and Paris and that seemed to encourage everyone to travel.

Yung-Su and Mi-Hyun also talked about their travels in Australia and how they'd had such a great time. After the wedding, they had spent time up and down the West Australian coast from Perth. Then the touristy activities in Melbourne and Sydney. Yung-Su had been to Melbourne and Sydney before. So, he was a good tour guide for Mi-Hyun in both these cities and their surrounds. By the sounds of it, Mi-Hyun had caught the travel bug and she assured everyone that this would not be her last trip away from South Korea.

Amy and Asha were able to spend some time with Yung-Su and Mi-Hyun before they went back to Korea. They took them to a number of places they had not been able to visit including the Blue Mountains and the wildlife park on the way. Mi-Hyun was so excited about getting so close to the Australian wildlife and the beauty of the Blue Mountains. She took so many photographs that would provide such wonderful memories.

On the Saturday before their departure, Amy took Mi-Hyun shopping while Robert and Asha met Yung-Su at the Woolloomooloo (Wool-loo-moo-loo) wharf for lunch at Asha's favourite seafood restaurant on the finger. They all had oysters and then shared a huge seafood platter of cold and hot delicacies. This was all washed down with some Sauvignon Blanc. Amy might have been jealous. But Asha was sure she was also enjoying a good meal with Mi-Hyun at the end of their shopping expedition.

Over lunch, Yung-Su told Robert and Asha about some of the things that had been going on in his life. Asha thought that this was partly to mend the bridges with Robert. As Asha had found out from Yung-Su, he had rejected Robert's insistence that he wear his leg braces and use crutches more often. And Robert had not been impressed. Yung-Su made a point of bringing this up to get this out into the open finally.

"So, Yung-Su, that was the main reason that you did not go to Sydney with me?" Robert queried. "I was only trying to do what I thought was best for you."

"I always knew that you wanted to do what you thought was best for me. Sometimes, I did not agree. We were both, and are perhaps still, very stubborn."

"Well times have changed and it looks like opinions have mellowed."

"Yes, maybe a little.

It took a while. But, Robert, I did take your advice. I am still wearing leg braces and crutch-walking at least twice a week at Mi-Hyun's insistence. I have also continued to do the exercises that you had prescribed. My favourite exercise was hand-walking, wearing leg braces and using your hands for support while you barked lift — push, lift — push, as I took one step after another across the hotel room. Even one time that Asha was with me in Korea, he helped me with hand-walking. Mi-Hyun still helps me with hand-walking."

Yung-Su had given up both tennis and basketball and was now concentrating on sit-skiing.

"Yung-Su, you are such a gifted athlete," Robert commented.

"I agree," confirmed Asha.

Yung-Su is in training to represent Korea at the winter Paralympics. While he was playing basketball and tennis, these Korean teams had never qualified for the summer Paralympics. So, this would be his first and much deserved Olympic debut.

Yung-Su said he is being sponsored by a major Korean hospitality company. He also does some public speaking. And, with Mi-Hyun's job as an English high school teacher, they are able to live pretty well. They hoped to start a family the following year. Perhaps, another 'grandchild' for Robert?

While waiting for taxis to take them to their respective destinations, Robert picked Yung-Su up from his wheelchair and gave him a huge hug before gently placing him back in the wheelchair.

The following day, Robert and Asha took Yung-Su and Mi-Hyun to the airport.

Robert had been a little apprehensive about meeting Yung-Su again. The time in Perth had quelled that fear and spending time with him in Sydney had been most satisfying. Robert liked Mi-Hyun. He thought she has a very strong personality and is an excellent partner for Yung-Su. Mentally, Robert wished them both well.

As Asha and Robert strolled back to the car after waving goodbye to Yung-Su and Mi-Hyun at the departure gate, Asha's eyes welled up. He was so happy that Robert and Yung-Su had made up after such a long time. Asha looked at Robert who had a smile on his face.

Chapter 32
Change

On the Sunday of the long weekend at the beginning of October, the quartet was at Robert's apartment for a lunchtime barbeque.

They were all gathered on the balcony when Andrew announced that Elisa and he would be moving to India in November. He said he had been able to secure a position as a GP in a practice in Nagpur.

Asha was very surprised as Andrew had never said anything about this to him. He remembered Andrew mentioning to him in 2004, when Asha took Andrew to India for the first time, that he wanted to return to India to live, to practise medicine and to help those in need. At the time, Asha had just taken that as a throwaway comment apposite for that particular setting and never, for a moment, thought that Andrew would follow through on it.

"Andrew, are you serious?" thundered Robert. "Do you know what it is like to live and work in India? In your condition, how are you going to survive?"

Andrew wheeled around, pushed his way into the lounge and stormed out of the apartment closely followed by Elisa.

Robert had realised how thoughtless his words 'in your condition' must have sounded. He had not been trying to be offensive, just realistic in his mind, based on his knowledge of India, where those in wheelchairs are not well catered for.

"I think that Amy and you ought to leave." Robert requested.

The following day Asha went round to see Andrew. He was still upset by his father's words, harsh he thought. Asha suggested that Robert had probably not expressed himself as best as he could. And Asha said he agreed with Robert that life would not be easy for Andrew in India, particularly rural India.

"How do disabled Indians get around in their country?" Andrew quizzed.

"With great difficulty. I had not found it easy pole-hopping or using crutches in India. I had not used a wheelchair in my home town. But I could imagine the problems. The footpaths and roads, with their seemingly endless potholes, were not built for wheelchairs. A lot of the poor and disabled beggars crawl around using bits of tyres on their hands and knees or sitting on makeshift little buggies, looking like a rough piece of wood on wheels. The monsoon season would add another problematic dimension with the torrents of rain and flooding that go on for months. Overall, Nagpur is not a wheelchair-friendly place and you need to be very watchful using crutches."

"I understand my father's and your concerns. But Elisa and I are still going."

Asha asked Andrew to go to see his father to make peace, which he did.

Robert told his son that he had been shocked by the sudden announcement. He apologised for his outburst and the heat of the moment callous comments. He said he was still concerned about how Andrew and Elisa would fare in Nagpur. Nevertheless, Andrew had his support and best wishes.

Robert invited the quartet to a matching food and wine event. It was held at a top-class restaurant in Manly and featured wines from an Orange winery that they liked. In some ways this was a goodbye dinner for Andrew and Elisa. With Robert and Andrew having made up, there were no bad feelings and the past was in the past, allowing father and son and the others to have an enjoyable night out together.

As they entered the restaurant, they could see rows of tables with crockery, cutlery and three glasses at each place setting.

They were given a glass of Sauvignon Blanc. This was the one that Asha had really liked at the wine bar in Orange.

The menu of food and wines looked very interesting. There were five courses. The first two were accompanied by white wines. After the second course, the winemaker gave a brief overview of the two wines that had just been tasted. Instead of moving straight onto the featured reds, there was a surprise blind tasting. Everyone had to stand up and answer questions about that wine. If you got the answer wrong, you sat down. The five stayed in the competition for some time but none of them won. The winner got a bottle of that wine. The consumption of food and wine continued. At the end, the winemaker, once again, gave a summary of the reds that had been tasted. What a great evening it had been.

"Thank you, Robert for inviting us for this," Asha exclaimed. "The food was smashing and the wines were first class and a good match."

"Dad, this was a fantastic idea. A chance to sample a number of wines with a very high standard of food."

"I am glad you all enjoyed it. I certainly did."

Robert, Amy, Elisa's parents and Asha saw Andrew and Elisa off at the airport. For Asha, this seemed very strange. Asha had moved to Andrew's country for a better life. Now Andrew was moving to Asha's country to make life better.

Robert was very stoic, not showing much emotion and staying in the background, having said his farewells to the couple in private. Elisa's mother was in tears as was Elisa as they embraced each other. Asha bent over and gave Andrew a huge bear hug. As Asha released him, he looked into Andrew's blue eyes, with tears welling up in Asha's eyes.

"Take care." Asha hoped.

Andrew smiled and turned around to follow Elisa through to departure. They looked back and waved. Everyone waved back.

A couple of days later, Asha went round to Robert's apartment for a chat and a glass of wine on the balcony, their irregular get-together. Asha did not want to mention Andrew and his departure for India. But Robert did.

"I regretted using the words 'In your condition, how are you going to survive'?' I had not meant to denigrate Andrew's abilities and capabilities. After all, his mother and I had raised him and had allowed him to find his feet and do whatever he could. We had not mollycoddled him. We had provided him with our support and love as well as external care that was appropriate. In these circumstances Andrew had blossomed. So, was there really any reason to worry?"

"From all the years that I have known Andrew and had spent a lot of time with him, it was clear to me that he was a very self-sufficient person, capable of looking after himself and Elisa. Don't worry," comforted Asha.

Asha decided to change the subject and talk about his work. Asha told Robert about how much he was enjoying forensic analysis. However, at the same time, it was laborious and time consuming. Being an impatient person, this frustrated Asha.

"From your background in information technology, Robert, is there anything out there that would help improve the process?"

Robert's eyes lit up.

"There is something that comes to mind that might be worth considering. I have not been directly involved in analytics or business intelligence as we call it, for some time. But I have kept track of developments in that area. There are a number of solutions on the market that analyse data and turn the data into decision-making information. This is done through a series of queries run against the database. That is more like looking at what has happened. It could help pinpoint, in your case, Asha, where fraud has taken place. An extension to that approach would be to do predictive analytics, based on models that would uncover possible fraudulent events."

This got Asha very interested and they continued their discussion on this subject for quite some time in the company of a lovely drop of Shiraz. What could Asha do with this new-found knowledge? The starting point would be to raise this with his boss at work.

What an odd evening. It had started off on a downer, but ended on a high.

When Asha got home, Amy was still up watching television. Asha told her about the talk with Robert. Amy was not surprised that Robert regretted what he had said to Andrew. But she was quite excited about the analytics opportunity.

Christmas was not the same as it had been over the past few years as Andrew and Elisa were in India. Robert joined Amy and Asha for lunch and they called Andrew and Elisa on Skype. It was great to see them and have a chat that seemed to go on forever. Both sides of the call toasted each other's health, wished each other a Merry Christmas and said goodbye.

Andrew's parting words were "Hope to see you guys next year. Take care."

Chapter 33
International Events

Robert's business was going very well, including expanding into New Delhi and Bangalore. This allowed him to spend more time in India. Robert made a point of visiting Mumbai at least once a quarter. And, more often than not, he would make a side trip to Nagpur to visit Andrew and Elisa.

On Robert's first visit back to Nagpur, Andrew showed him how he was coping. Apparently, he had taken some of Asha's comments on board in terms of the best way to get around. He had bought a second wheelchair, which he kept at the surgery. The other one was for normal use at home or when he went out. He had a car and driver that transported him between home and office as well as other places that he and Elisa wanted to go to. During the work week, he would wear his leg braces and use crutches, offering him the flexibility that he required for getting around.

"Well done Andrew," Robert confessed. "How could I have doubted your creativeness?"

It was on another of Robert's trips that Andrew and Elisa proudly announced that they were going to have a baby and that Robert would be a grandfather.

Robert smiled. "My first grandchild. I am over the moon for you and pretty happy myself."

Amy and Asha welcomed the news of Elisa's pregnancy with much excitement and enthusiasm.

Asha had been staying in touch with Andrew, in particular, by email and Skype. Amy was also in touch with Elisa. Elisa and Andrew had both seemed to have settled in.

Andrew was well established in the medical practice. He had also become involved in the local movement to eradicate polio. He had joined the Nagpur Rotary Club and was encouraging that group to educate the community about the importance of immunising their children against polio. This had become something close to his heart to the extent that he became personally involved in the government's campaign to prevent polio. He had gone out with volunteers to nearby villages to provide the oral vaccine drops. He had also organised clinic days at his practice specifically for the neighbouring families to bring their children in to receive the drops.

Elisa had managed to get a job as a music teacher at a high school not far from where they lived. She had also joined a local music society that gave the occasional concert.

They were well assimilated into their local community.

In March, Amy and Asha took Robert on a trip to Canberra, primarily to visit the National Gallery of

Australia for one of their bumper exhibitions, entitled *Masterpieces from Paris*. First stop was the Bradman Museum. Asha had kept the details of the trip secret from Robert other than the exhibition. As they approached Bowral in the Southern Highlands of NSW, Asha asked Robert if he had been to the Bradman Museum and he said no. Robert was quite excited when Asha told him that was where they were going. This had become a standard stop-off between Sydney and Canberra for Asha and Amy. A most enjoyable visit for all of them. They each bought a piece of the memorabilia from the gift shop. There was a book on Bradman for Robert, a bat for Amy and a stubby holder for Asha.

Asha was really struck by the Southern Highlands, simply beautiful countryside. He vowed for Amy and himself to have a couple of days in that area just going from township to township. But when would they be able to fit it in, contemplated Asha?

Their next stop was a winery between Yass and Canberra, where they did a little tasting and Asha bought half a dozen bottles of wine to add to their cellar. How long they would be there before drinking is a good question!

They stopped for a late lunch on the outskirts of Canberra before navigating their way to their hotel.

Dinner was a splendid occasion overlooking Lake Burley Griffin. They had a sumptuous four-course meal, washed down with some very good wines, local to the Canberra district.

The visit to the NGA exhibition the following morning was wonderful. Such an array of European masterpieces from the Musée d'Orsay in Paris, featuring artists such as Cezanne, Gauguin and Van Gogh. This was the cream on top of the cake, with layers of the Bradman Museum and their dinner underneath.

On the way back, they made a detour to cross the relatively new Sea Cliff Bridge near Wollongong and then up to the Bald Hill lookout with spectacular views down the coastline to Wollongong. This is also a popular spot for hang-gliders.

What a great weekend, bringing together many of Asha's favourite delights: cricket, wine, fine dining and culture! Plus sharing the experiences with Robert made it so special.

Robert pondered on such a great trip with Amy and Asha to Canberra. He enjoyed every aspect of the time with them. That was the most important part, just sharing time and experiences with them.

Asha got an email from Yung-Su to say that he did not medal in Vancouver at the Winter Paralympics. However, he said that the experience was beneficial and he would practise hard for the next one. Good attitude, thought Asha.

In June, Asha was posted to the office in Singapore for three months to gain international experience. Unfortunately, Amy was not able to go with him.

Asha got to the airport in plenty of time, checked in, went through passport control and security before making his way to the airline's lounge, where he had a glass of wine and a snack. Then off to the departure gate. The business class line was not too long allowing Asha to board in relatively quick time. Asha was directed to the side of the aircraft where his seat was. When he reached the row where his seat was, there was a gentleman sitting in the aisle seat. Asha said, "Excuse me" and sidled past him as there was plenty of room.

As Asha settled back into his seat, a crew member offered drinks and a bowl of nuts to him and his cabin mate. They both took a glass of champagne.

They then introduced themselves. His name was Tony, a Chinese Singaporean. He looked like he was in his mid-forties. But hard to tell. He was a member of parliament in Singapore, in fact the Minister for Tourism. He had been attending a regional tourism conference in Sydney.

After take-off, they both put up the leg rests. Asha noticed that Tony had callipers attached to both shoes. He was intrigued. He leaned over. "Tony, I hope you do not think that I am being rude. I noticed your callipers. Are your legs affected by polio?"

"Asha, that is fine. I contracted polio as a baby and wear full-length callipers. Interestingly, I see that your right shoe is built up."

"Yes, Tony. We have something in common. My right leg is affected by polio and is four inches shorter than my left leg. Hence the build-up."

Asha then proceeded to give Tony an abridged version of meeting Robert and how he had come to being where he is. Tony seemed quite interested, asking the occasional question or making a comment.

Their conversation continued over lunch, with Asha finding out more about Tony, his career and family.

Another thing Asha found was that Tony and he have a common interest in horse racing. Tony is a member of the Singapore Turf Club and goes to the races at Kranji regularly and offered to take Asha there. Need to keep that in mind, Asha put into his memory bank.

Although Asha had been to Singapore a couple of times, he did not really know the city that well. Tony gave him a good understanding of the touristy things worth experiencing, which Asha made a mental note of for him to sample, particularly with Amy.

They exchanged business cards and Tony said he would like Asha to visit his home for lunch one Sunday. He would call Asha to arrange the date and to give him the details.

After they landed in Singapore, they waited until the other passengers had gone and then they made their way to their chariots to wheel themselves to the baggage carousel, where Tony and Asha parted company. Tony had his driver to meet him.

What a fortuitous circumstance, thought Asha!

Asha was met at the airport by the Singapore practice partner, Sunny. Asha had warned him, if that is the right word, that he would recognise Asha by his wheelchair as well as his "Indian skin colouring".

After Asha checked in at the serviced apartment, he dropped off his bags and wheelchair. When Asha got back to the lobby, Sunny announced his surprise that Asha was not in the wheelchair. Asha explained that the wheelchair had two purposes, firstly to take the load off walking and secondly as a vehicle when he was not wearing his big calliper.

They then went out to dinner, where Sunny gave Asha some background on the local business, which was a great introduction.

Sunny and his driver picked Asha up on the Monday morning to show him to the office. Sunny pointed Asha to the room they had set aside for him. Once Asha had dropped off his bag, he made his way to the conference room where the staff members were assembled to meet him. Introductions over, Asha went with Sunny to his office where he gave Asha his first assignment.

Thereafter, Asha travelled by the Singapore Mass Rapid Transit Rail between Orchard and City Hall, about a five-minute ride. Very handy as the stations were pretty close to his apartment and office.

The Singapore office environment was a little different to the one in Sydney, being a little quieter. But it was still an enjoyable workplace. Importantly, it was a great opportunity to increase his network and to get used to a different culture. Asha's office colleagues were very keen to help him settle in and it became a habit for a number of them to go out together on Friday nights for a few drinks and a meal. Occasionally, they would also go to night racing. Asha really enjoyed the atmosphere at Kranji racecourse.

The weekends Asha spent mostly on his own. He tried to go swimming in the pool on the rooftop at least once during the weekend. The first time he went there was interesting. He could not use his wheelchair as the access was not wheelchair friendly. As he entered the pool area, wearing both his long and short callipers, he could feel eyes from around the pool looking at him. He had become accustomed to the stares of strangers in Sydney and elsewhere he travelled. What attracted their gazes? Was it his brown skin or his polio leg? It did not matter.

Asha just found a lounger, sat down, got ready, crawled over to the pool and in he went. Swimming was very refreshing in such a humid city and it was good exercise. Afterwards, he sat and read and had a beer and a snack. This became the habit for his time at the pool. Sometimes other ex-pat colleagues, living in the complex, joined him. It was good to have a mixture of time on his own and some company.

One time when Asha went to the pool, he noticed an ex-pat colleague from Melbourne.

"Hi Joe, I have not seen you here before."

"Asha, it is my first time."

Asha sat down on a lounger next to Joe and dressed down to his swimming shorts.

"Asha, I am fascinated. I knew from our previous conversations that you had been afflicted by polio from an early age. However, when I saw you walk over and then undress, I had not been aware of that device or whatever you call it that you wear on your right leg."

"Well, Joe, my right leg is devoid of muscle power and can hardly move on its own."

Holding up the calliper, Asha explained "Without this piece of scaffolding I would not be able to stand up far less walk."

"That is brilliant. Shall we go for a swim? Do you need any help?"

"Thank you for the offer. But I am fine crawling over to the edge of the pool."

When they came out of the water, Joe commented on how good a swimmer Asha is.

"A few years ago, in India, I used to do a lot of gym work and swimming. The gym work built up my upper body and my left leg. The resulting strength helped my swimming.

At one time, I contemplated trialling for the Paralympics. Unfortunately, India did not have a strong Paralympian federation, so they could not give much guidance. Also, the qualification trials were to be held in South America, a long and expensive way to travel. So, I decided against taking part in the trials. Pity. It would have been a good experience.

I still do gym work and swim to keep my body in good shape."

"Asha, what an interesting story!"

Tony did call Asha and he had lunch with him, his wife, Angie and their two teenage children. Their apartment was large and splendid with views over the city and out towards the sea.

"Tony, I am very impressed that a disabled person like you managed to get into public life and such a senior role. I need to learn from you. Was it difficult being accepted by your party and the general public?"

"Asha, in the main, there were no big issues. Whether you are able-bodied or have a disability, some people accept you and others do not. I made a point of wearing my callipers and using crutches so that I was on a similar level to able-bodied people and they did not look down to a wheelchair-bound person. When I was out canvassing, I would explain my physical disability and tell people that my brain and other faculties all worked fine. Then it was on to selling the policies of my party and why they ought to vote for me."

"Sounds like it worked. I will bear what you said in mind."

Asha thoroughly enjoyed the lunch and said that he would like to reciprocate when Angie and Tony are in Sydney, if the occasion arose.

At other times at the weekend, Asha would go sightseeing, again sometimes on his own and other times with one or more colleagues. These activities prepared him for the time that Amy would come for a visit for a long weekend.

When that weekend arrived, Asha borrowed Sunny's driver and car to go to the airport to pick up Amy. Asha looked through the glass into the arrivals hall expectantly looking for Amy. And then he spied her walking towards the carousel. His heart started pumping. It was great to see her, Asha beamed. He had missed her so much. This was the longest time that they had spent apart since they moved in together. Asha could not take his eyes off her. She grabbed her bag from the carousel and wheeled it as she skipped towards the exit. She ran into Asha's arms and they hugged and kissed fervently for what must have seemed ages, at least for the driver.

Amy and Asha sat in the back of the car holding hands and talking. What did they have to say? They had been speaking on the telephone at least once every day while Asha had been in Singapore.

Once inside the apartment, Asha caressed Amy and then dragged her into the bedroom. No time for a tour of the apartment.

One of the few things Asha did not like about his big calliper was the length of time it took to remove it. So laborious. Furthermore, he had to remove his left below-knee calliper as well. What must it be like for Andrew and Yung-Su if they needed to take two full-length leg braces off in a hurry? Why had Asha not just used his wheelchair to go to the airport? Asha complained to himself.

And why not keep both callipers on if he was in such a rush to make love to Amy? There was a very good reason. Asha had sex before with Amy, wearing the big calliper. That was in the back seat of a car. It was so cumbersome, weighing his leg down in its jail cell, making it very difficult to move around.

Just be patient, Asha kept telling himself.

What a gorgeous feeling it was to wake up on the Saturday morning with the beautiful Amy beside him. Asha nestled into her side and cuddled her and...

This brought back memories of their honeymoon.

Amy and Asha got ready and went down to a little cafe near the apartment that Asha frequented and had coffee and croissant and then it was on with the tour of Singapore.

The focus was just on spending time together.

They had lunch in Little India. Asha took Amy to a restaurant where the food was served on banana leaves and you ate with your hands. This was a new experience for Amy and she loved the experience, even suggesting they ought to do something like that in Sydney (if they could find a restaurant that does it).

They went to the casino. They took a cable car to Sentosa again and did some of the things that they missed out on doing last time. They went on the Singapore Flyer, which is a giant Ferris wheel, with the stunning views below as you circle above the city. They also had a corporate dinner. But they were not able to fit in racing just like Asha had not been able to go racing with Tony. Unfortunately, their time together was far too short.

At the end of Asha's three months, Sunny threw a farewell dinner for him and some of the colleagues from the office. Asha had thoroughly enjoyed the experience, had made new friends and had increased his network. Great memories.

Singapore is one of Asha's favourite places, where east meets west.

Singapore is a wonderful hub for travel by air, well placed geographically to get to Europe, the Americas, Asia and the Pacific. Singapore is closer to Perth in Australia than Sydney is to Perth! And easy to get to the airport from the city.

The transport in Singapore, particularly the SMRT train system, is very accessible for wheelchair users. That was very handy when Asha went into the office or travelled around the city using his wheelchair.

Singapore is a tremendous tourist destination, with the development of hotels and restaurants along its waterways.

Asha would like to spend more time in Singapore and even work there. Something to contemplate for the future. But, for the time being at least, Sydney is home.

When Asha got back to Sydney, Amy and he went house-hunting. They thought it was the right time to get into the property market. But it was not easy finding what they wanted in the Eastern Suburbs. After a few weeks of looking, they were becoming very frustrated. And then they were attracted to a house advertised in the newspaper. They went to the inspection and liked what they saw so much that they put in a bid. They had a tense day or so as they waited to hear back from the agent. It was theirs. They were relieved and over the moon. Their first house.

Causes for celebration kept coming. They found out that Amy was pregnant and due to give birth the following July. The telephone service rang wildly as they called their families with the news. Of course, Asha called Andrew. He and Elisa were so happy for them. They knew the joy they had felt when they found out that Elisa was pregnant. They wished Amy and Asha every happiness for a healthy baby.

Co-incidentally, Asha got an email from Yung-Su telling him that Mi-Hyun was pregnant, due around March the following year. Great news. Asha called Robert and told him. He seemed so happy.

Robert replied. "All my 'children' are producing. This is going to keep me a very busy grandfather, with one in Australia, one in India and one in South Korea. I am so happy for Yung-Su and Mi-Hyun. After not being in touch properly with Yung-Su for such a long time, I am now re-invigorated about our relationship."

Robert went on a business trip in October to Seoul and was able to spend time with Yung-Su and Mi-Hyun. True to what Yung-Su had said when they had lunched in Sydney, he did wear his leg braces and used crutches, which he did when he came to the airport to pick Robert up. Robert was a little surprised but also happy. Mi-Yun was looking very well, in fact glowing, and there was always a smile on Yung-Su's face. Such a happy couple.

One evening, Yung-Su came to Robert's hotel on his own to go out for dinner. Robert met him in the hotel's underground car park and took him up to his room. They sat down and talked for a while. He told Robert about his Winter Olympic venture. He was a little disappointed with his performance but accepted that he was still learning and would improve. And then he asked Robert to do something. Yung-Su hand-walked with Robert for about ten minutes. No need for Robert to bark out commands this time. Yung-Su was doing it with relative ease, no doubt due to Mi-Hyun's coaching.

After a rest, they went down to a Korean restaurant on the other side of the road from the hotel. It was very basic but the *bibimbap* was delicious. How Robert had missed enjoying Korean food with Yung-Su.

Yung-Su told Robert that he was looking forward to fatherhood. He said he was so happy being with Mi-Hyun. She had helped him become more confident. His health had improved, he was eating properly and he had lost some weight.

Robert went with Yung-Su down to his car and waved him off, wishing him and Mi-Hyun all the best with the impending new arrival. Yung-Su thanked Robert for everything and promised to stay in touch.

Asha was using his wheelchair more often than walking as had been recommended by my orthotist. In any case, he was finding walking more difficult as his left knee was struggling to handle the weight. So much so, he had resorted to using two walking sticks. This took him back to the time when he was recovering from the Achilles problem.

Asha went to see an orthopaedic specialist as recommended by his orthotist. He arranged for some X-rays to be taken of the knee. They showed a tremendous amount of wear and tear. The specialist thought that a knee replacement would help. That sounded a bit drastic to Asha.

Asha talked over the visits to the specialist with his orthotist. He came up with two other options, which were a full-length leg brace or abandon walking and just use the wheelchair. What a conundrum? Asha wanted to remain ambulatory and mobile.

Asha thought about the options long and hard, discussed them with both Amy and Robert. At the end of the day, it was his choice. He decided not to do anything, at least at this point in time. Just continue to use his wheelchair for the most part.

So, Asha, just get on with life and stop feeling sorry for yourself, he told myself. After all, there are many people in the world much worse off than him. This is not the Asha pole-hopping around. This is the Asha who has made a good life for himself, has a lovely wife with a home to share and a well-paid, interesting and challenging job.

It was during the time that he was using the two sticks that he had a coffee catch-up meeting with a friend in a city hotel. Asha had gone by bus. But he decided that he would go home by taxi. After they had finished their coffees, Asha asked the lady serving them if she could ask the concierge to bring him a wheelchair to use to get down to the forecourt.

The wheelchair duly arrived. Asha said goodbye to his friend and wheeled himself down to the forecourt to get a taxi. When the taxi arrived, Asha got out of the wheelchair and walked around the car and got into the front passenger seat.

When they reached Asha's home, he paid for the ride and the driver released the boot, which Asha thought was strange. Then the driver said he would get Asha's wheelchair out. Asha was surprised. Asha told the driver he did not have a wheelchair. The one he was using belonged to the hotel. The driver asked Asha what to do? Asha suggested that he call the hotel and let them know about their error of loading the wheelchair. The hotel concierge told him to deliver the wheelchair back and they would pay the fare.

Asha had not seen John and Eve too much other than at Andrew's and his weddings. Amy and himself had been very busy and, of course, Asha had been away in Singapore for some time.

Asha got in touch with John and invited him and Eve to their place for dinner. They had a lot to catch up on. Asha's and John's jobs were working out well. John had recently received a promotion.

As they were reaching the end of the meal, John announced that he and Eve would be getting married. Amy and Asha were overjoyed for them and raised their glasses in a toast. The weddings keep a-coming.

Andrew and Elisa travelled back to Sydney in late November to be with their families and friends for Christmas and for Elisa to give birth. Matthew was born in the early hours of December 25. This meant an interrupted Christmas lunch hosted by Robert for the quartet, minus Elisa this time, as well as Elisa's and Amy's parents. But, nevertheless, great timing.

Andrew returned to India a week later, while Elisa and Matthew stayed with Elisa's parents.

Chapter 34
Past, Present and Future

Andrew came back to Sydney in February for the christening and to take his family back to India. It was good to see Andrew again, even after such a short time away as well as for a very brief period.

Amy and Asha managed to fit in a weekend away in the Southern Highlands at the end of February. They drove down late on Friday afternoon and checked into a B&B in the Bowral Town Centre, handy for dining out and wandering around the next day. That night they had a fabulous meal at a top-class restaurant and then off to bed.

After a country breakfast the next day, they had a look around Bowral and then dived into the car for the drive to Moss Vale, where they enjoyed a light lunch before moving onto Berrima.

After checking into a Berrima B&B, they took a stroll round this historic town which goes back to 1831. Even the place where they were staying was steeped in history as it was a very old inn. They could not do justice to the various places of interest in one afternoon, partly due to being distracted by the arts and crafts shops. They earmarked a couple of places to visit the following morning.

Another scrumptious dinner in one of, if not, the best restaurants in the area. It was within walking distance of the B&B. However, just like their stroll in Bowral after dinner, they noticed a chill in the air again as they made their way back to the B&B.

In the morning, Amy and Asha finished off their sightseeing in Berrima, stopped for lunch in Moss Vale, finishing off a most enjoyable weekend in the Southern Highlands.

It was definitely worth the trip, not that it is so far from Sydney. It was good to have the flexibility of casually roaming around for a couple of days, something that they will not be able to enjoy to the same extent, once the baby is born. Nevertheless, Asha was really looking forward to being a father, something incredibly new.

Amy and Asha moved into their house in March. They took most of their furniture from the rented apartment and splurged out on some new essentials, at least that was how they justified what they were buying.

The house was in a leafy street with small gardens front and back. It had three bedrooms, a study, lounge/dining, a spacious kitchen, laundry and two bathrooms, one with shower and one with bath.

A few weeks later, Amy and Asha threw a house-warming party on a sunny Sunday afternoon. Amy's parents flew in from Perth. Naturally, Robert was there with a bevy of friends from university and their work places. And Eve and John were able to join them. Sadly, Andrew and his family were missing. Nevertheless, everyone had a great time celebrating the new house.

Amy and Asha attended Eve's and John's wedding in Sydney along with Robert. Naturally, Alice came over for the celebrations. Robert was very happy to see her again.

After the wedding, Alice and Robert were able to catch up in a less stressful environment. But, a couple of days later, Alice returned to Vietnam.

When Eve and John got back from their honeymoon, they had Amy and Asha over to their apartment for dinner. They had spent their honeymoon in New York and had a wonderful time sightseeing as well as taking in Broadway shows. Amy and Asha agreed that they ought to make an effort to visit New York and, perhaps, other parts of the USA... some day!

Yung-Su called Asha to let him know that Mi-Hyun had given birth to a baby boy, who they had named Chang-Su. Both mother and son were doing very well.

Asha called Robert to pass on the good news. He was ecstatic that he had another grandson.

"Who is going to give me a granddaughter?" was his question.

Robert telephoned Yung-Su to pass on his congratulations and wish them all good health. Yung-Su seemed happy to receive his call. Robert also spoke to Mi-Hyun, who was so excited and talkative. She described Chang-Su to Robert as having black hair and brown eyes with a small nose, just like Yung-Su. Mi-Hyun said that Yung-Su had been very supportive, but not quite to the extent of changing nappies.

Robert said to himself that he needed to plan another visit to Seoul.

Amy and Asha started preparing for their new arrival, decorating the room and buying some neutral clothes as well as the baby care necessities. They were not sure if it was bad luck. But Asha was not superstitious and told Amy that what was meant to be will be.

Asha believed that fate is in the choices people make and determines their future that is already preordained.

This is something that Asha had in common with Robert, who had previously relayed tales of what he felt were his fated experiences and interpretations.

"I am who God says I am.

My whole life has unfolded through a series of decision points. A decision not to go to university. A move to London and a change of hostels where I met my wife. Change of jobs into the nascent computer industry. Tossing up whether to move from London to Bristol, Malta or Sydney. The offer to emigrate to Sydney came first. Deciding to stay in Australia and to get into the housing market had given us a solid footing. Having a son was part of my maturing. Career changes ending in setting up my own business. The individuals with polio whom I have helped. Why them specifically? I felt that it was a very well-defined path that could have been much different. I'll never know and don't think about it.

Why Bristol, Malta or Australia and not, say, Canada? We discarded Canada as an option because of its extreme winter weather.

I was not sure about Bristol. Perhaps I just saw an advertisement for a job and felt that Bristol would be a good place to bring up a family.

Malta was a little more precise. I had friends from Malta and I went to the Mediterranean island a couple of times to holiday with them.

"They lived in a lovely village called Siggiewi, which is ten kilometres from Valletta, the capital. I stayed with Salv and his parents in their two-storey building with a patio for a roof. The stone floors kept the place cool in this warm tropical climate. Everything around seemed to be white including the walls of the houses, causing a very strong glare.

"The village was relatively quiet except for the peeping of horns from cars and scooters as the vehicles drove through the main square. Apart from that, there was really no hustle and bustle. People went about their business in a very casual way.

"We did not sit around except when we were at the beach. We would go to Valletta, the capital, and potter around, doing some gift shopping. On some days we would play football on what seemed to be a concrete pitch with a covering of sand.

"But the beach was the place to be. With the sun blazing down from a clear blue sky, you could not beat playing around in the light blues and greens of the Mediterranean Sea, which seemed so clean and clear. And the sea temperature was very pleasant.

"At night, after a hard day in the sun, we would relax in the village with a family dinner or go to the casino where we would have some food and beer.

"We did not drink to excess except on my last night on one of the visits. The result was a very uncomfortable flight back to London, ending with me sitting in the toilet as the plane landed. That would not be allowed to happen today, with much stricter controls in place.

"Such fond memories. Malta has such a beautiful climate, easy-going ways and the friendliness and richness of its people. I was well and truly looked after there. These are some of the reasons I would have liked to have lived there.

"As for Sydney, the attraction was the apparent quality of life and the very pleasant weather. An ex-colleague of mine had moved to Sydney about a year previously with his wife and his letters extolled the virtues of life in Sydney and how much they were enjoying being there.

"We had decided that whatever came through first would dictate where we would go.

"Australia won and we flew out to Sydney under the Australian government's assisted passage scheme, where we paid ten English pounds to migrate to Australia on the condition we remained there for at least two years. I refer to this as us being ten-pound tourists.

"This was a big risk but that did not seem to come into the equation. We did not have much money. We did not have a confirmed job to go to, just an interview set up for me. But we were young and seemingly adventurous. Or was this just our Fate?"

As Asha reflected further on what Robert had told him some time ago, he realised that his "Fate" had been unfolding in a similar way to Robert. He had also moved to Australia, the land of opportunities. Unlike Robert, Asha had gone onto further education and gained his degree. But this direction had been encouraged by Robert. Asha's career was in its infancy. Asha had done some charity work and wanted to do more. He had married and was now awaiting the arrival of his first child.

Here's another story from Robert about Fate that Asha remembered;

"In May 1999, Yung-Su and I went to Fukuoka for the wheelchair tennis Japan Open. We settled into the hotel and had a good dinner the first night together with some other Korean players. I was very much included.

"We would travel to and from the tennis centre in a coach. During one of these rides, there was one interesting and, in some ways, funny experience. The president of the International Wheelchair Tennis Federation asked me how I got into this, meaning wheelchair tennis. I said 'by accident'. His response, sitting in his wheelchair, was 'that is how most of us do'. It's good to have a sense of humour.

"At the tennis centre, Yung-Su would spend most of his non-playing time watching the games with the other Koreans and basically ignoring me. At night we would all have dinner together. Then, the next day, the same isolation for me at the tennis. I did not know anyone other than the Korean players and it was difficult to converse with them as my Korean was pretty non-existent and their English was not too good.

"I had been away with Yung-Su and the Koreans before. But this was the first time that Yung-Su seemed to be 'ignoring' me. I tried to spend more time with Yung-Su but he was more interested in being with the other Koreans. So, I had plenty of thinking time, which led me to the conclusion that I was wasting my time in Fukuoka. I was due back in Seoul for work in a few days. So, I decided to go there earlier and leave Yung-Su in Fukuoka.

"At three o'clock on the Monday morning as I was asleep in my Seoul hotel room, the telephone rang. It was my parents' next-door neighbour on the line to tell me that my father had passed away. In these days, I never bothered leaving my itinerary and contact details with family. But my mother remembered the name of the hotel that I was to be staying at in Seoul.

"If I had remained in Fukuoka until the end of the tournament, I would not have received that call.

Fate."

No point in worrying about If and If only as you do not know what would have happened – good or bad. Things are what they are, thought Asha.

Time seemed to be passing so slowly as Amy and Asha waited expectantly. Apart from work, they had kept busy with their interests; opera, horse racing and weekend lunches. In some respects, the only downside was that Amy had stopped drinking wine. Such a sacrifice. But that did not stop Asha from imbibing.

Asha's left knee seemed to be getting weaker and weaker. He was still using his wheelchair mainly. But he was not happy sitting in a wheelchair most of the time. However, even when he walked with crutches, the pressure on his left knee was becoming unbearable. Asha had decided that he did not want to have another operation. Also, he did not want to be in a position, at least not yet, of having to use a wheelchair as his only form of mobility. So, he succumbed to getting a full-length calliper for his left leg.

Asha went to the orthotist for the standard procedure of moulding plaster of Paris around his leg from toe to thigh as the template for the calliper. However, with the advances in technology, the fitting was for a leg brace that has an intelligent sensor system which measures the leg position while walking and controls the orthosis joint accordingly. This means that the knee joint is automatically opened while walking. it locks in the stance phase for safe support and unlocks in the swing phase for a more natural gait.

Two weeks after the fitting, Asha went back. The leg brace fitted very well, providing great support not only for his knee but also his ankle. The brace fitted inside his shoe. Asha walked up and down the room. Initially, it felt a little odd, walking quite naturally without a stiff leg like his right leg. After a little time, Asha felt quite comfortable and confident. That's good. I'll be able to do more walking, thought Asha.

The orthotist recommended that Asha use a walking stick in his left hand for balance and support. No need to use crutches.

When Asha got home, Amy was standing at the front door. She greeted Asha and commented on how well she thought he walked. "Thank you. Although I have been wearing the new device for a very short time, I feel extremely mobile."

That night they went out to a restaurant within walking distance, which was easy going. The restaurant owner was surprised that Asha was not using crutches or a wheelchair. "You look great," he said.

By the time they sat down in the restaurant, Asha had a very good appetite and thirst. The dinner was excellent and put Asha in a very good mood. But he was quite exhausted and ready for bed.

The following day Amy and Asha went shopping. Using the escalators was now easy and natural.

When Asha went to work, it was easy getting around. No crutches and no need for the wheelchair that Asha had in the office. His colleagues all seemed amazed at how well he was getting around, just like before he had the problem with his left knee.

Eve and John had become some of Amy's and Asha's closest friends, particularly with Andrew and Elisa being in India.

One Sunday, the two couples arranged to meet in Centennial Park for an autumnal picnic.

Fortunately, the sun was shining and it was quite warm. Eve and John had got there before Amy and Asha and had managed to secure a table. So, after Amy and Asha drove up and parked nearby, they got the picnic basket and food out of the car and strolled over to Eve and John

"Asha, what has happened to you?" John queried. "I am surprised that you are not using crutches or your wheelchair."

"Well. I have been having some trouble with my left ankle and left knee in particular. I had a number of options and the one I chose was new assistive technology that provides support while it helps me walk pretty normally. So, there you are — a new me or even the old me!"

The pleasantries out of the way and time to enjoy lunch, comprising prawns from Eve and John and chicken from Amy and Asha plus some salads. But they were careful with the wine, limiting themselves to just one and a bit glasses for everyone except only water for Amy.

One morning in late July, Amy waved Asha off to work. A couple of hours later, she called him at the office to tell him that her waters had broken and that Asha ought to return to take her to hospital. When Asha drove into their driveway, Amy was waiting a little anxiously on the front steps.

As it turned out, there was no need to rush. The contractions were reasonably spaced. They just had to be patient. About three hours later, Asha followed Amy as she was being rolled into theatre. Asha had never been a spectator in a hospital theatre before. He stood beside Amy, holding her hand, as she pushed, screamed and sweated. But not for long. The baby was placed on Amy's chest, held in her arms. Amy and Asha smiled at each other. It was a girl.

Amy and Asha had already chosen names for a boy and girl. Their new born was called Roberta Asha Kakkur.

The telephones went into meltdown as Asha called his parents, Amy's parents, Robert and Andrew with Elisa. Congratulations and best wishes chorused down the line from all the joyous parties.

Because Amy and Asha had not known what sex the baby would be, they had bought neutral-coloured clothes and furnished its room in pastel colours, neither blue nor pink.

Asha had two weeks off work on paternity leave from work as Roberta settled in and they endured sleep-broken nights. They did not care. They were happy that they had a healthy daughter.

Asha did his fair share of nappy changing. Just proud to help out.

Asha went back to work and Amy and Roberta enjoyed each other's company together. Asha always looked forward to returning at nights to see Roberta. The weekends were taken up with doing things with her. As the weather got warmer, they spent more time outside with her, going for strolls.

Sometimes, Asha would take her for a ride. Sitting in his wheelchair, he would put her on his lap, hook his right leg across onto his left thigh and push them around the house. She would lie there, looking up at him, laughing and gurgling, probably wondering what was going on. She seemed to enjoy this. Asha certainly did.

Christmas was approaching. So, Amy and Asha decorated the house again, just like the previous year. This time they had special presents to buy, although not sure if Roberta was going to appreciate them at almost six months.

Andrew and family had made the trip back to Sydney for Christmas and New Year. Amy and Asha had delayed Roberta's christening until they were with them.

A big family gathering took place plus friends, including Eve and John for the christening on Christmas

Eve followed by an informal gathering at Amy's and Asha's place for finger food and drinks.

Christmas Day was huge, not just in a religious sense, but because Amy and Asha were surrounded by all their families. Asha's parents, brother, sister and family had also flown in together from Nagpur. Amy's parents came over from Perth and Elisa's parents made the short trip from Manly.

Robert put on a splendid barbeque for the masses. The place was abuzz with chatter. Everyone was relaxed. Matthew and Roberta were being spoiled by the grandparents. What joy! A real day of celebration.

They all gathered a week later, again at Robert's apartment for New Year's Eve. Then, within the next couple of days, all the visitors were gone.

Asha had thoroughly enjoyed being with his parents and siblings again. It was also special to spend time with Andrew. He was fantastically happy in India and thought it was one of the best decisions he had ever made.

Chapter 35
Tragic

January 2012 marked one year without any polio cases in India. What an achievement. Asha called Andrew to thank him for his efforts in ridding India of polio. Andrew was very pleased for the nation. But he stated strongly that the work was not finished. The immunisation programme must continue. He said that he was committed to doing whatever he could to help.

It was the middle of March and Robert had been home all day. He had watched the horse racing on television in the afternoon and caught some of the qualifying laps for the Melbourne Formula 1 Grand Prix due the next day, Sunday. After dinner, he went back to watching more sport on television until he received a call from Elisa.

Asha's father called him and then Robert called. Asha rushed over to Robert's apartment. As soon as Robert opened the door, Asha hugged him. Then they moved to the balcony, neither of them saying anything.

They sat down but silence continued. Asha did not know what to say. Andrew had been killed.

Elisa had been so distraught that she could not explain to Robert what had happened properly.

Asha's father had provided him with more details, at least what he had understood from the initial police statement.

Andrew had been closing up for lunch when two youths entered the doctors' surgery where he worked. The police think that they were looking for drugs and had stabbed Andrew a number of times, presumably because he had refused to cooperate. Andrew had died immediately.

Robert and Asha were both in shock. But they knew they had to do something. Robert said he would go to India to be with Elisa and Matthew as soon as possible. Asha said that he would go with him. It was the least Asha thought he could do. Andrew had been like a brother to him. Asha also knew that Elisa would need as much support as possible.

Amy arranged for her mother to come over from Perth to Sydney urgently to look after Roberta so that she could go to India as well with Robert and Asha. Some feminine support for Elisa. After all, Andrew, Elisa, Amy and Asha had been very good friends for many years.

They managed to get flights booked for the Monday.

On the Sunday night, Asha was watching the news when a report from India grabbed his attention.

'An Australian doctor was killed yesterday in Nagpur, a town a few hundred kilometres east of

Mumbai. The cause of his death was not clear. There are suggestions that it might have been racism.'

Vision of a street scene, presumably in Nagpur and perhaps outside Andrew's surgery were flashed across the screen. And that was it. Asha was stunned. Where did they get this information? Who said it might be a racist attack? Was this just sensationalising some unfortunate event?

For some reason, this brought back memories of times when Asha had been picked on in his own country.

Once, Asha was lying beside a hotel swimming pool in his trunks when someone from security came up to him and asked him what his room number was. Asha was flustered by the question and could not splurt out the answer. Robert had seen what was happening and came over to find out what was going on. He told the security guy that Asha was with him. The guy left with his tail between his legs. This was Indian against Indian.

Another time, Robert and Asha had got out of a taxi in front of another hotel. Asha was ahead of Robert as they entered the hotel. There was no security scanner just the doorman who stopped Asha and asked him where he was going. Asha told Robert what was happening and Robert told the doorman that Asha was with him and they walked off into the lobby. Robert told Asha to stay where he was as Robert went back to talk to the doorman. Robert berated him for stopping Asha and told him not to do that again. Robert and Asha were both hotel guests.

"Asha, I cannot understand why you were stopped. After all, you are better dressed than me."

Asha was wearing a long-sleeved shirt, long pants and proper shoes, whereas Robert wore shorts, a T-shirt and sandals. Once again, Indian versus Indian.

Were these examples of racism?

Asha called his father and told him what he had seen on television. Ranjiv said a similar story had been broadcast on the local news. He did not know why they had suggested racism. He confirmed that, as far as he knew, the police were still treating it as a drug-related killing.

The trip to India was very sombre. None of them had the energy or inclination to talk much. Asha just listened to music, watched a couple of movies, ate the meals and slept a little. Robert and Amy seemed to do similar things. They changed planes in Dubai and then managed to get a flight to Nagpur soon after reaching Mumbai. Ranjiv met them at Nagpur airport.

Ranjiv was so soulful in expressing his condolences to Robert.

On the drive, Ranjiv gave them more information about what had happened. The police had arrested two youths and confirmed that they had been trying to get drugs from the surgery. Apparently, Andrew refused to tell them where the drugs were kept. So, they threatened him with a knife. A struggle ensued and Andrew was stabbed a dozen times in a frenzied attack on his upper body. The youths had then fled empty-handed. The police had found Andrew's body on the floor in a pool of blood. His wheelchair was up against the back wall. The contents of the shelves were strewn on the floor and the cabinets had been smashed.

Thoughts of a waste of a young life permeated the air!

By the time they arrived at the farmhouse, the sun was coming up and the household was up and about, including Elisa and Matthew who had moved there after Andrew's killing.

It was a very uncomfortable reunion for all. Words were difficult.

After breakfast, Robert and Elisa discussed what had to be done, in particular the funeral and her and Matthew's future. They agreed that the service and cremation ought to take place in Nagpur and they would then take Andrew's ashes back to Sydney. Elisa had also decided that Matthew and she would return to Sydney to live.

It was a small gathering at the funeral; Asha's family, Elisa, Matthew, Robert, Amy, himself and a few acquaintances that Elisa and Andrew had made in Nagpur. Both Robert and Asha spoke at the church service.

Robert was very eloquent talking about his love for his son and how Andrew had overcome some early setbacks in life to be a very successful young man in sport, academically and in business. Robert remarked on Andrew's efforts to help those who were less well off in India.

What amazed Asha, in some way, was that Robert showed no animosity to India and its people for what had happened to Andrew. He seemed to have accepted that, sadly, such things happen to innocent people, being in the wrong place at the wrong time. Or was that just a brave face?

When Asha spoke, he was shaking and his voice was trembling in anger. Asha was so sad and ashamed of his countrymen. How could they take the life of his mentor after all Andrew and Robert had done for him, an Indian?

Asha clearly felt sorry for the loss of his friend of ten years. But that was nothing compared to how Elisa must have felt. Andrew and Elisa had been married for less than four years and their son, Matthew, was not even eighteen months old. Furthermore, Elisa was three months' pregnant with their second child. That wonderful news only confirmed a few days ago was sadly affected by Andrew's demise. What was Elisa going to do without Andrew? How were Matthew and the unborn child going to grow up without such a wonderful father who would have used his worldly experience to guide them?

Amy and Asha made their way back to Sydney with heavy hearts. They poured all their energies into their work and, above all, into their daughter.

After Elisa and Robert returned to Sydney, Asha avoided them for some time as he did not know how to handle the situation. Amy was a little different. She made a point of meeting up with Elisa and Matthew with Roberta in tow. Usually a coffee morning. Yet, Asha's guilt grew primarily because he had not even bothered to spend time with Matthew, his godson. Asha felt that he ought to have been there as a father figure, but his excuse was that it was too early.

Asha had difficulty sleeping at night. He could not stop thinking about Andrew. Instead of going to bed he would sit in the study with a glass of wine and remember his times with Andrew. Every night Asha tried to recall a different moment: tennis, university, travelling, nights out. Asha missed Andrew so much.

But, in the end, it was just the anger that poured out. Of course, Asha was extremely sad that Andrew had passed away. And he was ashamed of the part his fellow Indian countrymen had in his death. But most of all he was livid. There was fire in his eyes and belly.

How could these two fucking useless Indians have murdered my best friend, cried Asha? What was the fucking point? Just a waste of a brilliant life.

Why had God allowed this to happen?

This was a similar question to the one Asha asked as a boy. Why did he get polio? Why him? What had he done to deserve becoming a cripple?

And, now, what had Andrew done to be cut down in his prime?

Asha had no answer then and did not have an answer now.

But could God be blamed? He had created mankind. Did that make him responsible for the future of humanity?

If everything was perfect, all good and no bad, would humanity function? The population would grow and grow and grow, with people born, maturing but not dying. Then the planet would explode, bringing to an end life as we know it. Would that be a good outcome? No.

God provides guidance and allows everyone, the good and the bad, to exist as preordained. This argument, however, did little to suppress Asha's anger, which was not aimed at God but at the villains responsible for Andrew's death.

Asha's state of mind was driving Amy insane. She told Asha to go to see a psychiatrist. But Asha did not think that was the answer.

After a couple of weeks, Asha decided he needed to get this whole matter off his chest. So, Asha worked up the courage to call Robert and to invite Robert to have lunch with him.

Robert was very happy to see Asha and had been disappointed that they had not met up since Robert got back. But, Robert added, that he was as much to blame as Asha. Robert had been having difficulties coming to grips with his huge loss. To get his mind off Andrew, he had travelled to some of his business centres other than India.

Now was not the time to re-open Robert's wounded heart, or was it? Asha needed to deal with his response to Andrew's death and, perhaps, Robert also had to face up to the reality that Andrew had gone and that he had to move on.

Over lunch, Asha told Robert what was happening to him and how he could not get Andrew and the murder out of his mind. Asha also told Robert that he had not seen Elisa since her return, although Amy had met with her a number of times. Also, the fact that Asha had not even made the effort to spend time with Matthew.

Robert suggested that they all get together to celebrate Andrew's birthday as they had been doing for the last few years. Asha was not sure about that. But he agreed to go ahead with the suggestion. Robert said he would take care of inviting Elisa.

The day arrived to celebrate Andrew's birthday. Amy and Asha had decided to have an afternoon tea. Amy had made some finger sandwiches and had bought some cakes.

As Elisa walked through the door of their house, Asha greeted her with a forced smile and hug. Robert arrived soon afterwards and they sat in the lounge with their glasses of champagne. Robert spoke up, and looked upwards:

"Happy birthday, Andrew."

The rest chorused, "Happy birthday, Andrew."

To Asha's surprise, Elisa was quite relaxed. This helped with the conversation. They enjoyed the afternoon, if enjoyed is the right word. But, for Asha, most of all, it helped him see that Elisa and Robert had been able to deal with Andrew's death and get on with their lives and that he ought to make an effort to do the same.

As the afternoon was coming to a close, Robert decided to share something with Elisa, Amy and Asha.

Andrew had known that Robert had planned to give most of his money away. Andrew was pretty well off. He had bought an apartment in Sydney before they had left for India and rented it out. Also, he had taken out a serious life insurance policy that meant that Elisa and Matthew were well taken care off with the proceeds after Andrew's death.

"I have something very important to tell you. I hope that what I have to say will have your full support. I had been thinking of a way to remember Andrew. As a result, I have come up with the idea of providing a scholarship in his memory. The scholarship will cover all costs associated with undertaking a three-year degree at a Sydney college. And it will be repeated every three years. The candidates for the scholarships will be disabled or students from a poor background who are performing at a high level from schools in Nagpur."

Asha looked at Robert in astonishment.

"Why?"

"A number of reasons. Firstly, you are a credit to the cause I described and fit the criteria perfectly. Secondly, and perhaps more importantly, Andrew wanted to help Indians in need. He went to India to try to achieve that. But things went sadly awry. This is a continuation of Andrew's journey."

Asha smiled. Amy thought it was a wonderful idea. Elisa said it would be a great way to keep alive Andrew's hopes for India's less privileged.

Asha was to be the local mentor for the Indian students. The selection team, back in Nagpur, would be Andrew's practice partner, someone from Rotary and the principal from Elisa's school. It was too late to start the process for the 2013 college year. So, they planned to award the first scholarship for the 2014 year.

When Robert went back to his apartment, he sat alone on the balcony, except for a glass of wine, and he thought about life with Andrew. Tears started running down his cheeks as he remembered him from his very first day, such a wonderful feeling to be partly responsible for bringing this little beautiful boy into the world. Robert marvelled at how Andrew had dealt with his disability, not letting it interfere with his zest for life. He had a very strong character that blossomed as he excelled at school and in sport. He was quite outgoing and had made many friends throughout his relatively short existence. Robert was grateful for how he had welcomed Asha like a little brother and had become his mentor. How Asha must be missing Andrew as well.

Robert had committed himself to being there for Elisa and Matthew providing whatever support. The men, Asha, Elisa's father and he, now had the responsibility to be Matthew's father figures.

"Dear Andrew, forgive me for any failings I had as a father. I love you," mouthed Robert to himself.

That night Asha repaired to the study with a glass of wine. But this time, there was no anger. Just smiles as he reflected on Andrew's life, from the time they had met, playing tennis and travelling. His birthday lunches were always one of the annual highlights. And, finally, Robert's commitment to Andrew's memory. Thereafter, no more sitting in the study on his own wallowing in self-pity.

Amidst all this sadness and tumult, there was a bright, shining light. John called Asha to let him know that Eve was pregnant. Asha congratulated him and asked him to pass on his best wishes to his wife.

Asha also told John that he had been side-tracked by Andrew's death and suggested that they get together for a drink in a couple of weeks, which they did. It was good to talk to a friend outside the family circle.

As time went by, Asha continued with his personal reflections. Amy and he were happy together, very happy. They were about to celebrate Roberta's first birthday. Work was going well. Yet there was something missing, a void.

Asha's mind was tortured as he tried to work out the missing element. He went back over his life, India, polio, Robert, Australia, Amy and, of course, Andrew. That was it. Asha wanted to follow in Andrew's footsteps. Not helping India. But doing something for Australia, his adopted country and the country that had adopted him. What were the options? Helping with a charity was a noble thing to do. But Asha was already doing something in that area. He wanted to do more.

Asha had joined Rotary, partly because of their efforts in driving towards a polio-free world. The catalyst for that was what Andrew had been doing in India.

And there were other projects in his local Rotary district where he was a member that he was able to get involved in around the community. But that was still not enough.

That's it. Asha decided he ought to enter NSW State politics. Initially, the thought had seemed strange. Asha was not really into politics. He'd had some discussions with Robert about politics, here and in India. Asha was not a member of any of the major political parties and did not really align with what they stood for. One seemed to be oriented towards the wealthier and the other to the working class. Where was the balance? Asha would want to help everyone and TREAT EVERYONE FAIRLY. The answer was to become an Independent candidate at the next NSW State government elections. When were they due, Asha asked himself?

The following morning Asha discussed this with Amy. She was a little surprised. Yet she thought it was worth giving it a go. She thought Asha had the right people skills, personality and ideals to make a good Independent member.

Asha then called Robert and asked to meet him. A couple of nights later, they sat on Robert's balcony with a glass of wine in hand, discussing Asha's plan, well more of an idea than a plan.

Robert challenged Asha. "Is this the career move you want? Do you know how much time is involved and the sacrifices, particularly relating to family, which will have to be made?"

Good questions, thought Asha. If I failed, I had law to fall back on. Amy had already offered her full support.

They discussed it more and decided to start laying out a plan.

Robert offered Asha his support. "Asha, you have a lot to learn about politics, what it is all about, how it works and what the main issues are. However, I think you can do it. It will be a lot of hard work. And I will help you as much as I can. Firstly, you need to apply to become an Australian Citizen and, hopefully, receive that honour on Australia Day next year."

Chapter 36
Tony

Since the fortuitous meeting with Tony on the flight to Singapore, Asha had stayed in touch with him by email and telephone.

When Tony and Angie visited Sydney for a vacation, they spent time with Amy and Asha, sightseeing and dining out.

They had a great time together and had settled easily into one another's presence. Angie and Tony enjoyed the ferry ride to Manly and the boardwalk stroll to Shelly Beach, culminating in a delicious seafood lunch.

Tony and Angie invited Amy and Asha to see the opera, *La Traviata*, performed on the harbour. Amy and Asha were very happy to be going to this opera again, particularly as it was in the open air, offering a vastly different experience. Asha had seen it at the Sydney Opera House with Robert and had not been impressed. At that time, opera was new to him. Then he went with Amy to see La Traviata at the same venue and enjoyed it so much that they bought a CD of the opera.

Amy and Asha met Tony and Angie in their hotel suite for pre-theatre drinks and nibbles. Angie answered the knock at their door and welcomed Amy and Asha.

"You are both looking splendid" Angie commented.

"Thank you, it is good to dress up in a tuxedo and to have such a beautiful partner by my side," Asha acknowledged.

"And, Asha, you are wearing new shoes," Tony entered the conversation.

"Very observant. I had them made recently, with the build-up inside the right shoe. So, it is less conspicuous, not that it really matters. But I also think it looks smarter compared to the addition of four inches on the outside."

"Also, you are walking pretty normally."

Asha explained what had happened resulting in him being fitted with the assistive technology brace.

"Looks good. What would the two of you like to drink? We have beer, spirits as well as red and white wine."

Amy had a gin and tonic and Asha had a beer. The same for Angie and Tony. Amy and Asha sat down while Angie got the drinks.

"Cheers," wished Asha. "Here's to an enjoyable evening. If you look over there, you can see across the harbour and the location for the opera."

"OK. Drinks finished, let's go," Tony beckoned.

When they reached the venue, Asha was blown away by such a magnificent setting with the opera to be performed on a tailor-made stage built over the water off the Royal Botanic Garden with the Opera House and the Harbour Bridge as backdrops. It turned out to be a wonderful production.

They were chauffeur driven to and from the opera, finishing the night off in style with supper back at the hotel.

Asha had already broached the subject of him entering politics with Tony in Singapore and had continued to discuss the subject during their regular telephone calls. So, on Tony's visit to Sydney, Asha asked Tony to have coffee with him to have a serious face-to-face discussion to learn from Tony's experiences and to seek his advice.

This seemed logical to Asha as Tony had become a sort of mentor to him in addition to Robert as his father figure.

"Asha, it will not be easy to get into politics and to stay a member. There is a lot of hard work and it is very time-consuming."

"I understand that and I am not afraid of hard work and am willing to put in the hard yards. Robert is committed to supporting me, as is Amy."

"That is tremendous. You will also have my support."

"Thank you. I asked you a similar question before. I just want to make sure that I will be putting my best foot forward. Did your disability have any negative effect on you getting into politics?"

"As I suggested previously, in reality we are all the same, whether we are able or differently able. People will either accept you for who you are or not as we do with others. You seem to be very confident. So, I am sure your disability will not get in the way as it seems not to have done so far in your business life. You are a very successful practitioner."

"Appreciate your comments, Tony. I do feel good about myself and am proud about what I have achieved. And I do want to make a difference in public life.

After Asha's long talk with Robert, this discussion with Tony just put the icing on the cake and convinced Asha to make the move into politics.

Asha had talked to Robert a number of times about meetings with Tony and their various discussions. Robert seemed happy that Asha was getting another perspective.

Robert invited Tony, Angie, Amy and Asha and, of course, Roberta over for a Sunday BBQ. It was interesting to watch Tony and Robert in discussion and get involved in them. This was a very blokey Australian time, with the girls left to their own devices as well as looking after Roberta.

"Robert, what a beautiful place and fantastic view! I have heard a lot about you from Asha. You have been a wonderful influence on him."

"Tony, thank you. It has been an interesting and enjoyable journey with Asha. I am proud of what he has achieved."

"OK guys, let's get on with lunch and enjoy the company of the three lovely ladies," Robert encouraged.

Asha was delighted that Robert and Tony got on very well.

Later in the year, Asha was in Singapore on business. Amy and Roberta went with him. It was Roberta's first trip overseas.

Tony invited Asha to observe question time in the Singapore Parliament chamber one day from the public gallery. The whole process intrigued him, particularly the vigorous exchanges. This was a new experience as Asha had not even seen any parliamentary sessions in Australia, not even on television. Afterwards, Asha spent time with Tony in his office.

"What did you think of question time, Asha?"

"I enjoyed it very much. Interesting that the debates got a bit heated at times with much shouting across the chamber."

"Well, this is the sort of interaction that you will be involved in once you become a Member of Parliament."

"I think I will enjoy the jousts. Thank you for inviting me and for your time. See you at the weekend for lunch on Sunday."

Later that day, Asha reflected on political views. Robert's were more left wing. Tony's were to the right. And his were quite centric. Asha thought it had been interesting how balanced the discussions the three of them had on the current issues of climate change and the global economy when they were together in Sydney.

On the Saturday, Amy, Roberta and Asha had a good day on Sentosa Island. Not sure how much Roberta will remember as she was only fifteen months old. But you have to start somewhere and some time.

On the Sunday, lunch with Angie, Tony and their children, was most enjoyable. Their daughter took to Roberta and essentially looked after her for the whole time, keeping her occupied and out of trouble.

Then it was back to Sydney after a good, productive and varied series of activities.

On the flight home, Asha's mind could not stop thinking about politics and the contribution he could make. Asha was becoming impatient.

Chapter 37
Reminiscing

Another Christmas arrived, the first without Andrew. Amy and Asha invited Robert over to their place for Christmas lunch. Elisa and Matthew were spending their Christmas with her parents as well as Andrea, Andrew's and Elisa's second child, who had been born in October. A beautiful little girl, Robert's second granddaughter.

The positive mood was sparked by Roberta. This was her second Christmas. She was very excited to see all the presents under the tree. One by one she ripped open the paper, looked at the gift and moved onto the next one until all had been opened. She did not seem to be sure what to do next. But her favourite seemed to be a pretty dressed doll.

When Robert arrived, Roberta rushed up to him and jumped into his arms. This brought a smile to Robert's face and a screech from Roberta.

Robert gave his 'granddaughter' her gift. It was a beautiful silver charm bracelet with two charms, one an elephant and the other a koala. So thoughtful. Roberta hugged and kissed her 'pa' and said thank you.

Lunch was more of a traditional Australian fare with seafood being the centrepiece, washed down with Australian wines. Most enjoyable. Robert was really appreciative of being able to spend Christmas with Amy and Asha as well as Roberta. They had touched on Andrew's memory but did not dwell on it, just making the most of the festive day, with the focus on Roberta.

When Robert got back to the apartment late in the afternoon, he settled on the balcony with a glass of wine to keep him company and sat back in deep contemplation —

Andrew, I miss you so much. I miss your smile. I miss your understated humour. I miss your individualism. I know, in recent times, we have been separated by distance and only able to get together occasionally. For that reason, I miss you even more.

Could things have been different? We could have gone to Bristol or Malta, even Canada instead of Australia. Now Canada would have been very different.

Although we never emigrated to Canada, I went there on business and holiday a number of times.

There was the one with Yung-Su when we had a short stay in Vancouver.

My other visit to Vancouver had been a little more challenging. I had left a warm Sydney day in January to attend a conference in Vancouver. I did not usually bother about cold weather gear on the basis that, in a colder climate, I was never outside for too long. I arrived in Vancouver, but my luggage did not. So, after checking into the hotel, I went in search of a clothing store for some warmer clothes and ended up buying a tracksuit. That would be useful in any case and not only on this trip. Fortunately, my luggage turned up before the start of the conference.

Missing luggage, another memory trigger. Always an interesting experience when your luggage does not come off the carousel.

On one trip, I was flying from Singapore via Hong Kong and San Francisco to Portland, Oregon in the USA.

The first issue was that, when we got to Hong Kong, we were told that there would be a five-hour delay for our onward journey. What to do? It was a Saturday. So, I called a work colleague and arranged to meet him and a couple of others on Hong Kong Island for lunch. A great way to spend the time.

Back to the airport and all aboard heading for San Francisco. I had checked in two bags. But only one arrived in San Francisco. That was frustrating in itself, but it was always compounded by the need to wait until it was confirmed that the last bag had reached the carousel and mine was missing. I went to the airline desk to report the missing bag and was given a form to fill out on the way up to Portland. I was also told that, in all probability, my other bag would be there as well. Highly unlikely, I thought. Well, would you believe it, both my bags were in the baggage hall in Portland? How did that happen?

On another trip, I was due to fly from San Diego via Los Angeles and Hong Kong to Seoul, Korea. A storm delayed the flight out of San Diego. As a result, I missed the connecting flight in LA.

At the LA airline desk, I was booked on the following evening's flight. I left my luggage with them and asked them to make sure it was on the next day's flight, which they assured would be taken care of.

I checked into an airport hotel for the night, spent a lazy day there, bought a sweater, returned to the airport, checked in, confirming that my luggage would be on the flight, and boarded the aircraft.

In Hong Kong, I was upgraded to first class, a bonus. Well, something had to go right. But not everything. When I got to Seoul, no bag.

In the airline's office, they gave me the equivalent of 100 Australian dollars and told me that my bag would be delivered to my hotel that evening, which did happen.

The joys of air travel!

Back to my visits to Canada. I also had an interesting experience on the other side of Canada.

In 1980, I was responsible for purchasing a mainframe computer in my role as data processing manager for a local government council.

In the northern summer of that year, I was invited to accompany the senior salesman, who had been instrumental in winning the deal, on a world tour. My role was to explain to all and sundry in his company, in various locations, why they had been chosen. It was also an opportunity for me to investigate local government systems.

The itinerary was interesting, taking in some business and some non-business locations. We flew to San Francisco and then onto San Diego, a couple of days later.

The next stop was Atlanta. There I found one drink I did not like. We were in the self-service canteen, picking up our lunch. When we sat down, I had a sip of my drink and almost spat it out. I was expecting the taste of Coca-Cola, but it was iced tea. I hated it.

We hired a car and drove to Nashville, where we managed to take in a show at the Grand Ole Opry.

Then onto Cincinnati for an overnight stop before getting to Dayton for our next meeting. I do not know why we stayed in a motel on the outskirts of Cincinnati instead of just driving the fifty miles or so onto Dayton.

A couple of days later we were on the move again, flying to Boston for an overnight stop before our morning flight to Halifax, Nova Scotia, Canada.

A strange thing happened in Boston. When we were checking in, I could not find my passport. Yet the check-in agent and other officials still let me board the flight.

And when I arrived in Halifax, they let me in on the condition that I located my passport or got a new one.

In today's environment, this would not have been allowed to happen. I would have had to stay in Boston, thus missing one of my key meetings of the trip, in order to address the issue.

After some detective work, I tracked my passport down to the motel in Nashville. It must have fallen off the bed when I was packing. I arranged for my passport to be freighted to Halifax. Problem solved and back to business.

Only London and Perth in Western Australia to visit and the trip would be finished.

In one of my later jobs, I struck up a good relationship with my counterpart in Canada.

One year, I visited him and his wife in Toronto and stayed with them. It was summer and I really liked the city, in some ways a little like Sydney. I had a great time with them, being shown the sites and enjoying great food in their bungalow, sometimes outside by the pool, and in restaurants.

I'm not sure if I would have liked the city so much in winter, much too cold for me. I had clearly grown softer since leaving the United Kingdom.

So, perhaps, Canada would not have been too bad, winter weather excepted. But it did not happen and that was part of my Fate and the Fate of Andrew.

I was not feeling lonely, just alone, sitting on the balcony.

I had not made many close friends over the years. I don't know why. Perhaps, I did not think there was a need or I just did not want to invest time.

In my school days at primary and high schools, nobody really stood out other than Bert who had played cricket with me.

I got on with a number of people through the local football team, including John who became my best man. He moved to Sydney after me and we got together socially occasionally for some time before that relationship petered out.

Living in London, again only one person stood out and that was Fred at whose wedding I was best man. I stayed in touch with him and his wife, Janice, after we moved to Australia. But that also went into limbo before being resurrected after a few absent years of correspondence. Then I had a couple of holidays with them in the USA, separated by them visiting me in Australia. We still communicate by email.

For the first holiday in the USA, I met Fred and Janice in San Francisco. We hired a car for the drive to Las Vegas.

The first stop at Napa Valley was disappointing. We had planned to do wine tasting until we found out they charged for the pleasure! I was not used to being charged for wine tasting in Australia. After some thought, we decided against tasting the Californian grape.

We had two lovely days in the Yosemite National Park area, coinciding with Fred's and Janice's twenty-fifth wedding anniversary. The Park was magnificent with its giant sequoias and steep cascading waterfalls.

To celebrate the anniversary, we lashed out in an upmarket restaurant in Oakhurst, washed down with a bottle of chardonnay from Cloudy Bay in New Zealand. The wine was superb. But I was taken aback when I told the waiter that my fish was not cooked all the way through and his response was that I should have asked for that!

We had another stopover in Death Valley. Just magnificent colours.

Then onto Las Vegas, where we met another couple we knew from London. We walked the strip, dined out and went to a show. One day we went up in a small plane to the Grand Canyon and back. I am not a strong flyer, except for my grip on the armrests. Unfortunately, early in the trip, a little girl threw up, filling the plane with unpleasant odours. I did not know how long the trip was and so could not work out how long I would need to hold on and how long I would need to endure the rank-smelling air. Anyway, we made it back safely and into the fresh Nevada air. It was still worthwhile viewing the Canyon.

The second trip started in New York as Fred and Janice wanted to go to the US open tennis, for which we had tickets to two-day sessions and one-night session. Unfortunately, the night session was washed out but we managed to get an exchange for another day session instead.

I had never really wanted to go to New York. Well, as it turned out, the city amazed me and I was hooked.

I got there a day before Fred and Janice. After checking into my hotel near Times Square, I went onto the Square to look around and then into a bar for an ice-cold beer. The following morning, I walked up towards Central Park, stopping for breakfast in a real American diner and then onto the Metropolitan Museum of Art. Thoroughly enjoyed wandering around the galleries.

The tennis was enjoyable, easy to get to Flushing Meadows by train. The night after the rearranged day session, we went across to watch a Mets baseball game, dining on hot dogs and beer. I'd been to a number of baseball games before in Cincinnati, Toronto and San Diego. But this was the first baseball experience for Fred and Janice. They must have liked it because they went to a game in Boston after I left them later in this trip.

We also took in *Sweeney Todd*, a Broadway musical. I thought it was a great performance. Not sure that Fred and Janice agreed.

We then hired a car and drove north, staying a couple of nights at Rhode Island, which included a visit across the water to Martha's Vineyard. This was just after Labor Day and it was quite quiet. But we enjoyed the colonial village atmosphere. Then we drove to Boston. I was only there for one day, during which we walked the Freedom Trail, a 2.5-mile walking route of historic sites that tells the story of the nation's founding. It was good exercise and most informative. Then back to Sydney for me. Fred and Janice would return to England after their stay in Boston.

In Sydney, Pauline and I had a few couples with whom we were friends, largely through my work. We would have dinner parties as the main social activity. However, after Pauline's death, I lost touch with them.

Later on, in work life, I enjoyed social friendships with a number of colleagues, mainly in Korea. We would go out to dinner occasionally on my visits. They would send me back to my hotel after dinner whilst they went "out on the town". Then, one afternoon before I was due to make a visit to Seoul, I got a call to tell me that one of Korean team, Jun-Seo, had drowned. He was playing golf and the buggy he was riding went out of control and ended up in the lake. He could not get out regardless of the efforts of his playing partners. I still made the trip to Seoul. As I walked into the office, I was greeted with a huge display of white chrysanthemums, standing in the office of Jun-Seo. That brought tears to my eyes. After that, when I set up my own business, I did not see any of the team as I was not travelling to Korea anymore.

I did, however, strike up a friendship with one of the Australian workers, who reported to me. That has continued up until now. I remember Martin, his wife and three children, coming to my apartment when Asha was there. When we were sitting on the balcony, I was getting a little concerned with the youngest one, George, who kept standing up on the chair by the balustrade. I thought he was going to bungee jump over the edge without any attachment. To ease my concerns, I suggested we go down to the pool, where Asha spent time with George and his floaties. Martin and I still get together regularly even since we went our own way with work.

On reflection, I think that the lack of a number of close friends is due to me being very selfish and enjoying my own company.

Well, Andrew, enough reminiscing for now. Good night.

Chapter 38
What's Next?

Around eight a.m. on Monday, 21 January 2013, Robert called Asha.

"I am in hospital. They plan to take out my gall bladder later on today."

Asha told his boss what was happening and he told Asha to take as much time off as was required. When Asha got to the Accident & Emergency area, they were about to move Robert to the pre-op ward on a different floor.

Robert had woken up around three o'clock on Sunday morning with a very strong pain across his stomach. He tried to get into a comfortable position in bed but to no avail. Robert kept getting up trying to force himself to be sick and to open his bowels. But nothing happened. He'd go back to bed, get up again, have something to drink, ranging from Berocca to water to Coca-Cola and tea. Back to bed and the cycle continued with no relief from pain.

Around ten thirty a.m., he struggled to get dressed and went to the nearby chemist to get a laxative. He took two tablets and went back to bed. He'd already taken a couple of stomach ache tablets he'd bought on the previous Friday when his stomach had been playing up then. That ache passed quite quickly, but not this one.

When Robert had been travelling to India in late 2012, he got food poisoning on one visit. At least that was what he thought. And on two occasions, he had felt a lot of discomfort on the return flight and had been physically sick when he got home. After a further episode, Robert had gone to see his GP. The doctor's summation was that the cause could be one of a hundred things. He gave Robert a referral to see a specialist if the symptoms came back. Nothing happened in the next month so Robert threw the referral out. Then the episode on Friday and this most uncomfortable situation. Was there a connection to the so-called food poisoning in India?

Robert lay in bed thinking what to do. Asha and his family were away for the weekend. Andrew might have been able to help but he was no longer around. That took Robert's mind off his own condition and made him think of Elisa, Matthew and Andrea and how they were coping without Andrew. It was now almost one year since Andrew had been murdered. Robert had thought about him every day since and missed him so much.

When it got to four o'clock in the afternoon, Robert decided he was going to hospital. He showered, got dressed, put toiletries and underpants into a backpack and called 000. He was put through to the ambulance services and his particulars were taken. Robert was asked to let the concierge in the apartment know that an ambulance was on its way, which he did. A few minutes later there was a knock on Robert's apartment door. The ambulance officers had arrived.

Robert took them to his bedroom where he sat on the side of the bed. A series of questions then followed.

Where was the pain? How does it rate on a scale of 0 to ten? Robert said nine. When did it start? Any history of diabetes, heart disease...? No. Any allergies? No. Do you smoke? No. Do you drink? Yes, one and a half bottles of wine per day.

Various measurements were taken; blood pressure, pulse and temperature, which was a little high. Robert was given a shot of morphine and then sat in the small chair with wheels that the officers had brought. Robert was then wheeled out of his apartment into the lift that had been kept on his floor by one of the guys from concierge who had brought the officers up. They went out to the ambulance where Robert climbed into it and onto the bed. The pain had eased a little.

They drove slowly to the hospital about one kilometre away. But there was no siren roaring, which disappointed Robert. Robert was rolled into the Emergency Ward and attended to almost immediately.

More questions: name, date of birth... More morphine. A cannula was inserted into Robert's left arm for the saline drip and other drugs that needed to be administered. Blood was taken for some tests to try to isolate the problem. A little later Robert went in a wheelchair to get chest X-rays. Neither the blood tests nor X-rays were conclusive. It was then determined that Robert needed to have a CT scan either that night or the following morning. In the meantime, Robert continued to get shots of morphine. During all this time Robert had been on Nil by Mouth.

A decision was taken to do the CT scan around midnight. Prior to that, Robert had to drink three glasses of 'gunge' that would help with the process. This was a muddy semi solid concoction.

After the CT scans, it was just a matter of lying back in bed and trying to get some sleep. That was near impossible. Robert thought that hospitals were meant to be places of quiet. Not where he was and it was the staff making the noise, chattering amongst themselves and clattering equipment.

Around seven a.m., Robert was told of the CT results that his gall bladder was the problem and not the liver. The liver was enlarged but there were no signs of cirrhosis. Robert thought the consultant, who was guiding his treatment, was disappointed because he felt it ought to have been Robert's liver due to the regular amounts of alcohol intake. A surgeon was found to operate on Robert to remove the gall bladder and the surgery was scheduled for after five o'clock that afternoon.

Asha stayed with Robert for most of the day. Asha had a break for lunch when he also went back to Robert's apartment to pick up a few things for him, including his iPad.

Early in the afternoon came a change of strategy. Analysis of blood tests had led the attending team to think that a gallstone was blocking the bile duct. They felt that if they could release it, some of the "rubbish" would follow, easing the pain and the urgency to remove the gall bladder. However, an ultrasound of the gall bladder area failed to detect the gallstone blockage. On to Plan C, a course of antibiotics for five days and then remove the gall bladder, allowing the a-n-g-r-y one to settle down.

Asha was back by Robert's bedside on the Tuesday morning by which time they had moved onto Plan D. Blood tests had shown that the alleged gallstone may have passed and that they would operate to remove the gall bladder after four o'clock in the afternoon.

All Robert and Asha could do was wait. Asha went to the cafe to get a snack and left Robert to rest.

There was plenty running through Robert's mind—

I am not frightened to die. I am more concerned about how other people, particularly family and friends, would feel if I did not make it. How has my life been? What will be left behind?

I found it interesting that, as youngsters, we think we are invincible and that life will go on forever. As we get into middle age, we try to make the most of every moment. Then, as the sunset approaches…

In my mind, I started planning my funeral. I would like it to be a celebration, with people in colourful clothes, not black. As for music, so much to choose from. This is going to be very difficult, from pop music to musicals, onto classical and opera.

There is the whole set of recordings of the Beatles. This reminded me of being at a Beatles concert, which also featured the Moody Blues, making me think of their mournful and beautiful song *A Whiter Shade of Pale*. Around the same time, I went to see Roy Orbison twice, this solo figure in black. His recordings are amongst my most cherished. My favourite musical of all time is *Les Misérables*, with the tension offset by some wonderful songs. Violin concertos by Bruch and Mendelssohn and Puccini's operatic masterpieces of *La Bohème, Madama Butterfly* and *Tosca* fill out the list of the sounds that I have savoured most. Yet, I have decided not to use any of them during the service. I have chosen:

- *Abide With Me* — Bryan Terfel

I wanted this played at my wedding. But I was outvoted. I also wanted a blue buttonhole, the colour of Chelsea's strip. Again, I missed out. So, perhaps, the flowers could feature blue and yellow.

- *Morgen* — Placido Domingo and Itzhak Perlman

- *Flower of Scotland* — Kenneth McKellar

How would my obituary read? Born to loving parents; Alex and Faye. Was not keen on study, preferring to play cricket and football. Probably did not push himself as much as he could have, being a little shy. Married and migrated to Australia. Had one child; Andrew. Was a caring person. A finely balanced life.

Enough of that for now.

When I had my last major surgery to repair my left Achilles tendon, I remember the pre-op very clearly. The below-knee part of my left leg had been shaved. I was given a hat, a little like a hairnet but without the holes. Then an injection to calm me down. This was great. I felt so at peace and floating on air. What an extraordinary feeling.

Around five p.m., Robert was taken to the anaesthetic area to be readied for the operation. And Asha went home to await the outcome. Robert mouthed the words of the Lord's Prayer to himself.

Our Father which art in heaven, Hallowed be thy name.

Thy kingdom come, Thy will be done in earth, as it is in heaven.

Give us this day our daily bread.

And forgive us our debts, as we forgive our debtors. And lead us not into temptation, but deliver us from evil: For thine is the kingdom, and the power, and the glory, for ever.

Amen.

Asha had left a message at the hospital for someone to call him once Robert was back in the ward. All Asha could do was wait. Easier said than done for someone impatient like Asha.

Asha paced around, unable to settle, just thinking and thinking and thinking.

Asha's mind was in overload—

What a life I have had! A life that may not have started off well for me. But I have always had people in my life who cherished me and for whom I cared, both able-bodied and differently able.

That started with my immediate and extended family, including my aunt and uncle. Ranjiv, my father, carried me around on his back up until I was around five years old and went to school. That was the catalyst for me getting my first pole and independence, hopping around. Now that I have spent time in Australia, I can relate to the kangaroos and their hopping.

I made friends at school, particularly Rajesh and Manosh. Although they could be nasty at times.

Then the big development when Robert stopped me in my tracks. He encouraged me to go to university in Sydney. Then I met his son, Andrew. We became very close, like brothers and we did many things together without living in each other's pockets. Through Andrew, I was introduced to his then girlfriend and future wife, Elisa, and later mother of two children: Matthew and Andrea.

At university, I met the love of my life, Amy. We hit it off from the very beginning. We had many things in common. Also, it was Amy who encouraged me to enjoy opera. And, of course our gorgeous daughter, Roberta.

At university, Philippe from Denmark and Scott from Canada became wonderful friends. Sadly, Scott was tragically killed in a car accident.

I had heard a little bit about Yung-Su, mainly from Andrew as Robert was reluctant to talk about him. However, I was very happy to meet him when Andrew and I went to Japan to play wheelchair tennis. Yung-Su and I got on straight away. After that we met a number of times on tour and, over time, Robert became more comfortable talking about Yung-Su. Robert and Yung-Su met for the first time after many years at my wedding in Perth. He was with his wife, Mi-Hyun. Robert and Yung-Su seemed to get on well and over the coming months and years met, including on a visit by Robert to Seoul. Yung-Su and Mi-Hyun had a baby boy, Chang-Su. Robert was delighted with the arrival of another "grandchild".

I met Alice, who Robert had invited as a friend to Andrew's and my apartment. She mentioned that she had two children, Annie and John. Alice told us that Andrew and I had something in common as John went to the same university. Then, on New Year's Eve, we met Annie and John at Robert's apartment. I had a good chat with them and they seemed like normal people. One day I invited John to have a coffee with me. It was then that I found out that John was also disabled as a double amputee below the knees. John and I became very close friends. As Amy and I did with his eventual wife, Eve.

Amy's parents, Ella and Roger, accepted me unconditionally. They did not seem to have any issue with my disability. We all got on very well and enjoyed one another's company, fortunately.

Then Tony and his wife, Angie, as well as their two children, came into my life. Such a chance meeting on an aeroplane that developed into a close family friendship and Tony's mentorship.

What would have happened if I had not had that chance meeting with Robert in Powai almost twelve years ago? Who cares? It happened and I know it had a huge impact on my life.

Not needing to hop around using a pole, but being more mobile and more independent with a calliper.

A life in Sydney, Australia, offering so many opportunities that I would not have been able to get in Nagpur, Powai or other parts of India.

Being introduced to fine food and wine, initially in India, leading to an eclectic taste for wine from French champagne to dessert wines and a love for food from various cuisines around the world.

Being introduced to wheelchair tennis and travelling the world.

Studying at university, which I could have done in India. But I don't think it would have been the same experience, having the opportunity to mix with students from other countries and cultures.

Showing Westerners, Andrew, Elisa, Amy and Robert, my native place and being proud of my background and family.

Developing a real interest in horse racing.

And last but not least that great bunch of people who enhanced my very being.

What a life, so far!

These memories all have their roots in that auspicious day in March 2001. What a wonderful twelve years for which I will always be grateful to Robert.

I had flown Robert's nest but we had remained close. I know our time together has to end but I don't want it to be now.

That had been my Fate. What was Robert's?

We still had lots to do together, particularly my campaign to become a Member of Parliament.

I could not stand to lose another person so close to me. My best friend and Robert's son had passed away less than twelve months ago.

Asha made a cup of tea for himself.

Amy and Roberta had gone to Perth to visit Ella and Roger. Asha telephoned Amy just for something to keep him occupied.

And then what, Asha asked himself? He turned on the television. But nothing interested him. He checked email, Twitter and Facebook. But could not concentrate.

Asha decided to go for a walk down to the local cafe and get something to eat.

"Hi, Julia. I'll have a piece of vegetarian quiche and a glass of Sauvignon Blanc please."

Asha sat down and put his mobile phone on the table. The quiche and wine arrived. Asha kept looking at the phone, wishing it to ring. The food and drink were fine, more something for him to do than it was to satisfy his appetite.

"See you later, Julia."

Back home, Asha took off his callipers and then proceeded to wheel himself backwards and forwards along the hallway, still unable to settle. His brain was running at a hundred miles an hour. Asha was torturing himself.

Ring… Ring… Ring…

"Hello?"